Sunflower

Marilyn Sharp is the wife of Representative Philip Sharp,
Congressman from the district of Indiana. She lives with her
husband and three-year-old son Jeffrey in Arlington, Virginia.

Marilyn Sharp

Sunflower

Pan Books in association with
Macmillan London

First published in Great Britain 1979 by Macmillan London Ltd
This edition published 1979 by Pan Books Ltd,
Cavaye Place, London SW10 9PG
in association with Macmillan London Ltd
2nd printing 1980
© Marilyn Augburn Sharp 1979
ISBN 0 330 25850 8
Made and printed in Great Britain by
C. Nicholls & Company Ltd, The Philips Park Press, Manchester

to Phil,
for advice and consent.
And for order in the house

one

Malcolm stood with his back to the castle, pacing uneasily and keeping an eye on the road where it curved up from the village of Knaresborough.

The castle rose up behind him, bleak and broken, a snaggled-toothed relic etched against the leaden sky of a wet April dawn. Its grim dungeons were padlocked now behind heavy wooden doors, its history reduced to a line or two in the British tourist guides. The fortress stood silent, harmless, a brooding shadow of terror dimly remembered across the boundaries of time. But to Malcolm, standing there alone in the fading darkness, with mist rising wet and cold against his face, the ghosts of Knaresborough Castle were strangely alive. Not that he was seeing things – there were no ghostly images mounting the battlements, no mute spirits clanking weightless chains in his mind's eye, nothing as graphic as that. It was just a feeling he had, a sense of mystery provoked by broken walls and empty, staring windows, like so many eyes peering at him out of the past.

And so he turned to face the present, keeping an eye on the road and an ear cocked for the hum of a motor. Instead, all he heard was the sound of water rushing over rocks – a gentle, hypnotic sound, desolate, like the steady scrape of the windscreen wipers as he made his way north from London through the lonely night. He turned his collar up against the chill of the air, then reached for the packet of sunflower seeds in his pocket.

It had to be sunflower seeds. Graham had been quite specific. Not peanuts or cashews, but *sunflower* seeds. The signal Graham would recognize: the code name for the subject.

He tore open the cellophane wrapper at the point where a red arrow said 'open here' and began to eat the seeds slowly, one at a time, careful not to drop any.

Malcolm was a tall man, but not tall enough to carry so much weight. Mere overweight had given way long ago to genuine obesity. His eyes were pinpoints in a florid face, surrounded by lines of age, yet alert and watchful under the brim of his black bowler. His coat was also black – surely the proper colour for this sort of meeting – and a vintage style, bought to last for years, like everything else Malcolm owned. Under the coat, his shoulders sloped forwards, collapsed after too many years of supporting the burden of his huge head. Yet, in spite of his bulk, his pale fingers were long and slender. They might have been folded across a body with a lily in their grasp.

He yawned and shrugged off the fatigue of a sleepless night. He had worked straight through, rolling the last sheet of the report out of his typewriter just in time to get rid of the evidence and be on his way. There had been no time for early tea, much less a nap; but now, standing in the open air, with the report safely zippered into the black case under his arm, he felt like a man on the threshold of a new day. His full lips curved into a smile. It was appropriate that Graham had chosen this time, daybreak, for their first face-to-face meeting.

Through the old stone gate – all that was left of the castle walls – he could see the other side of the road and the café, a small white-frame building with chintz curtains crisscrossed behind bone china teacups in the windows. Beyond the café lay the sleeping village, where a night of steady rain had left the air sweet smelling and the colours all deeper in tone. Green trees were greener. Curving blacktop roads were blacker. And sturdy old houses built of drab Yorkshire stone – rough, uneven blocks edged in black, like mourning cards, after centuries of exposure to the air – these were a little less drab in the deep, wet silence of dawn.

Like the rest of the village, the café was still locked for the night, but the sun was already beginning to throw pink and yellow rays of dawn up into the eastern sky. And if Malcolm knew anything about cafés done in chintz and bone china, he knew they were operated by plump, apple-cheeked ladies who got up to greet the sun with pastries fresh from the oven. But still no car. No foreign sound to intrude upon nature's own. No Graham.

Malcolm didn't know precisely who Graham was, only that he was top echelon and had never before risked the cover of his own good name by venturing out into the field. Like Graham, Malcolm had a safe job; he worked behind the scenes, never on the front lines. But while the Grahams of the world sat in plush offices, issuing orders and making policy, the Malcolms worked out of draughty cubicles, ploughing through detail after tedious detail, seeking out that rare morsel of information that was worth the attention of the Grahams. Or so Malcolm thought.

He pressed the black case a little closer, feeling the comforting presence of the report that was so much more than just details, more even than some abstract policy that might or might not work. It was his *piagrece de resistance*, the crowning glory on a career of service his superiors had taken for granted too long. Now, the long-deserved honour would come. Not publicly, of course; it was all too top secret for that. But privately – new respect among his colleagues, the people who had ignored him all these years, the people who simply didn't see him when he passed them in the halls, who always seemed a trifle annoyed if he interrupted their work with a question, or a suggestion. All of that would be different soon – very different, very soon – and for that, he had mostly himself to thank.

Of course, Graham deserved some credit, too. It was Graham, after all, who had asked for the best research analyst available, Graham who had chosen Malcolm over the rest. Graham who had given Malcolm this key assignment.

For a moment, Malcolm stopped pacing, eyeing the ground at his feet with peculiar interest. Then he dampened one pale finger against his tongue and stooped to retrieve a single sunflower seed that had somehow eluded his grasp. As he straightened up, he caught sight of someone moving off to his right. A man appeared on the path that skirted the lower level of the castle grounds and began to move slowly around the walk that framed the broad lawn. Even from this distance, Malcolm was grudgingly impressed. This stranger coming towards him did not appear to be Mr Top-Echelon Graham, whose working clothes no doubt ran to Savile Row tweeds and shoes of Italian leather. This was a common man, in faded denims, with a blue seaman's cap pulled low over his brow. He was in character right down to the way he walked, with the rolling gait of a sailor. And he appeared from the one direction Malcolm had rejected as unlikely.

9

Malcolm stuffed the sunflower seeds back into his pocket and moved to head the man off where the walk came closest to the castle. '*All human things are subject to decay,*' he said as the man approached him.

'*And when fate summons, monarchs must obey,*' Graham replied.

The two men fell into step, saying nothing as they made their way past the castle and down to the promenade, where the ground fell away sharply to the river below. Graham paused there for a moment, calmly inspecting the distant viaduct that carried the main road across the river into the village, and the tiny houses grouped along the water's edge.

'Well?' he said at last.

It annoyed Malcolm to notice that Graham was younger than he – mid-forties, maybe fifty, he guessed, as he studied the lean, unworried face that testified to nothing except lack of experience.

'I've given this problem many long hours of thought—'. he began.

But Graham cut him off. 'I'm not interested in technique, just results. Can it be done? That's what I want to know.'

'Yes, sir,' Malcolm replied quickly. 'Yes, it can be done.'

Graham turned away from the scenic view below and towards the path that led down to the lower level and eventually wound its way back to the place where he had first appeared. Malcolm followed a respectful step behind. The sound of rushing water grew louder as they descended the steep riverbank.

'How?' Graham wanted to know.

Now that the time had come, Malcolm wasn't sure where to start. Graham would want it straight – neat and concise. On the other hand, Malcolm knew he had to be careful what he said.

He quickened his pace to move abreast with the other man, then plunged straight into it. 'We begin,' he said, 'by stealing this from the White House.' He handed a folded newspaper clipping to Graham.

Graham unfolded the clipping. 'You mean—?'

'Yes, sir, that's what I mean.'

For a moment, Graham's expressionless face came to life. He clearly liked the idea. But then he frowned.

Malcolm spoke up quickly before Graham could verbalize his doubts. 'We use the best possible person,' he said, 'a top-notch professional who can do a clean job, leaving no evidence behind. Not a single clue to who or what he is, nothing to—'

'Yes, yes, I know all of that,' Graham broke in impatiently. 'But what's the point of it all?'

'The point is, sir, that *we* provide the clues,' Malcolm said, spacing the words to give them their proper importance. He was all civil servant now, strolling along with his hands clasped behind his back, keeping the black zippered case pressed close to his large body, delivering his report efficiently. 'We choose key trouble spots around the world, places where US prestige is already an issue, and we launch a campaign of befuddlement and apparent bungling. If we choose carefully, we might accomplish a few specific goals, as well as the broader one. In any case, we give them nothing to help them recover the stolen item. In fact, we do all we can to prevent it.'

'Ah, yes, I'm beginning to see where you're going,' Graham said. He chuckled. 'In the end, I presume, we save the day and reap the rewards.'

'Yes, sir. But not without placing blame where it's due.'

Graham didn't say anything for a moment. He continued on down the path, stroking his chin thoughtfully, mulling over Malcolm's words. 'It's good,' he said at last. 'I have to hand it to you, Malcolm – it's very good.'

'Yes, sir.'

'But it's all predicated on one questionable point. Is it possible to steal the item you have in mind?'

'There's the rub, of course,' Malcolm replied. 'I should think it can be done. Nothing is ever completely impossible, you know.'

Graham stopped where he was and turned on Malcolm with an angry glare. 'I didn't tell you to bring me *possibilities*, I told you to—'

'There is one man who can do it,' Malcolm broke in quickly.

No comment, only a raised eyebrow from Graham.

'His name is Richard Owen.'

Yes, of course. Richard Owen. Malcolm hardly needed to say

who he had in mind. Whenever there was just one man for the job, it was always Richard Owen. Graham resumed his leisurely pace down the path towards the riverbank. 'Convince me,' he said.

'Do you know Owen?'

'Of course. And I don't think I trust him for this. You tell me, why does it have to be Owen?'

Malcolm cleared his throat. 'Well, sir, I should say he has all the necessary qualities. He's competent. He's intelligent. He's extremely clever. As far as I can determine, his track record is without blemish. And, apparently, he's immune to fear. Frankly, sir, I'm not sure anyone else would be willing to accept this assignment.'

'When I give an assignment, Malcolm, acceptance is not a question.'

'Of course, sir. I didn't mean to suggest otherwise. But we must have someone who is up to the job, and Richard Owen has one unique qualification: he's an absolute genius with languages. He speaks eight of them fluently, you know.'

'Yes, I know that.'

'Actually, to say he is fluent is rather an understatement,' Malcolm added. 'He's also a master of dialects. For example, he can speak English as an Englishman, or an American, a Scotsman, an Irishman, even an Australian. And he can break the language down to dialects within those countries, as well. I daresay it's a gift, though it's not so surprising when you consider his background. His father was in diplomatic service, and they lived all over the world. Young Owen had tutors, always the best. Later, he attended university at Oxford and the Sorbonne. Quite a good student.'

'You don't miss anything, do you?'

'It's my job, sir,' Malcolm replied. 'It's odd when you think about it,' he added, staring into empty space somewhere over the river. 'I mean, how much you assume you know a man just by the way he speaks. Nationality is part of it, of course – one does tend to generalize – but that's no problem for our Mr Owen.' His eyes shifted back to Graham. 'Owen is literally a man without a country. It would be quite impossible for anyone but the most highly trained expert to determine his native tongue. In fact, I question whether any expert is Owen's equal.'

Graham merely nodded.

'His value for this assignment is obvious, I think,' Malcolm went on. Then, the good civil servant, leaving nothing to chance, he explained: 'Owen is able to surface and re-surface, time and time again, in the same place or an entirely new location, each time as a different person. Physical disguise helps, of course, and he does need the full line of false documents, but those can always be supplied. His command of languages is the main thing.'

They rounded a curve in the path and came out with a good view of the river at close range. Graham stopped, again seeming to study the view. 'Where is Owen now?' he asked after a moment.

'In Brussels. And I don't believe we'll have any trouble with him, sir. He's a bloody cold bastard, if you'll pardon my saying so. And he does his jobs without much concern for the motives behind them – not out of anything as noble as patriotism, mind you. It's the *challenge* that motivates Owen. It's meeting the challenge that gives him his satisfaction. He has never failed. He's simply the best there is.'

And that, thought Graham, summed up the problem of Richard Owen. Intelligent, Malcolm had said. Extremely clever. The words were hardly adequate. Owen was brilliant. Ingenious. More than that, independent. And that combination made Graham nervous.

He turned to Malcolm. 'Obviously, you've done your research on this man.'

'Yes, sir.'

'Then you tell me, what makes him function?'

'That's no simple question,' Malcolm replied. He was silent for a moment, pulling his thoughts together. Then he said, 'Owen is a complex sort of person – on the one hand amoral, on the other a moral purist. He's a master of deception, but incapable of hypocrisy. He'll kill one of our kind without a moment's remorse, but he doesn't like to hurt innocent people and tries to avoid it. In fact, he rather *likes* people, as long as they give him no reason not to. But liking and trusting, to Owen, are two very separate things.'

'Precisely,' Graham said. 'You're *not* easing my fears. If Owen

13

should care about this, if he should ask too many questions—'

'Ah, but he won't. He never does. He'll ask *some* questions because he likes to work from knowledge and not from ignorance. But policy doesn't interest him. Policy decisions require a position to start with – this side is right or wrong – and Owen doesn't take positions on that sort of issue. He doesn't care about ideology. He's not attached to the traditional values, if you will. He simply does his job, and there you have no worries. Owen believes in one thing absolutely, the value of his word. If he gives you his word, he'll keep it. He'll go to incredible lengths to keep it.' Malcolm glanced away to the river. 'Of course,' he added, 'he may just turn you down.'

Graham did not reply, but he knew Malcolm was right. There it was again, the problem: unlike most of his agents, Owen could not be predicted. Yet Owen was the only man for the job.

'On the other hand,' Malcolm said, 'I don't see how he can. It goes to his motivation, the challenge. Owen will do almost anything if it interests him. And this assignment, I think you'll agree, could hardly fail to do that.'

Malcolm's heart began to beat a little faster. He opened the black zippered case. 'It's all right here,' he said. 'I've put together a complete dossier on him.'

Graham said nothing. His placid features were frozen, his eyes glued to the document in Malcolm's hand.

Malcolm failed to notice.

'I have something else for you, too, sir,' he said, digging deeper into the black case. 'I've put together a rather detailed outline of the plan we were discussing. It's complete with suggested places where clues might turn up, and the trouble they might cause. I've also outlined my thinking on the climax and denouement, if you will. Of course, you didn't give me all the details of what you had in mind. I had to fill in a few holes – make some educated guesses, you might say. But if you will just read it, sir, I think you will see it has merit.'

Graham no longer tried to hide his dismay. His expression ran from astonishment to outright anger. 'You put all of that into writing' he demanded.

'Don't worry,' Malcolm assured him. 'I worked at night when there was no one there to see me. And I shredded everything, *everything*, except what you see right here.'

Graham glanced down at the neat, typewritten notes in Malcolm's hand. His mind ran through the possible pitfalls. Shredded notes could never be reconstructed, but there were other possibilities – words etched into a typewriter carriage, for instance. Yet, he knew instinctively that the old man's typewriter would be an ancient model, with so many years of Malcolm's bureaucratic verbiage run through it, no expert could hope to make sense of a single word. Anyway, there would be plenty of time to reinforce instinct with a thorough search of Malcolm's home and office. He glanced down at the notes. 'Copies?' he said.

'Just two, one for you and one for me. They're both right here – quite safe, I assure you.'

Graham's face relaxed into a smile: 'Good job, Malcolm. Let me see what you've done.'

He took the report and began to read it. They continued down the path to the river's edge and sat down on a wooden bench. Malcolm lowered himself on to the opposite end of the bench. He glanced back over his shoulder. From this point, the castle was completely hidden by the steep slope of the riverbank. The café was well out of range, and even the cluster of houses at the base of the viaduct was separated from them by a thick growth of trees, budding with new leaves. The sky overhead was bright with the promise of a clear spring day, and the rising sun began to burn off the mist and draw the chill from the air. Malcolm took a deep breath and reached into his pocket, then hesitated. One did not 'nibble' in the presence of one's superiors. But was Graham still a superior? Malcolm thought not. He brought out the sunflower seeds and began to eat them, one at a time. It was a fresh new day, a new beginning, and he was glad to be alive.

Graham noticed the pathetic gesture of equality but continued to read. When he was finished, he turned over the last page and looked up, but not at Malcolm. He was looking at the river rushing by – muddy green water bursting with new strength, breaking over the rocks with savage force, tumbling over itself and spitting

15

up foam. He was looking at the river, but he was thinking about Malcolm – and his plan.

Malcolm had been a good choice. He was loyal and hard working and, more than that, above suspicion. He was everything Richard Owen was not – a drone, a plodder who would never be credited with anything close to imagination. There would be no reason for anyone to connect him with this. But Graham had underestimated him, had given him too much information, and now the old fellow had drawn himself right into the inner circle. *Two people* would share this secret; there should not be three.

Yet, it was an excellent plan.

Graham turned to Malcolm and said, 'It's all here.'

'As I told you.'

'And you're quite sure there are no other copies? Nothing left carelessly on your desk? Nothing accidentally thrown into the trash?'

'If you'll pardon my saying so, I'm not daft,' Malcolm replied. 'And I'm no newcomer to this business.'

'No, you're not,' Graham conceded. As he spoke, he took a fountain pen from his pocket, routinely removed the cap and aimed it at the other man. A kestrel hawk dipped low in the sky and hovered, motionless, seemingly without effort, over the river. Then in a single, graceful move, it banked away over the trees and disappeared out of view. That graceful, gliding motion was the last thing Malcolm ever saw. He uttered a brief cry, but the sound was lost in the noise of the river. His arm jerked up to his face, but it was too late.

Graham quickly searched the dead man's pockets, then rolled the body over into the scrub growing beside the river. When someone stumbled on to it later in the day, all traces of the poison would have vanished, and the late Mr Malcolm would be nothing more interesting than a government clerk on holiday, the victim of a heart attack.

Graham placed Malcolm's report back in the black zippered case, tucked it under his arm and walked away into the trees. Behind him lay an open cellophane wrapper, with sunflower seeds spilling out over the ground. Soon, a stray wind scattered the seeds and lifted the wrapper into the river. For a moment, it bobbed along the surface, fighting to stay afloat. But finally a swirl of white foam washed over its bright red letters, and the wrapper, too, disappeared from sight.

two

The Rendezvous Bar in Athens was all polished wood and old leather, small and cosy, with soft lights glowing under a crystal chandelier. Along one end ran a carved mahogany bar where, it was said, the bartender made smalltalk with cabinet ministers, diplomats, and spies – a tour-book exaggeration that was not entirely false. At six o'clock on an April evening the room was beginning to fill with groups of men in business suits and others more casually dressed, tourists who apparently knew that spring was the only time of year to visit Greece. There were women, too, in bright spring dresses, scattered at tables around the room as if they'd been placed there for colour, like the sprays of gladioli that came from the flower stalls around the corner on Avenue Vassilissis Sofias. There was no music, only the sounds of subdued conversation, some laughter, ice clinking against glass. And one dignified waiter in immaculate whites who moved noiselessly through the room, like an old family retainer, serving drinks from a silver tray.

Hovering over it all was the Grande Bretagne, the queen mother of Athens hotels, a stopping place over the years for monarchs and millionaires, even Winston Churchill, who escaped an assassin at the end of the war through the subterranean corridors of the hotel's cellar.

Richard Owen had never seen the cellar, but if the rest of the hotel was any indication, he guessed it was probably done in Parisian marble and gilded bronze.

Owen smiled his approval as he crossed the lobby and entered the bar. While the rest of Athens was going to neon and plastic, the Grande Bretagne had retained its nineteenth-century charm. It was almost like coming home for a man who had no home. He chose a corner table with a clear view of the entire room and summoned the waiter with a gesture that was both subtle and commanding.

'Glenfiddich, on the rocks,' Owen said.

The waiter nodded and moved away again, sizing up his new patron. An American, quite obviously – mid-thirties, tall, with a slender, athletic build and brown hair cut fashionably long. His face had a rugged quality, but his features were even and well defined, and his eyes were young – full of trust and confidence, as clearly American as if they were stamped 'Made in the USA'. Yes, this was an American, the waiter thought as he went to get Owen's drink. An American with rare good taste who ordered malt scotch by brand and his clothes from a quality tailor. An unusual American, but clearly the real thing.

Only Richard Owen was not American. Or British, or French, or Russian. Or anything else. He belonged to no country beyond the one named in his current passport, and that would be different tomorrow. Over the years, he had carefully erased all traces of his native accent and the personal mannerisms that are just as much of a giveaway. With each new name, he became a complete new person – for an hour, or a day, or a month or more. When one name died, the person died, too, and a new one was born. Between names, he became Richard Owen, a person as carefully planned as the others. His real identity was buried in the past. All that was left was a face without fire in its eyes, a solitary figure without friends or family and one who preferred it that way. For a reason. Attachments meant vulnerability. It was safer not to care.

The waiter brought his drink and Owen looked up, then focused his eyes on the wall across the room, over the heads of the other people. He wanted only voices, floating to him like so many points of information to be rejected until the right sound came through.

Mostly, they were speaking English. A little French. Some German. Hardly any Greek.

Some *German.*

The voice was a man's, but it was followed soon after by a burst of feminine laughter, then her reply. Her accent was American, her German book-learned. But she would be in real trouble if she ever had to fool a German who was less her slave than this one. Or so it seemed to Owen.

He let his eyes scan the room, moving slowly but certainly to a table where a young woman was holding the full attention of a handsome young Deutschlander. She smiled sweetly as the man held his lighter to her cigarette, then met his eyes over the flame with a look that could have melted the buttons off his shirt. Owen smiled to himself. He knew the type. As toddlers they were precocious, as teenagers little flirts, and as grown-up women they were capricious nymphs, modern-day Aphrodites who tallied broken hearts like notches on a gun, while Daddy paid the bills. And Daddy, of course, was rarely the natural parent.

She, alone among the women in the bar, was wearing a plain black dress – very plain, very chic, and very expensive. She was a sleek blonde, with delicate colouring and gay, laughing eyes. Owen could guess at the intimate details – her make-up would be flawless, her fingernails perfectly manicured, and her undergarments, such as they might be, colour-matched.

The German, made bold by drink – or proximity to such willing charm – made no effort to keep his voice down. He was telling Blondie how beautiful she was. Beautiful, but smart. He hadn't met anyone like her for a long time.

American women have been liberated, Blondie told him.

Liberated?

We're no longer chained to the kitchen, she explained.

I see. He nodded. That should leave you time for other rooms.

'*Aber naturlich,*' she replied with a knowing smile.

Indeed, Owen thought. Blondie chained to a kitchen was a picture his imagination refused to produce.

He listened a while longer and, in the end, decided that Blondie's American accent was very good, but not good enough. She was a natural-born fräulein if ever he'd heard one, a German woman *pretending* to be American, and speaking her native tongue as if she had learned it in school. Owen smiled. A lesser ear for language would have been fooled; his was not.

Blondie was the right fräulein, too. Even from across the room, he could hardly miss the splendid ruby earrings that adorned her lovely earlobes like a pair of polished red dice. As he watched, she raised her hand to one ear and slipped the ruby off. For a moment, she held it in her hand. Then she returned it to its rightful place and removed its opposite number.

Yes, Blondie was the woman he had come here to meet, and how she was going to detach herself from the German was her problem.

Owen tuned out the seduction scene across the room and lit a cigarette. He exhaled slowly, watching the smoke as it curled in the air and vanished into a cloud hovering near the ceiling. He was thinking about dice, the man in Brussels rolling a pair of red dice in his hands like Captain Queeg come ashore. He was a bland-faced man whose only distinguishing characteristic was a pair of dark-framed glasses he probably changed as often as he changed his socks.

Owen was finished in Brussels and ready to leave for Oslo on schedule when the bland-faced man intervened. It was a simple encounter, the most basic approach: 'Pardon me, sir, do you have the time?'

Time was the first key word.

As Owen answered, the man fell into step beside him, heading towards Owen's hotel. 'I have *to* meet my wife in an hour,' he said. *To* could also be *two* or *too*.

'Are you *going* my way?' the man went on. And when Owen said he was, 'Well, *now*, that's just fine.'

Time to go now.

Then he brought out the dice, and Owen knew the bland-faced man was no ordinary courier. It had been years since anyone had given him a double red alert. A single red was common enough and only meant to get in touch with the nearest station as soon as possible. Usually it was a matter of extravagant expenses or some such detail. But a double red was something else. Under a double, you talked to no one, especially not the local station. A double came direct from the top. No questions asked. Just follow orders until someone cares to enlighten you. And trust no one, not even your own granny, unless she's sporting a pair of something red.

Owen didn't trust anyone anyway, and his granny had been dead for years.

So he listened carefully to the bland-faced man, and by the time they parted three blocks later, he had acquired a new name, an American passport, a one-way ticket to Athens, and orders to go to the bar at the G.B. and wait for contact from a German woman travelling under cover as a young American socialite. Now, here was Blondie, in her double red ruby earrings, looking very Saks Fifth Avenue in her chic black dress and speaking German like a second language instead of the one she was born to.

Owen downed the last of his drink and signalled the waiter for another. He noticed Blondie looking at him. Her expression was uncertain, and for a moment he thought she was going to interrupt whatever the German was saying. But when Owen's eyes met hers, she turned away. She repeated the same performance a few minutes later, and finally she made her move. The German was digging into his pocket to pay the bill when Blondie made a clear, but silent decision. Her voice floated across the room:

'*Entschuldigen Sie mich bitte.*' (Excuse me, please, I think I see someone I know.)

Without waiting for the German to reply, she stood up and came towards Owen's table. Owen watched her long, slender legs moving across the room with the kind of graceful strides she was supposed to have learned back at Miss Polly's Prep in Boston, or maybe New York. He started to get up as she approached him.

'Pardon me,' she began, all American now. 'Aren't you—' Then she answered her own unfinished question. 'No, I'm afraid I've made a mistake.' There was just the right touch of embarrassment in her voice, just the right shade of emphasis on the correct word. 'I thought you were someone I met another *time*.'

When contact was not expected, as in Brussels that morning, the person making contact was required to give the whole phrase as identification. But when contact was prearranged, as in this case, Owen had to reply.

'I'm sorry I'm not who you thought I was,' he said. 'But do you have to go now?'

She flashed the sweet smile, and for just a moment her hand lingered on the table. 'My friend is waiting for me. I'm sorry I bothered you.'

'Not at all.'

So, just like that she walked into, and out of, his life. Owen and half a dozen other men watched her exit from the bar. Like the others, Owen was smiling, but not for the same reasons. Her physical charms had not escaped him, but he was even more impressed by the skilful way she had dropped the small, folded piece of paper unseen on his table. Without taking his eyes off the door, he lifted his glass with one hand and dropped the other into his pocket. The hand that came out of the pocket was holding his cigarettes. He lit one and settled back to finish his drink.

It was dark when Owen left the hotel twenty minutes later. The open cafés in the square across the street had filled with people, mostly couples, as oblivious to the bright spring flowers and gently rustling trees as they were to the noise of the city around them. Hotel waiters in white jackets balanced their trays overhead and plunged into the traffic, an occupational hazard when you have paying customers on both sides of the street. A warm breeze touched Owen's face, like the hand of a gentle woman, and for a moment he allowed himself to wish that the meeting with Blondie had been a little less professional, a little less brief. Then he plunged into the traffic after the waiters. He bisected the square at an angle and came out facing the American Express office across a wide avenue. He stopped at a kiosk for a newspaper, glanced at the headlines, then crossed the avenue into Ermou Street. He walked slowly, his hands in his pockets, just another tourist on the lookout for a good taverna with *bouzouki* music and gay *syrtaki* dancing. After a block or two, he made a left turn, then a quick right into the darker, less travelled Petraki Street.

There, stopping to light a cigarette by a shop window, he read the message:

8 Kiristou St. Tomorrow 8 am Ask for icons, St Paul.

Owen moved away from the shop window and headed on down the street. As he walked, he tore the paper into tiny bits and threw them into a sewer.

three

Breakfast brought a chink in the Grande Bretagne's armour of elegance – a pot of Nescafé. Room service offered a choice of Greek or American coffee, and Owen opted for the latter. He liked nothing better after dinner than the thick, bittersweet Greek coffee, with a side of Metaxa brandy, but he preferred something a little milder to start the day. At least the Nescafé was steaming hot.

He poured a cup and settled back in bed to study the maze of lines indicating broad avenues and twisting side streets that called itself a map of Athens. He didn't remember Kiristou Street, and it took him a good ten minutes to locate his destination in the Plaka, the old town section of Athens that rambles up the slopes of the Acropolis. He glanced at his watch and decided to walk. The sight of the Acropolis sitting over the city in the morning sun, or at any time of day for that matter, was one that never palled.

After a shower and shave, Owen left the hotel and headed through Syntagma Square, the same direction he had taken the night before. The cafés under the trees were empty now, and the fleet-footed waiters had disappeared, along with the hand holders and the romantic lighting of the square by night. Apollo was kind to the Greeks at this time of year, allowing a gentle breeze to take the edge off his bright morning sun. Later, the day would be warm, a hint of summer. In the distance, the pure Greek air gathered into a visible white haze, a phenomenon Owen had observed in only two other parts of the world – the faraway highlands of Scotland, where the air was sweet and clean, and in a different form over the

23

industrial megalopolis that runs south from Boston on America's east coast. Through the haze, he could see the tops of mountains where people still lived as they had for centuries. But here in the city, beyond the colourful square, daylight unmasked the night-time sparkle of neon signs and cast a harsh light on the unimaginative architecture of the postwar building boom. Traffic was buzzing along the busy avenue, and the air was full of the sounds of a modern city getting a start on the day.

Ahead of him lay the Plaka and an abrupt change of pace – primitive whitewashed houses and shoebox buildings, nestled together like children's blocks along narrow, twisting streets that were hardly more than alleys. At night, the Plaka was full of music and people and bright, garish lights, like Greenwich Village or the King's Road. At this time of day, however, there were only occasional signs that people actually lived here – a woman in a kerchief shaking a rug from a second-storey window, a pair of children laughing and kicking pebbles on their way to school – but basically, the old town was deserted.

Owen passed the Orthodox cathedral at Plateia Mitropoleos and turned left into Mnisikleos Street, leaving modern Athens behind. In front of him, the narrow street ascended the hillside in a series of broad steps and plateaux. Here, the only sign of life was a stray cat observing the siesta early in a bright patch of sunlight.

At the top of the steps, a path skirted the ruins of the Agora and led around to the entrance of the Acropolis, which was hidden from view here by its own steep slope. But Owen was not out to commune with the ancient gods. A block before the steps began their ascent, he turned right into Kiristou Street.

The building at number eight was ordinary enough, sandwiched between a *souvlaki* stand and a tiny hotel. A sign over the door read *Theodorous Likas, Souvenirs*. The shop itself was dark and quiet, like the others on the street, but Owen tried the door and found it unlocked. He paused for a moment in the doorway to let his eyes adjust after the bright sunlight, and he heard the voice before he saw the speaker.

'*Kalimera.*'

'Good morning,' Owen replied.

A small, stocky man came into focus. He was probably fifty, with a thick head of curly black hair and the sun-leathered face of a Greek fisherman, and he was looking at Owen across a counter-top cluttered with cheap reproductions of ancient sculpture and mass-produced, 'hand-painted' pottery. On the wall behind him was a picture of King Constantine and his Danish bride.

Owen absorbed all of this in a single glance as he approached the counter. 'I wonder if you could help me,' he said affably. 'I'm looking for icons of St Paul.'

A broad smile broke over the suntanned face, a boyish grin full of the camaraderie of a shared secret. Clearly, Likas was not Owen's contact. He was another innocent, one of thousands around the world who were called on from time to time to estab-lish a convenient one-shot cover for something they knew nothing about. Blind faith. Unquestioned devotion to flag and country. But whose flag? Whose country? They didn't always know, and it wasn't Owen's job to enlighten them. An image of Blondie flashed into his mind. She was surely no innocent, and that was another point for her side. Owen feared nothing more than the idealistic zeal of a rank amateur out to serve his country.

'You will find what you are looking for upstairs,' the Greek said in slow, carefully pronounced English.

Owen followed his gesture to a flight of narrow wooden stairs that led to the upper floor. The door at the top was open a crack, and Owen assumed it was not left that way accidentally.

'Go on,' Likas urged him. 'I haven't seen him, but I know he is up there.'

He is up there. That evened the odds a bit. On the other hand, if the good *kyrie* hadn't seen him, he had no way of knowing how many hims there were.

Owen unbuttoned his jacket and he started up the steps, feeling for the revolver he carried nose down in his belt. When he reached the top, he pushed the door slowly back against the wall. The room beyond was heavily shuttered. It ran the full length of the shop, with barely enough headroom for a grown man. The shapeless shadows along one wall were packing crates. In the centre of the room was a table with two chairs, and at the far end, a doorway outlined by a narrow strip of light, probably connecting by outside stairs to the street behind the shop.

More important, there was a man standing behind the table. He was only a silhouette against the shuttered window, a man of average height, slim, otherwise featureless.

Owen noticed an odour of dust and disuse as he crossed the threshold and closed the door quietly behind him. The other man spoke to him out of the darkness.

'Good morning, Owen.'

The voice struck a note in Owen's memory, but he couldn't pin it down. 'Are you allergic to light, or what?' he said.

'Just cautious,' the man replied without moving away from the window. 'Come closer. Let me see your face.'

Owen didn't answer. For a moment he stayed where he was, calculating the distances between himself and the other man. Then, slowly, he moved away from the door and around the table, until he was facing the dark figure at arm's length. He reached for the shutter and opened it just enough to let a beam of light split the room and give shape to the unseen face. And when he had seen it, he was not amused.

'Macklin, you bastard,' he said coldly and snapped the shutter back into place.

Howard Macklin was some kind of junior assistant at the US Embassy in Athens, or had been the last time Owen had seen him. That was where you looked for the professionals, among the junior-grade officers. The big fellows were too busy doing what they were supposed to be doing to get much involved with dirty tricks. Or maybe they just didn't want to get any mud on their starched shirts and diplomatic sashes.

Macklin had two regular sources of income Owen knew of and had managed to keep them from knowing about each other. One paycheque came from the US Army, intelligence branch, the same boys who dreamed up the idea of stuffing empty whisky bottles with anti-communist propaganda and dropping them into the Danube, where currents would pick them up and sweep them behind the Iron Curtain. The idea was the local peasants would fish them out of the water, read the message and rise up in revolt.

The other came from Her Majesty's Secret Service, Britain's MI6. Probably Macklin ran a little freelance operation on the side. Of all the people Owen didn't trust, Howard Macklin was high on the list. You could never be quite sure who he was working for. Owen understood him all too well.

'That's not a friendly greeting for an old friend,' Macklin was saying.

'You're lucky I didn't kill you. Cigarette?' Owen produced a pack of Greek Papastrados.

Macklin declined in favour of his own filtertips, lit up and held a match to a small oil lamp on the table. The lamp was a cheap copy of a museum piece, and Owen smiled as the flickering light cast deep shadows over the room. 'Aren't we carrying secrecy a bit far?' he said as he lowered himself into a chair.

Macklin sat down on the other side of the table. 'Maybe. But this light will never be seen from the outside. The overhead might be.'

Owen conceded the point, though he doubted that floodlights would be noticed outside with bright sunlight bathing the white-washed walls that surrounded them. Macklin, he noticed with some satisfaction, was acquiring the beginnings of a middle-aged bulge. His hair was thinner, too.

The American had the kind of face security agents are supposed to have. You could spend the night drinking with him and not remember what he looked like the next day. He wore his hair short and his suits darkly conservative, but half of Athens knew at least vaguely what he was. On reflection, Owen decided the precautions of this meeting weren't so overdone after all. He certainly didn't want to be seen in public all pal-sy with the US Army or MI6.

Owen drew on his cigarette. 'All right Macklin what do you want from me?'

'I don't want anything from you. I have something for you.' Macklin produced a leather pouch but left it lying unopened on the table between them. 'We're working the same side of the street this time,' he added with a smile.

'Whose street?'

'Yours. I'm here for your man Simon.'

27

Owen shrugged.

'He told me to tell you, "the time is now".'

Owen didn't know Simon, at least not by that name, but he did recognize the variation on the code – and the street Macklin was talking about.

Macklin produced a deck of playing cards and turned up a pair of red kings. Owen smiled to himself as he thought of Macklin trying to figure out the signal. 'All right, I'm listening,' he said with a curt nod.

Macklin stubbed out his cigarette halfway to the filter and immediately lit another from the flame of the lamp. It was an annoying habit of his, like the habit of people who take non-fattening sweetners in their coffee, then order chocolate mousse. 'You're being put on special assignment,' he said at last. 'It's top secret.'

'Most of my assignments are.' Owen started to put out his own cigarette, then thought better of it. He decided to keep it burning right down to the end.

'I'm only repeating what Simon told me,' Macklin insisted. 'This assignment is so secret that your identity must be hidden even from your own people. I gather that's why they're using me instead of one of your own couriers.'

'Among my own people, my identity is fairly well established,' Owen said.

'Is it?' Macklin shot back. Then, with a wave of dismissal and a glance at his watch, he went on. 'It doesn't matter any more. In another ten minutes, Richard Owen will have been dead for twelve hours.'

Owen didn't comment. He smoked his cigarette and waited for Macklin to explain.

'For the record, you left Brussels yesterday morning, flew to Oslo and were checked through customs, but you met with an unfortunate accident on the way to your hotel. You died two hours later in a local hospital.'

'Very neat,' Owen said. He wondered who was the lucky bloke who got to stand in for him.

'It was a rented car – rented by you, of course.'

'Of course.'

'The point is, it's all official. Richard Owen is *dead*. The post mortems are in motion. Your files have been stamped closed, or they soon will be. Anyone trying to trace your movements will come to – you should pardon the expression – an abrupt dead end. Do you understand?'

'Certainly.' Owen understood, all right. Someone, somewhere, was going to a lot of trouble to cover his tracks.

'Good.'

Macklin was in charge now and enjoying it. He wore authority like a man who was not born to it but wished he had been. Owen refused him the satisfaction of questions. He knew silence would produce more answers.

'You leave Athens this afternoon,' Macklin was saying. He opened the leather pouch and handed an envelope across the table. Inside, Owen found a Swedish passport made out to a fur trader by the name of Lars Hansson. There were also some letters, a driver's licence and a wallet-size photo of a pretty young woman with two boys.

'Your family,' Macklin said.

Finally, there was an airplane ticket, one-way from Athens to London. Departure date, that afternoon.

'I've taken care of everything you'll need,' Macklin went on. 'When you return to the G.B., you'll find new clothes, all from shops in Stockholm – luggage, shaving gear, the works. There's even a novel that's all the rage in Sweden right now.'

'Very thorough.'

'I'll clean up after you've gone. Everything you brought into Athens stays behind. You must take nothing with you that might identify you as Richard Owen. Nothing. I trust you'll see to that?'

But Owen knew he didn't trust at all. The procedure he was explaining in such singsong detail was kindergarten stuff. 'And when I reach London?'

'Go to the Colony Hotel in Piccadilly. After that, your guess is as good as mine.'

four

Franz Heinemann twisted in his chair to see the clock on the wall behind him. Then he turned, glaring, to the younger man beside him.

'Find out what's happening,' he said.

It was not a request, nor even a simple directive. It was an order, delivered with all the courtesy of a military command.

Hans Muller jumped out of his chair and hurried across the departure lounge to the desk, where a man and woman in brown uniforms had finished checking in passengers and were looking as bored as those who were waiting to leave Vienna. As Muller approached, the uniformed bodies snapped to attention. Their faces were all smiles now, their manner sympathetic, if edgy.

Heinemann caught snatches of the conversation: 'So very sorry ... unfortunately, can't be helped ... is the maestro uncomfortable? ... A lounge for our VIP passengers ...'

If the lounge were truly reserved for men of distinction, Heinemann might have been interested. But airlines calculated personal worth in numbers of miles flown. Very important had nothing to do with superiority or birthright; anyone could qualify.

VIP lounge? Ridiculous! It wasn't worth the effort it took to move.

Heinemann's thoughts slipped back to an earlier time, when travelling had been a pleasure. Trains were slower, but they left on time; and they ran separate cars for people of class and the rest.

Air travel had changed all of that. A matter of mass transportation – with a purpose, perhaps, but leaving no place for passengers such as himself. First-class passage today offered little more than free cocktails and a slightly wider seat. The airlines were too impersonal, everyone treated the same. 'Where are you going, sir? To New York? Here you are.' Zip, zip, zip. The computer handed over your ticket. 'I'm sorry, sir, but we'll have to open your bags. And if you'll step this way?' Zip, zip. The machines told them you didn't have a gun in your pocket or a bomb in the sole of your shoe.

Of course he had no gun in his pocket, no bomb in his shoe! How dared they *question* that?

Yes, Heinemann still preferred to travel by train, but trains didn't run between Austria and America. A train couldn't get him to seven cities across the United States in the short span of ten days. And American trains, he had heard, offered fewer comforts than airplanes.

He had no choice but to fly.

But he did draw the line at one thing: the preflight inspection that was yet another sign of inefficiency, of inability to control a gang of international thugs who understood power better than the world's leaders. 'I will not have you putting my Stradivarius on that conveyor belt,' he had asserted in a tone that left little doubt about the life left in his old bones. The young woman who worked for the airport looked terrified, but she had agreed; and she handled his violin as gently as if it had been a bomb.

Muller returned to his seat and said, 'It won't be long now, Maestro.'

'That's what they said twenty minutes ago.'

'This time I think they mean it.'

'I don't pay you for your opinion,' Heinemann replied. 'I pay you to get things done. We're late. There's no excuse for that.'

'It seems it's a question of safety—'

'Safety? Nonsense! They appeal to our fear to cover their own ineptitude.' He glanced at Muller. 'I suppose it's not your fault.'

Muller started to speak, but Heinemann cut him off.

'Never mind. If we must wait, we will put the time to good use. Give me the itinerary.'

Muller produced a sheet of paper, unfolded it, handed it to the old man.

Heinemann took it without a word, and looked it over with a critical eye. His first stop was in New York City, a recital at Fisher Hall. Then he would go on to Chicago, Denver, Los Angeles. He would play in Houston and Atlanta. And in Washington, DC. At the White House, with all the trappings of a command performance. That, after all, was the prime reason for making this trip.

He glanced up at Muller. 'There's no hotel listed for Washington,' he said. 'You know I insist on advance approval.'

'Well, sir—' Muller cleared his throat. 'The President intended to give you the use of Blair House, which is the official guest residence of—'

'I know what Blair House is. I *don't* understand indecision.'

'It seems there's a scheduling conflict. A visiting prime minister—'

Could there be any choice, Heinemann wondered. World leaders came in two varieties these days: common men elected for mass appeal and dictators who were tougher than hoodlums. There was no strength of will in leadership any more. No character. No high purpose.

He didn't have time to voice the objection further. The uniformed man approached them. He spoke to Muller. 'If you'll follow me, we'll get the maestro settled before the other passengers board.'

Deference, Heinemann thought, was often very close to condescension. Nonetheless, he pulled himself up, took Muller's arm, and followed the uniform across the lobby and into the waiting plane.

It was after ten a.m. in Vienna when Heinemann's plane broke through the clouds and levelled off at 35,000 feet. About the same time in London, Richard Owen left the Colony Hotel on his way to Heathrow Airport.

He had arrived the day before and settled in his room to wait for something, someone – for a small, dark girl with sad eyes, and a shy smile, and set of fresh towels folded over one arm. She was Indian, or possibly Pakistani, and Owen double-locked the door behind her when she was gone. He knew there was clean linen in the bathroom, and the Colony wasn't the kind of hotel where you could expect extra service.

In the folds of the towels, he found what he was looking for, a manila envelope thick with new documents. There was a French passport in the name of André Bouchard, whom the accompanying papers identified as a freelance journalist. There was also an airplane ticket. And a locker key. And the passport photo looked exactly like Owen as he might look in another ten years.

That night, Owen wrapped Lars Hansson's personal belongings in brown paper and took a cab to Waterloo Station. He matched the number on the key against the locker numbers until he found the right one. Inside, he found a worn canvas suitcase. The luggage tag said André Bouchard and gave a Paris address. He swapped his brown paper parcel for the canvas bag and left the station.

He walked back, choosing the scenic route that took him across the Thames, and he stopped on a bridge to admire the view – Parliament standing proud against the lights of the sprawling city. Big Ben was just striking the hour, launching into another round of the familiar Handel tune. He dropped the locker key into the surging black water below.

Owen stopped at a chemist's shop in Charing Cross, then returned to his room, where he dropped the Swedish passport and Hansson's papers into the bathroom sink and set his lighter to them. When the flame died out, he turned both taps on full and watched the ashes disappear down the drain.

Next, he propped the French passport open to the photo page and unwrapped the hair preparations he had bought from the chemist. And the next morning, the French journalist André Bouchard left the hotel unseen. At Heathrow, he boarded TWA's morning flight from Vienna, bound for New York City.

five

Richard Owen made his way through the crowded TWA terminal at Kennedy Airport, stopped at a news-stand for a copy of the *New York Times*, and headed for the glass doors that led to the taxi stand outside. New York offered its own brand of culture shock for incoming travellers used to the old-world manners of Europe. In London, they formed polite queues wherever there was any waiting to be done, a nice orderly version of first come, first served. But here it was more like survival of the fittest, a tough game played with pushing, shoving crowds of glassy-eyed professionals who tossed out rude remarks from behind the I-don't-give-a-damn veneer of their stone faces with as much grace, and about as much compassion, as a toreador moving in for the final thrust.

Richard Owen loved New York. More than any other city in the world, he thought, this one had a heart of its own – a cold heart, maybe, but one that never stopped beating, even in the dead of night. As he emerged from the terminal, he took one look at the tangle of people fighting it out for a firm grip on a passing door handle and knew he had arrived in the New World. It was raining lightly, but dark clouds over the unseen skyscrapers of Manhattan threatened a real downpour. He sidestepped a young couple who were looking in vain for a porter and threw himself into the mêlée. Then a yellow Checker cab came to a short stop beside him, and he grabbed the door, claiming it for his own.

The driver leaned across the front seat and wound down the window. 'Where you going, buddy?'

'Manhattan.'

The cabbie nodded and pushed open the front door for Owen to lift his bag in.

These days, Owen had heard, you had to ask the driver's permission before you got into the cab. They were required by law to take you anywhere you wanted to go, as long as it was within the city limits, but Owen knew the law didn't mean much and that it wasn't easy to find a cab if you were heading for some outlying district – or, worse, a ghetto.

'To the Regency,' he said.

This was a privately owned cab, and it didn't have its bullet-proof partition. One good thing about those partitions: they made driver-passenger conversations next to impossible. And without that protection for himself, Owen could only hope this driver wasn't the chatty type. He didn't feel much like a harangue on New York traffic, the Mets, or what a lousy job the mayor was doing. Whoever the mayor was now.

He settled into the back seat and picked up the *Times* while the driver nosed the cab around a cloverleaf and pulled out on to the Van Wyck Expressway. He scanned the headlines on the front page, then turned inside. Halfway through the first section, he stopped short. It was a small item, buried below the fold, and Owen might have missed it if the name Howard Macklin hadn't jumped out at him.

ATHENS (AP) – Howard Macklin, 35, assistant first secretary of the US Embassy here, was accidentally drowned yesterday afternoon when he fell from a yacht in the Saronic Gulf off the Attic coast of Greece.

The yacht belonged to friends of Macklin who said the American official was known to be a poor swimmer. His body was discovered several hours later, washed ashore near Lagonissi, 20 miles south of here.

So, Macklin dead, one convenient day after he met with Owen on a double red alert. And the verdict was death by accidental drowning. Owen thought of the bland-faced man in Brussels. Was he dead, too? And the Indo-Pakistani maid? And Blondie?

'Rest in peace,' he murmured as he folded the newspaper and tossed it aside.

'What's that?' the driver asked.

'Nothing.'

Without meaning to, Owen found himself staring at the driver's hack licence in its plastic case on the dashboard in front of him. Anything was an improvement on the passing landscape: Queens fogged in under a drizzling sky. Suddenly, the licence came into focus and roused him out of his thoughts with a jolt. The name: Aaron Rosenberg. The picture: a round-faced man with thinning black hair and a good sixty years to his credit. Owen's eyes swung back to the driver. He was at least twenty-five years younger than the man in the picture, with wide shoulders and a strong neck. His hair was blond, his eyes pale blue, his features sharp – a perfect stereotype, out of Hollywood war movies. From the looks of things, Owen thought the driver's father might have led Aaron's father off to the ovens.

And where, thought Owen, does he think he's taking me?

Then he noticed something else. The driver's hands were placed firmly on top of the steering wheel, and his shirt sleeves, extending beyond the cuffs of the plaid wool jacket, were fastened with a pair of flashy red cufflinks. He was studying Owen through the rearview mirror, and the hint of a smile crossed his face.

'You happen to have the time?' he said matter-of-factly.

'I have two o'clock,' Owen replied. It was more like ten a.m.

'Two o'clock,' the driver repeated. 'Bad time to go into Manhattan. Lots of traffic right now.'

'No doubt,' Owen said.

The driver was German, all right. His English was good, but Owen detected a distinct Prussian tone in the accent. His mind scanned an imaginary map of the Fatherland and settled on Berlin.

'Where did you send Aaron Rosenberg?' he asked. 'Argentina?'

'That's close enough.' The German smiled. 'I slipped up on the licence. Sorry.'

Owen didn't return the smile. 'Forget it,' he said. But he filed the mistake away in his own memory bank.

'I'm Simon, by the way,' the other man went on, extending his hand over the back seat without taking his eyes off the road. He didn't say Simon – he said See-mone, giving it a French pronunciation. But Owen knew the French-sounding *Simon* was a common German name, like Smith or Jones in America. 'The double red ends with me,' Simon ended. 'I'm authorized to tell you why we've brought you here.'

Owen gave the hand a perfunctory shake and waited for Simon to explain. But for the moment, Simon was busy with the cab. An accident on the road ahead had narrowed Manhattan-bound traffic to one, slow-moving lane. Simon was in the wrong lane. He waited briefly for a driver to let him in, then, that failing, he stepped down on the gas and forced his way into a small gap between a Volkswagen and a long black limousine. The limousine driver came down hard on his brakes, setting off a discordant symphony behind him. In that moment, Owen caught a glimpse of a small white-haired man sitting with a companion in the back seat of the limousine. The man's face was calm, even cold, untouched by the racket around him. And Owen recognized him as the famous violinist, Franz Heinemann.

Simon nosed the cab around and took his place in the long line of traffic. 'If I didn't know better, I'd swear I'd been doing this all my life.' Then he was quiet again, drawing his thoughts back to the subject at hand. When he finally spoke, there was a trace of amusement in his voice. 'We're sending you out with your garden shears,' he said. 'We want you to pick us a sunflower. That's the operative code name, by the way – *Sunflower*.'

Owen sat in the back seat listening to what Simon was saying, and as he listened, the German began to come up in his estimation. He was a friendly sort, with an easy manner and a ready smile. But Owen observed an edge of cold reality in Simon's pale blue eyes. He began to get a different picture of the man, a kind of x-ray view of a body where all the nerve endings connected up with a stainless steel spine. The perfect stereotype. All he needed was the long leather *Uberzieher*, with a pair of brass lightning bolts stapled into the neckband.

They were crossing the Triboro Bridge, with its postcard view of the city. But Owen didn't notice. His attention was fully focused on the words coming over the seat.

'Sunflower,' Simon was saying, 'is our code name for Anne Easton. I assume you know who she is.'

'Of course,' Owen replied. A bit of an understatement. Anne Easton was four years old and an international celebrity. In newspaper parlance, hot copy – a household word, a real charmer, a tiny waif of a girl with big brown eyes and a dimpled smile that rarely failed to produce a smile in return.

She was also the only child of the President of the United States.

Yes, Owen knew who Anne Easton was, but Simon told him anyway: 'Matt Easton's daughter.'

Owen lit a cigarette. 'So what's the job? Protection? I don't do protection.'

Simon chuckled. 'Hardly. But it's not what you'd probably consider your usual line of work.' He glanced at Owen's reflection in the rearview mirror. 'Ever read *Mary Poppins*? If you haven't, you probably ought to.'

Simon raised a hand for silence as they approached the toll booths on the Manhattan side of the bridge. He eased the cab into a correct change lane, tossed three quarters into the basket, then raised his window and followed the signs towards the East River Drive.

His amusement had faded. 'You'll need to know more about Anne Easton than just who she is,' he said when they had pulled free of the bridge traffic.

Owen drew on his cigarette. His face was calm, his hand steady, but his mind was racing ahead. He thought he knew what Simon was going to say. An impossible challenge thrown up against all good sense. And he smiled.

'Why?' he said. 'What is it you want me to do?'

'We want you to kidnap her,' Simon replied, as calmly as if he were suggesting a good place for lunch. 'We want you to kidnap President Easton's daughter.'

six

The apartment where Simon dropped Owen was on Riverside Drive. It was spacious and tastefully furnished, with plenty of comfortable chairs. A man's apartment, and a good place to hole up for a while. Not quite the Regency, where Owen had planned to spend his first night back in New York. Better than the Regency. More private.

Furthermore, the kitchen was well stocked and the bar offered all the choice Owen wanted – three fifths of Glenfiddich and a fifth of Courvoisier VSOP.

He dropped his things in the bedroom and was pouring himself a scotch when he heard the sound, from behind – the sudden creak of a floorboard muffled by thick carpet.

His body tensed and his hand moved to the gun at his waist, but he didn't turn around. He stood motionless, seeming to study the lithograph hanging over the bar. Then he relaxed and reached for another glass.

'Not as light on your feet as you once were,' he said without turning around.

The other man came up behind him. 'How did you know it was me?'

'Not as observant, either,' Owen replied. He gave a nod to the lithograph, which was neatly framed under glass, reflecting back two faces. Then he turned to look at the man – at the faded jeans, the old cap, the day's growth of beard. He raised his glass. 'To my old friend, Graham,' he said. He tasted the scotch, then asked, 'What can I get for you?'

They settled themselves in the living room, where heavy curtains closed out the bleak day and muted the steady sound of rain against the windows. Soft lamplight gave the room a dark glow.

But there was nothing cosy about the look on Owen's face.

He lit a cigarette and leaned back, staring at Graham across the table between them. 'So,' he said, 'you want me to kidnap President Easton's daughter. *Why?*'

'I thought you might ask.' Graham picked up his drink but didn't taste it. Anger flashed in his eyes. 'I can't tell you everything,' he said. 'I'm not authorized to.'

Owen's face softened, almost smiled. 'You're not authorized to? Or you don't trust me to know?'

Graham looked up sharply. '*Should* I trust you?'

Owen shrugged. 'As far as I know, my loyalties have never been suspect.'

The flash of anger again. 'Your loyalties, Owen, are nonexistent. You're right, you've never betrayed us – but that's not the point. You'll do it because it's impossible, and that's good enough.'

Owen raised his glass. 'And you'll trust me to do it because no one else is sufficiently foolish to try – or brash enough to succeed.'

It was not a boast, but a simple statement of fact. Owen smiled when Graham failed to reply. He drew on his cigarette. 'What *can* you tell me?' he said.

Graham looked at him for a moment. Then he got up and began to pace the room. His face was troubled, his eyes still angry, his forehead creased into a deep frown.

'We have a security leak,' he began. 'Someone passing classified data to the Soviet Union. Someone inside the Agency, someone high-level.' He turned and caught Owen's eyes in a direct gaze. '*Very* high-level,' he added. 'We know that from the nature of the data passed.'

Owen nodded but didn't comment. This was not startling news. It happened from time to time. The CIA had a section full of agents who sought out just such potential traitors around the world. So did every other intelligence agency. He stubbed out his cigarette and picked up his drink as Graham resumed his pacing.

'In the beginning,' Graham said, 'we had four suspects. We set up tests for them, each of them individually. They passed, all of them, with no margin for doubt. None of them is the leak.' He nodded to himself as if to confirm the truth of the statement. 'That meant we had to look to a fifth man, someone we'd not considered in the beginning because of his position. It was unthinkable! He's a man with *instant* access to the Oval Office – *second only to the President himself.*'

Owen didn't move. He stared at Graham across the rim of his glass, his expression hovering somewhere between amusement and disbelief.

'You're joking.'

Graham shook his head.

The amusement faded. '*Ed Nichols?*'

'Ed Nichols,' Graham confirmed. He looked down at Owen, his eyes now cold with anger. 'Ed Nichols, the Director of the CIA.'

Owen leaned back in his chair to let this news sink in. No wonder the double red . . . No wonder Graham was upset! The man they all worked for, the head of the CIA. That much was bad enough. But Ed Nichols was a lot more than that. He was the President's campaign strategist. His chief policy adviser. His hatchetman.

More, even, than that. He was the President's best friend.

'Touchy,' Owen said.

'Touchy? It's *dynamite*!'

Graham picked up his glass and stared down into the amber liquid, swirling it angrily in his hand. The clinking of ice formed a counterpoint to the rain beating against the windows. There was no other sound in the room. Then he raised the drink to his mouth and finished it off in a swallow. When he looked back at Owen, his face was calm once again, his anger under control.

'The President, of course, will require absolute proof,' he said. 'He's not going to take my word for this. Or yours. And that brings us back to his daughter.'

Now, Owen saw the connection. The trap baited with an irresistible lure.

'Yes,' Graham confirmed, 'the kidnapping is Nichols' test. Anne Easton, ostensibly in enemy hands. Nichols will have to find her.' The hint of a smile appeared in Graham's eyes. 'We'll give him leads to work on. Our own leads. They will all prove abortive. Confusing. Even disastrous. We must force him into a corner of desperation. We must force him to *act*.'

'To contact the other side,' Owen nodded slowly. 'It's audacious,' he said, 'and appealing for that. But it's also extremely dangerous.'

'Precisely. It *must* be audacious. It has to be something that affects the President directly and personally. With his own daughter missing, he can hardly fail to take interest. He won't accept vague reports passed to him through the bureaucracy or various levels of White House staff. He'll insist on exact information, as it develops, straight from Nichols himself. Furthermore, he'll accept no excuses. He'll permit no mistakes. He will require nothing less than a total success. Nichols, of course, will know this. When failure occurs, as it will, he won't be able to write it off as a rare bad job and hope to do better next time. He cannot fail on this. Everything he values will be at stake. His relationship with the President. His job. His power.'

'Not to say Anne Easton.'

'Yes, of course.' Graham shrugged. 'That, too. In any case, when all else fails – and we will see that it does – he will have just one choice left. His friends behind the curtain. He'll *have* to go to them.'

Owen nodded. An excellent plan. The trap baited with a crisis so personally threatening to the President, it would have priority over everything else.

And for Owen, the ultimate challenge. A greater risk than he had ever known. He drank his scotch, his mind already shifting from motives to operations. *How* was always of far greater interest than *why*. *How* in response to *never*. Graham was right. Owen didn't really care who was working for whom. He had to know because knowing prevented mistakes, but if he kidnapped Anne Easton it would be for one reason.

Because it couldn't be done, he would do it.

'It will have to be done my way,' he said.

'Naturally,' Graham replied. 'If I knew how to do it myself, I wouldn't need you.'

'And without *any* harm to the girl.'

'That goes without saying. Anne Easton cannot be hurt. She must never be in any real danger. The same goes for the people around her. Family, servants, staff, Secret Service. None of them can be hurt.'

Owen smiled. 'You mean, don't kill off the President in the process.'

'I'd rather you didn't.'

Graham hardly needed to say so. There were few things Owen believed in absolutely, almost nothing beyond his own commitment to a quality job. He expected the same from others.

But he had no delusions that his cause was any more just than another. He didn't *have* a cause, just a job – the same job he'd have had if he worked for the other side. He preferred the side he was on for one reason: he needed breathing space, and in Moscow he wouldn't get it.

Nonetheless, he did believe in one thing. The freedom he required for himself was not a privilege he, alone, deserved; it had to be granted to others as a matter of self-preservation. That was the problem in Russia. *Special* privilege could always be reversed. Without a broad base, freedom had little value. People had to be allowed to choose their own way of life and live it. And innocence was one choice.

The killing of innocents, Owen believed, was too often the easy way out. An intelligent person could find a different solution. Killing became an option only when the victim, like Owen himself, had forfeited innocence by choice. And a four-year-old child, by definition, was strictly off limits. And, in this case, so was her father.

'I do have one requirement,' Graham said.

Owen raised an eyebrow.

'Once you have her, you must move her out of the country.'

Owen's gaze became steadily more incredulous. He was thinking about the White House, with its iron fence, its electronic security systems, its army of agents and special police. Somehow he had to break through all of that to kidnap the President's daughter. *Then* he had to sneak her across a well-guarded US border!

'Don't make it too easy for me,' he said. 'I might get bored.'

Graham smiled. 'We wouldn't want that.'

'It's a tough order.'

'I know. The toughest I've ever given you. But this thing has to look international. Otherwise, Nichols will have no reason to believe the Russians could help him.'

Owen nodded.

'You can take her wherever you want,' Graham said, 'as long as it's in Greece.'

'Why Greece?'

'Because I have people there I can trust in case you need help.'

'All right, so I take her to Greece. Then what do I do?'

'You wait until you receive my signal, at which time we'll meet, you'll turn the girl over to me, and I'll take her home. In the meantime, you do nothing – just keep her out of sight. It will be at least two weeks, maybe more.'

Two weeks . . . Simon wasn't kidding about Mary Poppins.

But Owen knew where he would go. A nice little holiday on the Cretan Sea. What he didn't know was how he was going to get there, with the President's daughter.

'What about the false leads?' he said.

'Simon will handle those. As soon as Simon gets here, we can go over what you will need. Simon will be your contact with me, by the way. After I leave here today, I don't want to see you again until it's time to bring Sunflower home.'

Owen smiled. 'You make me feel unloved.' He got up to refill his drink.

'Yes, well, don't forget, you're supposed to be dead.'

'It's not something I'm likely to forget,' Owen replied. He poured the scotch, recapped the bottle, turned back to Graham. 'I'm only sorry I didn't go to the funeral. Tom Sawyer rushed to Aunt Polly's arms.'

'You'd have run into Aunt Polly's switch if you'd tried it.' Graham smiled. 'It was a quiet affair, actually. Hardly anyone there.'

'Pity.'

'Yes.' The doorbell rang, and Graham looked up. 'That should be Simon now. Let him in, will you?'

Owen crossed over to the door and pushed aside the peephole. It was Simon, still wearing the plaid jacket and carrying a black attaché case. Owen flipped the lock and let him in. The door moved silently on recently oiled hinges.

'How's the apartment?' Simon asked once he was inside.

He was tall and thin but powerfully built, and Owen could see the clear line of a scar jagging down to his eye from the temple on the left side of his head.

'Comfortable,' he replied.

Simon nodded. 'We tried to accommodate all your needs,' he added, noticing the drink in Owen's hand. 'Unfortunately, the little redhead next door is away for a few weeks.'

'And not by chance.'

'No, not by chance. She broke her legs. Skiing. A collision with another skier.'

Simon gave him a thin smile that stopped just short of his pale blue eyes. It was more than insincere; it was menacing. The scar showed red against his fair skin and blond hair.

A scar to match on the other side, Owen thought, and Simon wouldn't need flashy cufflinks to prove he was in on a double red alert. He was glad to see that the German walked instead of goosestepping.

Simon dropped the attaché case on the floor beside a chair and sat down. He looked at Graham. But Graham was looking at Owen.

'You can have whatever you want,' he said.' I mean that quite literally. Anything. *Carte blanche.* You have unlimited credit in terms
of resources – personnel, false papers, technical services, anything.'

'Money?' Owen asked.

'As much as you need.'

'Thirty thousand dollars in cash.'

'No more?'

'That's pin money,' Owen said. 'I'll let you know later how
much more it will cost. Meantime, thirty thousand in a combination of large and small bills. No new money. Nothing traceable.
The total package compact enough to carry in a money belt.'

Graham nodded to Simon. It would be done.

'I'll need a lot more than money,' Owen said.

Simon pulled the black case up on to his lap and flipped open
the locks. 'This should be a good start,' he said. 'Our files on Anne
Easton. Everything we know about her from the time she gets up
in the morning until bedtime at night. Names and addresses of
friends she might be expected to visit. Her doctor and dentist.
Some general material on her personal habits – not much for a
four-year-old – but quite a lot on security.' He looked up at Owen.
'Six Secret Service agents on permanent assignment. More as
needed. They work in shifts. It's all there.'

Owen took the files and glanced through them. 'You have good
sources,' he said.

'Excellent sources.'

'They're accurate?'

'Extremely.'

Owen nodded and put the files aside for the time being. He
would read through them carefully later. 'Now,' he said, 'let me
tell you what else I want. The girl isn't my problem. It's the people
around her. *Those* are the files I need. I want everything you can
give me that comes from the Secret Service, and I must have
advance schedules for everyone in the family. Daily.'

Graham glanced at Simon. 'You'll have them.'

'I also want a tap into the White House mail surveillance. Retro-
actively. As far back as you can go without arousing suspicion.'

Graham's forehead creased into a puzzled frown. 'Why?'

Owen shrugged. 'I don't know. If I did, I could tell you exactly what to bring me. Since I don't, I need it all.'

'Can't you be more specific than that?' Graham asked. 'They get seventy-five thousand letters a week at the White House.'

'Then pare it down. Eliminate the fan mail and the hate mail, the photo requests, the autograph requests, and everything on the issues. Eliminate the routine, but bring me everything else.'

Graham looked back at him for a moment, then nodded to Simon.

'Newspapers,' Owen added. 'Both Washington papers, and not two days late in the mail.'

'No problem there,' Graham replied.

'And I'll need to know how big Anne is.'

Graham shrugged. 'She's small for her age.'

'I need to know precisely,' Owen said. 'Her exact height. Her exact weight. Her exact age in months and days.'

Graham nodded. 'Anything else?'

'Yes, one other thing. And it's critical.'

Owen leaned back and lit a cigarette. He was thinking about the risk. Not the risk of his life; he faced that every day. Death was an occupational hazard in this work. But here was something Owen feared more than death – the loss of his personal freedom. And he didn't care to guess the years he would spend in jail if he were *caught* with the President's daughter.

Normally, the CIA gave him sanction to break the law. There were no threats to disavowal. To the contrary, he knew he could count on extraordinary measures to prevent official action against anything he did on assignment.

But this assignment was a big one. It went well beyond the usual realm of the CIA. It was far more dangerous than anything he'd ever been asked to do. And the sanction, obviously, didn't come from Nichols.

He looked at Graham and said, 'Who authorized this?'

Graham shook his head. 'I can't tell you that.'

Owen shrugged. 'Then I must refuse the assignment. I won't take the risk, not on your say alone.'

There was a long moment of silence as the two men looked at

each other across the table between them. Outside, rain continued to beat against the windows. There was no other sound in the room.

Finally, it was Graham who spoke. 'You may be right. I suppose you deserve to know what kind of protection you've got. And you've got it. The highest possible protection. From the President.'

Owen was stunned to silence. Whatever he had expected, it wasn't this! He stared at Graham, his expression running from disbelief to shock.

'The *President*?' he said finally. 'The President has agreed to have his *own daughter kidnapped*? *By the CIA*?'

'The President,' Graham said, 'understands what's at stake.'

'I daresay he does!'

Owen leaned back and took a drink of his scotch. Anne Easton, he thought, was about to learn an extremely valuable lesson. Trust *no one*.

'Well,' he said. 'Is that enough to suit you? Will you do it?'

'Of course I will,' Owen replied. He looked down at his glass, then back up at Graham. And he smiled. 'I just want to be sure I send the bastard a card – next Father's Day.'

seven

Elizabeth Easton felt a sudden shiver of fear, a sense of panic swelling inside her chest and spreading coldly down her back. Like the chill of a fever. No, like waking up in the night and knowing an intruder is there.

She shook it off as she dropped her paintbrush into a jar of turpentine and stepped back from the canvas to study her daughter's face from a different angle. It wasn't right yet. She hadn't caught the smile that was uniquely Anne.

She picked up a rag and started dabbing absently at the paint spots on her fingers, reminding herself that she'd never claimed to be a portrait painter. Her professional work ran mostly to landscapes and still lifes and usually brought five figures at the New York gallery where she sold her work on consignment. But she didn't intend to sell this portrait of her daughter. She was doing it as a gift for her husband to hang in his White House study.

Elizabeth dipped the rag into the turpentine, still trying to shake the sense of foreboding that lingered on after the chill had gone. Parent love, the ultimate vulnerability . . .

Then, suddenly, she realized how quickly the light was fading. It was five o'clock. She pulled off her smock and left the studio, heading for the bedroom she shared with the President of the United States.

An hour later she emerged again, fresh from a hot bath and dressed for a state dinner. Short dark curls framed her face. Brown eyes, full of life, set wide over good cheekbones. Fair skin, a straight nose, and a smile that lit up her face with happiness.

She *was* happy here in the White House – with Matt, with Anne, with her work. Never mind what some people said she neglected . . . With little more than an hour before the official guests arrived, the state rooms of the White House would be bustling with activity. Tables to be set up, linen laid out, fresh flowers and candles arranged. Formal china and silver to be set into place. The chief usher was perfectly able to handle all of that.

The social secretary would take care of last-minute adjustments in the seating charts. The calligrapher would make up new place-cards and programmes as needed. The chef was in charge of preparing an excellent five-course meal.

Elizabeth didn't know what was on the menu tonight. She didn't care who was sitting with whom. The White House was Matt's work, not hers. She would attend the dinner – she would be there with Matt, and she would enjoy it – but for now she had better things to do.

She bypassed the elevator and made her way down the hall to her daughter's room, where she slipped quietly inside.

Time with her daughter, *plenty* of time with her daughter. That was a must every day.

Mrs Haskins, the governess, looked up and smiled. So did Anne. Elizabeth looked down at the round little face surrounded by dark curls, a face so much like her own. Anne was delicate, petite, vulnerable. The sense of foreboding returned. It sharpened.

Dear God, she thought. She would *die* if anything ever happened to Anne . . .

'Do you take much interest in your husband's work, Mrs Nichols?' the senator asked.

Vanessa smiled and glanced across the State Dining Room to the table where her husband was sitting between the Yugoslavian ambassador's wife and a famous columnist.

'Yes, of course,' she replied. 'But beyond generalities, I don't really know what he does.'

It struck her once again that Ed didn't look like a CIA director. Whatever that meant. Grey and distinguished? Small and furtive? Ed Nichols was neither.

He was a big, slightly awkward man with the candid face of a country lawyer, eyes bright behind loose-fitting bifocals in wire frames so old they had come back into style. It was a face quick to smile, suggesting an easy manner, a relaxed view of the world – suggesting a man for whom guile and cunning were as alien as foreign intrigue.

Vanessa smiled. She knew just how deep the apparent innocence ran. Guile and cunning were the staff of her husband's life long before he took over the reins out at Langley. Ever since Matt's first campaign a hundred lifetimes ago. For as long as she'd known him and, probably, long before that.

The senator, mistaking the direction of her smile, returned it. 'A very good answer,' he said. 'The perfect political wife – loyal without knowing too much.'

Dear God! Vanessa took a drink of her wine. Why, she wondered, did so many men who stumped the country defending women's rights still think Washington wives had no existence apart from them? And why did she, a personal friend of the Eastons, always get the worst dinner partners at the White House?

'I'm glad you approve,' she said, avoiding his eyes.

The senator was only slightly more interesting than the presidential assistant – a perfectly dreadful young man – who was

49

seated on her other side. If only Elizabeth would pay some attention to these things!

'But surely your husband shares some of his secrets with you,' the senator persisted.

Vanessa looked at him. 'May I ask you something? Why do you insist upon talking about my *husband's* work?'

The senator didn't reply. Someone on the other side of the table drew his attention away with a question. And since the young assistant was also occupied – thank heavens! – Vanessa took advantage of the chance to finish her soup in peace.

It was eight o'clock. The evening had barely begun. Four more courses. Two more wines. Speeches and toasts and strolling violinists in formal army dress. (Bound to impress the communists, someone would say. One of our crack combat units!)

Vanessa glanced at the head table in its usual place in front of the Adams mantel, under the Lincoln portrait. Elizabeth was chatting easily with the Yugoslavian President, probably in Serbo-Croatian. Elizabeth, stunning as always, and so damn good at these things. And Matt, dark and slender, a naturally elegant man who wore the power of the White House as easily as he wore the well-cut formal clothes.

Vanessa felt a warm surge of affection. Grace and style were part of the Eastons' appeal; and yet she knew their life was seldom as easy as they made it seem.

As she watched, Matt's eyes shifted into the room, scanned the crowd, stopped to look at someone at a table not far away. An expression passed over his face fleetingly – a dropping away of the public mask, a brief glimpse of the private man inside. Then he picked up his wine glass and turned, smiling, back to the guest of honour.

Vanessa frowned. She wasn't sure what it was she had seen in that moment. Was it anger? Suspicion? Hurt? But she did think she knew who the target had been.

Unless she was mistaken, Matt had been looking at *Ed.*

Sam Wycoff, the head of the Secret Service, was working late in his office. He glanced at his watch – eight o'clock – remembered he had promised his wife a movie, and attacked the papers on his desk with new energy.

Promises aside, he couldn't leave until he had approved the security plans for the President's Mexican trip.

The trip was routine, but the security plans were not. Two US businessmen had been kidnapped by terrorists in Mexico in the last year, and an embassy official had barely escaped the same fate. Wycoff, whose main concern was protecting the President, had recommended cancelling the trip. But the State Department, whose concerns were broader than that, wouldn't have it.

That's just what the terrorists want, they had argued at State. This trip is routine, but important. They would love to see us back out . . .

So would I, Wycoff thought.

But the President didn't worry much about personal threats. He had sided with State. He was going. And it was Wycoff's job to make sure he came back.

At the same time, Wycoff initialed another plan, assigning two special agents to the six who made up Anne Easton's Secret Service detail. Then he returned to the more pressing problems of the President's trip.

At eight o'clock Richard Owen picked up a new batch of mail Simon had sent over earlier in the day. There were hundreds of letters, all with one thing in common. They were addressed to, or written from, the White House.

Owen rifled through them, scanning, discarding quickly. Then one of them caught his attention. He read it again, and the others attached to it. Then he reached for a clipping he had torn from the *Washington Post* and matched one date with the others.

It was perfect.

He would need more: dossiers for background, photographs for the face, movie film for the mannerisms, tape recordings for the voice and the style of speech. But those things were easily had. The important thing was the set-up. The opportunity. The timing.

Owen smiled. He knew, now, how he was going to kidnap the President's daughter.

He lit a cigarette, then moved across the room to the stereo, flipped through several albums, selected one and put it on to play. A Vivaldi violin concerto performed by the master, Franz Heinemann. Owen smoked his cigarette in silence as the music came to life – bold, dynamic, uplifting.

He also knew how he was going to smuggle her out of the country.

eight

The car was a plain black sedan with no frills. Government plates assured it would be there, without a ticket, when Owen got back.

He double-parked and made his way through the crowd to Pier Ninety-two at the west end of Fifty-second Street, where the lights of the *QEII* brightened the night sky like a giant Yule log ablaze in its hearthside berth. Outside, the air was cool and damp, a wet spring night in New York. Inside the pier building, it was not just damp but chilling.

Owen pulled up his collar and took up a post outside the customs area, near the band whose musical welcome bounced tunelessly off the concrete floor and into the open ceiling of the long, barnlike building. He was wearing a blue suit under a dark burberry, his hair neatly combed, his expression suitably noncommittal. His manner and appearance were designed to match the car outside. Standard government issue.

The passengers were starting to disembark now, and Owen studied their faces with detached interest. He was looking for one face that was etched into his memory by a few hundred feet of film and as many photographs, shot with the flick of a cigarette lighter and without giving the subject a chance to pose.

Owen's mind scanned the man's dossier: Edward Drake. Born Manchester, England, thirty-six years ago. Height, six feet.

Weight, one eighty. Hair black, eyes brown. Occupation, photographer. Physically not unlike Owen himself – taller and darker, except for the fair skin, otherwise much the same. But Drake was also a gentle man, an artist, an unsuspecting man whose knowledge of weapons was limited to his cameras.

A camera bag was slung over Drake's shoulder as he came off the ship, suitcase in hand. He made his way through the thickening crowd to the traffic jammed up outside.

Owen headed him off before he could hail a cab.

'Mr Drake? Mr Edward Drake?'

Drake turned, surprised. 'Why, yes—'

'Frank Jackson, US Secret Service.' Owen flashed a wallet ID.

Drake glanced at the card, then at Owen. 'Is something wrong?'

'Nothing's wrong,' Owen assured him. 'But we need some more information before we can give you a clearance for Indian Springs. I have a car. If you're willing to answer some questions along the way, I'll drop you at your hotel.'

'Be glad to,' Drake replied as he fell into step with Owen. His English was cultivated, Manchester to London by way of public school. 'I've booked a room at the Algonquin,' he added when they were in the car.

Owen nodded and pulled out into the traffic. 'I know.'

Drake grinned. 'Yes, I suppose you would.' He turned to look out the window. 'I must say, I never expected you fellows to be running a limousine service.'

Owen returned the grin goodnaturedly. He was a government agent, yes, but not part of the Executive Protection Service, not one of the steely-eyed types who surrounded the national big shots.

'We don't,' he said, 'but this kind of clearance takes time. I had to see you tonight, and this is faster than trying to find you in at the Algonquin.'

Drake nodded. 'Is it far from here?'

'The Algonquin? Normally, no – but there's a big fire on Sixth Avenue. The streets over there are jammed. I'm afraid we'll have to go a rather long way around.'

It was excuse enough for a roundabout route. Owen knew this was Drake's first trip to New York, but any tourist pre-armed with a map of Manhattan would likely place the locale of his own hotel.

Drake produced a silver cigarette case as Owen stopped for a red light on Forty-second Street. He offered one to Owen.

'Thanks,' Owen said. 'We're interested in the period from 1967 to 1969. You weren't in England those years.' He leaned forward to accept the light from Drake's matching silver lighter.

'No, I was in Australia.'

Owen looked at the face on the other side of the car, at the fair skin, the full cheeks. Then the light changed and he moved ahead, not across town but south.

'Doing what?'

'Mostly bumming around. Taking pictures, of course.'

Owen listened enough to interject the appropriate questions. He wasn't interested in the answers; he knew them already. He was only interested in filling the time, and keeping Drake's attention occupied, between here and his destination.

Another fifteen minutes brought them to lower Manhattan, where the streets were no longer laid out in neat, numbered sequence. Here they twisted and turned into a maze that would disorient anyone but the most seasoned New Yorker – or a man like Owen who had studied the route beforehand and knew precisely where he was going. He turned left on Canal Street.

'I think that's enough,' he said as Drake finished detailing the years he had spent in Australia. 'We'll have to confirm it, of course, but as long as you've told me the truth there won't be any problems.'

'I hope not. How long will it take?'

Owen shrugged. 'A day or two. Final clearance has to come from Washington.'

Drake nodded.

'We're getting into an interesting part of the city, by the way,' Owen added then. He made a right turn at the next intersection, into a wide avenue lined with seedy bars and walk-up hotels that advertised their rates on signs tacked up beside dark holes that passed for doorways. Derelicts shuffled along the sidewalk, the lucky ones clutching their brown-bagged bottles. Others lay sprawled like dead men in the gutter.

'The Bowery,' Owen said.

Drake made no comment. He stared, wide eyed, at the world's most famous skid row.

Owen turned right again, leaving the Bowery behind, and by-passing Chinatown. Then he turned left into Little Italy. He stopped for another red light.

Drake was all tourist now and fully absorbed by the scene on the other side of the window. 'This is fascinating,' he said. 'I wish I could spend more time here.'

'Yes,' Owen agreed. 'You need time for New York.'

The light changed.

Ahead of them, the street darkened dramatically. On the left, an abandoned warehouse. On the right, a row of shops that were closed and barred for the night. Straight ahead, tenement build-ings with shades drawn, black silhouettes backlit by the lights of the city beyond.

Above it all, the lights of the Empire State Building glowed against the sky some forty blocks away. Somewhere ahead and behind there were people milling in the streets. But not here, on this dark stretch of pavement, where even the overhead street-lights fell victim to teenage vandals.

One light was burning now, cutting a corner out of the dark-ness. Owen spotted the van just ahead.

'I hope we're not getting close to the hotel,' Drake said. 'This looks like a rough neighbourhood.'

'It is,' Owen replied. 'And no, we're nowhere near the Algon-quin.'

Drake turned to him sharply. There was no fear in his face. He was puzzled, confused, something more than that. But not yet afraid.

'Where are we? I thought we were—'

He left the thought unfinished as Owen pulled into the kerb behind the van and shut the motor off.

Now the fear was plain on his face.

Owen looked at Drake, at the eyes that recognized a danger he couldn't define. Owen's hand moved.

'God, no! Let me out of here!'

Drake swung around, groping blindly for the door handle, his eyes desperately sweeping the street. But there was no one to see, no one to help – only the dimly lit, outstretched arms of a plastic saint behind the glass window of a storefront church.

Owen raised his arm and brought his hand down hard against Drake's neck.

Drake froze against the car door, and a sound escaped from his throat, a deep cry muted by rushing air. Then his eyes closed and his body slumped over sideways, hitting the dashboard hard.

He wasn't dead, just unconscious. Owen had no intention of killing Edward Drake.

Simon climbed down from the back of the van as Owen got out of the car. He was wearing two days' growth of beard to blunt the square line of his jaw, and a thrift shop suit that was shiny and shapeless from many years of wear. His blond hair hung limp and uncombed, and his shirt, like the suit, looked as if it hadn't been cleaned since last year.

The two men said nothing but moved quickly to the far side of the car, where they pulled Drake out by the arms and lifted him into the rear of the van. Simon sealed the door and switched on a light as Owen began to change clothes.

Then Owen turned to a black metal box, from which he produced a mirror, a comb and brush, a towel, a bottle of black hair rinse, a pair of silicone pads to flesh out his cheeks, and a replacement for the photo page in Drake's passport.

The new page had been chemically treated to match the rest of the passport. On it was a man who looked not quite like Edward Drake, but not like Richard Owen either.

In thirty minutes, Owen had become that man, with brown eyes set in a full face under a head of thick black hair. His clothes, including the thick-soled shoes that made him a full inch taller, were not Drake's clothes, but they came from London shops Drake was known to frequent.

Owen looked at himself in the mirror and smiled. It was close enough. As long as he didn't run into a long-lost American cousin, he would have no trouble passing for Edward Drake.

*

Simon watched Owen drive away, then closed the door of the van and turned back to Drake, still unconscious on the floor.

Sit on him, Owen had said. Just *sit on him* until the danger was over. And when would that be, Simon wondered.

Owen might not worry about being identified. Who could Drake name, a Secret Service agent named Jackson? But Simon didn't share Owen's confidence – or his mastery of disguise.

Nor did he share Owen's weakness for the innocents of the world. Drake was a threat, simply that, not worthy of further concern.

Simon moved quickly. He propped Drake's body into a sitting position against the wall of the van and produced a bottle of whisky. He forced open the mouth, held the bottle to the lips. Then he pressed a knuckle against the throat, activating a natural reflex. Drake swallowed. The whisky began to go down in small sips. Next, Simon pulled off Drake's suit, his shirt and tie, his shoes and socks, and replaced them with a suit of clothes like his own. Salvation Army rejects. By the time he was finished, enough time had elapsed. The whisky had mixed with the blood.

Simon turned and picked up a plastic syringe. There was nothing in it but air. The needle was finely ground steel, honed to a sharp point; it would leave no bruise. He inserted it carefully into Drake's arm, taking care not to apply too much pressure. Then he pushed in the plunger and released the bubble that would travel through the blood and into the heart.

A tiny bullet of air.

By the time Owen was halfway to the Algonquin, Simon and Drake had made their way back to the Bowery, where they slumped into a dark corner to stare at the passing world with sightless eyes, like so many others before them.

Later, Simon got up and walked away, leaving behind the nameless shape of a man – another drunk, another soul for the city morgue. And, when no one came forward to claim him, another tenant for another pauper's grave.

Edward Drake was dead. Irrevocably, untraceably dead.

*

The desk clerk at the Algonquin Hotel accepted Drake's altered passport without question.

Upstairs in his room, Owen locked the door and stretched out on the bed to reread the files on the man he had become.

He had left the tapes and movie film with Simon; they would be destroyed. Here, he had the dossiers, the still photos, a copy of the FBI report and the Secret Service clearance, which had been processed and signed three days ago.

And the letters, culled from the 75,000. It was through the letters that Owen had discovered Drake.

Dear Mrs Haskins,

We've never met, but I am Rowena Drake's oldest son, and I spent a good half of my childhood years listening to Mother's stories about her schooldays, and you. She insists I must write to you now that I'm planning a trip to the United States.

I'll be arriving 19 April on the *Queen Elizabeth II* at New York City, where I've booked a hotel for two nights. After that, I'd like to come down to Washington.

I know you're governess to the President's daughter, and naturally I would love to see the White House, but if that's not possible I'll be happy to meet you elsewhere.

In any case, please let me hear from you as soon as you have a chance. I'm anxious to meet you. Mother sends her love.

Sincerely,
Edward Drake

Mrs Haskins' reply followed by a few days:

Dear Edward,

Rowena's son! She's mentioned you so often in her letters, I feel as if I know you. And of course I would love to see you while you're here.

Unfortunately, I won't be in Washington during your visit. President and Mrs Easton are going on a trip to Mexico – they leave while you're in New York – and I'm taking Anne to visit her aunt and uncle in Michigan.

Of course I can still arrange a special tour of the White House for you, but is there any chance you might come to Michigan?

Please give your dear mother my love.

Sincerely,
Emily Haskins

Dear Mrs Haskins,

Yes, I could come to Michigan. I'm planning to fly on to California and assume Michigan is somewhere along the way. Let me know where and when.

Sincerely,
Edward Drake

Dear Edward,

I'm delighted to hear you will come. Michigan isn't on the direct route to California, but it's not too far out of your way.

Mrs Easton's brother has a summer home on Lake Michigan, at Indian Springs, which – if you're looking on a map – is close to Petoskey. I've asked Mrs Wainwright, Anne's aunt, if she would object to your staying a night or two, and she says it's fine. I've also given your name to the Secret Service. I hope you don't mind – it's necessary, of course – and I assume you have no black secrets in your past to prevent immediate clearance.

Let me know when you'll be arriving, Edward. I'm truly looking forward to your visit.

Sincerely,
Emily Haskins

There was one more reply from Drake, but Owen shoved it aside with the others. He was satisfied; he knew everything he would have to know when he got to Indian Springs. But for now, two days in New York – two days to do nothing except what Drake would have done. He pulled a quarter from his pocket, flipped it into the air, caught it on the back of his hand. The Statue of Liberty. He would start with the New York harbour.

He lit a cigarette. Then he burned the files on Drake, one piece at a time, in the bathroom sink.

Marine One appeared over the Washington Monument, blunt nose tilted slightly skyward as it moved in on the south lawn of the White House.

Clusters of people gathered against the black iron fence, unaware that the helicopter's landing pads were positioned precisely to block their view of the President when he came from the White House. Traffic was halted all the way back to E Street.

No one could move until after the helicopter had taken off again, in a direction known only to the military pilot and a handful of security agents. Its destination: Andrews Air Force Base, where *Air Force One* was fuelled up for the flight to Mexico City.

Inside the White House grounds, press and staff ducked their heads against the sudden blast of wind coming off the powerful blades as the helicopter came to rest perfectly on target. Then, in an instant, the wind died and people began to move.

Military aides opened the hatch and locked the steps into place. Two key staff men appeared through a break in the West Wing hedge, all business as they trotted across the lawn and climbed aboard.

Next, the First Lady emerged from the canopied Diplomatic Entrance. She smiled and waved for the cameras, then turned back to her daughter, who was standing with Mrs Haskins shyly back from the crowd. A few words, a smile, a quick hug, and Elizabeth Easton boarded the helicopter.

Finally, the President appeared to a round of applause barely audible over the noise of the idling engine. He flashed a smile, then reached down to gather Anne up in his arms.

Cameras clicked.

The President's smile faded as he looked at his daughter's face for a long moment. Then he glanced up at Mrs Haskins.

'Take good care of her,' he said.

The governess nodded. Everyone who worked in the White House knew how deeply attached the President was to his daughter, that he didn't like these goodbyes, however temporary. Mrs Haskins knew it better than most.

She touched his arm. 'You know I always do.'

'Yes.' The President cleared his throat, and his eyes shifted back to Anne. 'Behave yourself.'

She nodded solemnly, smiled, gave him a hug and a kiss.

The President hugged her, too. Then he put her down and headed for the helicopter without looking back.

Inspector Martin Schweitzer, who headed the Homicide Division for Manhattan South, looked at the uniformed officer on the other side of his desk.

'Why should I give a damn about another Joe Doe who killed himself on booze?' he demanded.

The patrolman was a beat cop on the Bowery. 'Because,' he said, 'there's something funny about this one.'

The Inspector raised an eyebrow.

'Let me put it this way,' the patrolman added. 'When was the last time you heard of a Bowery drunk wearing a pair of undershorts from a swank Regent Street men's shop?'

'Regent Street, where's that? Brooklyn?'

'*Regent* Street. *London.*'

Schweitzer popped a cigarette into his mouth but didn't light it. 'London, England, you mean.'

The patrolman nodded. 'Listen, Inspector, this guy was dressed like he hadn't seen soap for six months. And yet there they were, underneath all that filth, a pair of *clean* undershorts. From *London.*'

Schweitzer reached for a book of matches and lit his cigarette. He inhaled, staring thoughtfully at the other man.

'Interesting,' he said. 'I think we'll order an autopsy. And while you're at it, let's check his prints with Scotland Yard. I'd like to know who this John Doe really was.'

nine

The Wainwright house was an authentic Victorian structure of mismatched parts, full of gingerbread and turret rooms and oddly placed windows and doors. It sat on the slope of a hill, surrounded by trees, overlooking Lake Michigan and enclosed by an iron fence running all the way down to the white sand beach below. The other houses along the road were equally large and secluded, separated from each other by distance as well as the trees.

There were two points of access to the property – the beach and the front gate, which opened on to a driveway that connected the road and the house. With the President's daughter in residence, both were guarded around the clock by the US Secret Service.

It was Wednesday morning, two days since Owen had assumed the role of Edward Drake. He stopped his car at the front gate and rolled down the window as a man came forward from the gatehouse.

A big man, in an ordinary business suit, with a small lapel pin painted red and white. There was no bulge under the man's arm, but Owen knew he was wearing a shoulder holster.

Owen also knew about the transmitter clipped to the agent's belt, and the two wires attached to it. One ran up under his jacket, emerging at the collar and connecting with a plastic plug, like a hearing aid, in the man's left ear. The other came down through his left sleeve, ending with a microphone at hand level. The microphone was switched on. Permanently.

'Good morning,' Owen said. Another man, he noticed, remained inside the gatehouse, watching them through a large glass window.

'May I help you?' the agent said.

'I'm Edward Drake.'

The agent leaned forward, his eyes probing deeper into the car. 'Yes, Mr Drake. May I see your identification?'

Owen produced Drake's passport and handed it through the window.

The agent glanced at it, then said, 'Just a moment, please,' and turned back to the gatehouse.

Owen strained to hear what they were saying inside but caught only the murmur of voices. Then one of the agents picked up a telephone.

This was a vulnerable spot, the primary point of acceptance, and Owen was unarmed. He hadn't dared risk being caught with a gun, not here.

The man on the phone finished his conversation, and now the first agent was coming forward again. Owen noticed a subtle relaxing of the face muscles.

'Everything seems to be in order, Mr Drake,' the agent said as he handed the passport back, 'but I'll have to take a look at your luggage.'

'Certainly.'

Owen got out and led the way around to the back of the car, where he fit a key in the lock and opened the boot.

The agent unzipped his suitcase and ran a practiced hand through its contents, then turned to the camera bag. He advanced the film on the cameras, one at a time. He examined the strobe attachment and the extra rolls of film. Then, finally, his hand came to rest on a bulky, paper-wrapped package wedged under the window ledge of the back seat.

'What's this?'

'A present for the President's daughter.'

The agent pulled the package forward. 'Good thing you didn't pay for gift wrapping,' he said. 'You'll have to leave it with us, I'm afraid. Procedure. We examine all gifts.'

Owen shrugged. 'Whatever you say.'

The agent lifted the package out of the car and carried it across to the gatehouse. Then he turned back to Owen. 'You can go in now,' he said. 'Turn left at the end of the driveway. The garage is in back. They're expecting you.'

Inspector Schweitzer read through both reports and tossed them back on his desk.

The first came from Scotland Yard. John Doe was a British national, all right – a professional photographer by the name of Edward Drake – and his fingerprints were on file because he'd served in the RAF. He had no criminal record.

The second was the autopsy report. No evidence of death by unnatural causes. On the other hand, no evidence of heart attack or stroke. No damage to the brain or the nervous system. And while the alcohol level in the blood was well past the point of intoxication, there was no indication of liver damage or anything else that normally accompanied a pattern of heavy drinking.

The autopsy reached just one conclusion, in fact: a thirty-six-year-old man was dead, and the medical examiner couldn't say why. Or how.

That, alone, was evidence.

Schweitzer nodded. He knew who John Doe was; now he wanted more. He opened a drawer and pulled out a government form – an official request for information from the FBI computer bank in Washington.

A housekeeper met Owen at the door and showed him to his room upstairs. She was a small woman with a pleasant face and a steady line of chatter. Mrs Haskins would be pleased to know Mr Drake had arrived. She was busy with Anne now, of course, but would come along as soon as she could get free. Anne slept from one to three most days. That part of the day – and after seven, when Anne was in bed for the night – were just about all the time Mrs Haskins had to herself. Such a nice woman, Mrs Haskins, and a fine lady.

Owen agreed.

'Ring if you need anything,' the housekeeper added at the door. 'And while you're waiting, feel free to wander wherever you like. It's a nice walk down to the beach, if you like that sort of thing.'

'Thank you, I may do that.'

Alone, Owen lit a cigarette from Drake's silver case and moved across to the window, which looked down over the lawn towards the lake. He could see the roof of the guest house through the trees to one side and placed it in his memory. There, he knew, Anne Easton's Secret Service detail maintained their operations centre, and their link with the Washington headquarters.

The housekeeper had confirmed two important pieces of information for him. First, the time Anne went to bed at night – seven o'clock. Second, that he was free to move about the premises at will, to see for himself what he had previously seen only on paper – the lay of the house and the land, and the position of each of the guards.

He drew on his cigarette as he turned back into the room. Then he picked up his suitcase and began to unpack his clothes. If he didn't, he was afraid one of the servants would; and he didn't want anyone to examine the suitcase too closely.

Not that a servant was likely to detect a secret that had already passed muster with the professional agent outside. The false bottom wasn't really false; it was merely a second layer – or a third, to be precise. It lay flush against a large, flat brown paper bag, which was itself flush against the outer layer. Undetectable, even by x-ray, and not easily opened. No secret formulas, no hidden levers – this one required a knife to break the stitches.

But Owen wasn't taking any chances.

Inside the brown paper bag was the one thing he had to have if his plan was going to work. It wasn't a gun, or any kind of weapon.

On the other hand, neither was it a toy.

The FBI reports came back to Inspector Schweitzer on another official form: they'd never heard of Edward Drake until three weeks ago, when the Secret Service ordered a security investigation on him. Drake had passed with no problems; the FBI had reported as much to the Secret Service.

The Secret Service?

Schweitzer lit a cigarette. Where in the hell did channels begin with *them*?

Owen's gift was a great success.

It was waiting in his room after dinner the day he arrived, and he gave it to Anne the next morning.

Her eyes widened with astonished delight as Owen tore the paper away. 'A panda bear! He's bigger than I am!' she cried.

'Almost.'

Anne pounced on the bear with unrestrained glee, and Owen knew whatever affection he hadn't earned for being Mrs Haskins' friend, he'd obviously earned now.

He sat back to watch, smiling with pleasure and shrugging off Mrs Haskins' polite objections to such a generous gift. 'I saw it in the window at F.A.O. Schwarz and couldn't resist it,' he said.

Mrs Haskins smiled back at him and objected no more. 'It was thoughtful of you, Edward.'

'My pleasure. Look, Anne, the arms move.' Owen bent over to show her how they worked.

Anne flashed her dimpled smile and attacked her bear with new enthusiasm, bending the arms forwards and backwards, and in other directions they were never meant to go. But the bear was built to take it.

Owen lit a cigarette and turned back to Mrs Haskins. 'Do you suppose you'll ever come home to England?' he asked casually.

'Probably not.' The old woman's eyes shifted to the child. 'I'm so attached to Anne now, you know. She's almost like my own.'

'I daresay, she is in a way. But I should think you'd—'

A cry of alarm suddenly rose from the floor.

Across the room, a Secret Service man looked up sharply, then – assessing no danger – settled back in his chair and returned his gaze to the paperback book in his hand.

Owen looked down at Anne, on the verge of tears, holding one fuzzy black arm in her hand and staring unhappily at the bear. A tuft of white stuffing protruded from a hole where the arm had been.

'Look at that, will you?' Owen said. 'She's had it ten minutes, and already the arm's come off!' He got down on the floor beside Anne. 'There's a good girl. Let me have a look.'

Owen studied the arm a moment, then poked a finger into the white stuffing and, finally, shook his head. 'Whatever this was attached to, it's gone now,' he said. He tested the other arm, which came loose at his touch.

Anne was inconsolable.

'Don't worry, I promise we'll have him fixed,' Owen assured her. Then he looked up at Mrs Haskins. 'Fixed, my eye!' he added. 'I'm taking it back. They can jolly well send her a new one.'

Later the same day, when Owen knew Mrs Haskins was outside with Anne, he slipped upstairs to his room, where he brought the suitcase out of the closet, ran a knife around the false bottom and removed the brown paper bag. Then he left the room and moved quietly down the hall.

Mrs Haskins' room was adjacent to Anne's and they shared an adjoining door. Owen stepped through the door from the hallway and closed it behind him, then crossed over to Mrs Haskins' dressing table, which he pulled out from the wall. He produced a roll of strapping tape from his pocket and fastened the paper bag to the back of the dresser, checking to make sure it was secure. Then he shoved the dresser back and opened the door to Anne's room.

The bear was sitting on the floor at the foot of her bed, like a fat little Venus de Milo. But unlike the Venus, the bear's arms were resting on a table nearby.

Owen nodded and closed the door, then headed back downstairs.

Ken Russell found a message on his desk at the Secret Service headquarters in Washington. He was supposed to phone an Inspector Schweitzer of the New York City police. Important, the message said.

Russell reached for the phone.

Then he glanced at his watch. His meeting with the deputy director was important, too. Schweitzer would have to wait.

Owen spent two days inside the Wainwright house. He talked politics with Anne's uncle and theatre with her aunt. He talked family with Mrs Haskins. He talked to the servants and, whenever they would, with Anne's security men. With Anne, he took pictures.

He was a thoroughly charming and thoughtful guest. By the end of the second day, everyone in the house was sorry to see him go.

Anne's aunt and Mrs Haskins were waiting for him in the front room when he came downstairs with his bags at eight o'clock.

Mrs Wainwright extended her hand. 'It's been a pleasure to have you' she said. 'I hope you'll come back some time.'

Owen shook her hand. 'I'd like that.' Then he put his arms around Mrs Haskins and gave her a kiss on the cheek. 'I can't wait to tell Mother all about our visit.'

The governess smiled up at him. 'Give her my love, Edward, and tell her to come with you next time.'

'I will. Take care now.' He picked up his bags and started towards the front door. Then he turned abruptly, remembering. 'I almost forgot the bear!'

'Oh, Edward, don't bother—'

'No bother,' he replied. 'We can't have Anne disappointed now, can we?'

He dropped his bags and turned back to the stairs.

Anne was asleep as Owen entered the room. He closed the door and stood there a moment, listening to the regular sound of her breathing. Then he crossed the floor to the bed, pulling a fountain pen from the breast pocket of his jacket as he moved. He removed the cap and the writing point and pressed the pen against the soft part of Anne's upper arm.

The pen concealed a tiny cartridge that worked like a hypodermic syringe. When the sharp point punctured the skin, pressure forced the plunger in and the drug out. Sodium pentothal. The dose exact. The effect immediate.

Anne's arm jerked at the sharp prick of the needle, but Owen held it firm. Her eyes opened, then instantly closed again as her brain dropped to a medium level of unconsciousness. Anything more would be dangerous without medical equipment to monitor vital signs. But the dosage was geared to Anne's precise age and weight. At this level, she was safe.

Now Owen retrieved the brown paper bag from the back of the dresser and ripped it open. Inside lay a panda bear, armless, a replica of the other except for two special features. This one had a zipper opening, hidden deep in the plush, running from the head down to the top of the legs. And this one was flat, unstuffed, with a balloonlike inner lining that was set to expand with pressure.

It also had air holes punched into its plastic nose.

Owen spread the bear out on the floor and lifted Anne in, feet first.

Behind him, the door opened.

'Edward, I—'

Mrs Haskins stopped where she was, face frowning, eyes puzzled. Then her mouth dropped open and her eyes widened in horror.

'*Edward?*'

Owen leaped to his feet before the scream could emerge. He clamped a hand harshly over her mouth as he grabbed her around the waist. She fought against him vainly, her fragile strength useless against his.

Owen's thumb found the line of her jaw and the pressure point just below it. Still she glared back at him, her face contorted with rage. Then, slowly, her eyes went dull, the muscles of her face relaxed. She felt no pain as her body sagged, dead weight in his arms.

It was seven-thirty before Secret Service Agent Russell heard what Inspector Schweitzer had to say.

'You're right,' he said when Schweitzer was finished. 'It could be important. I don't know why we ran a security check on Drake, but I'll find out. Thanks a lot.'

He disconnected the line and called the Records Division, gave the man who answered Drake's name and waited until the information came back. Edward Drake was a friend of Emily Haskins. He'd been given clearance to Indian Springs.

And the President's daughter was there.

Russell punched out another number, urgently now. The line was busy. He got up and made his way quickly down the hall, turned into the office of the Protection Service, bypassed the duty officer without a word and pushed open the section chief's door.

'We've got a problem,' he said, and quickly explained what he'd learned about Edward Drake.

'But that's not possible,' the other man replied. 'Edward Drake isn't dead. He arrived at Indian Springs yesterday morning.'

Then his eyes widened as the obvious became clear and he grabbed up the direct line to Michigan.

Anne's aunt was still in the front room, talking to one of the Secret Service agents, as Owen came back down the stairs, holding the panda bear securely, but lightly, under his right arm.

He stopped in the doorway. 'I'm afraid I awakened Anne,' he said, 'but Mrs Haskins is with her.'

Mrs Wainwright smiled. 'She's so good with Anne.'

'Yes, she is, isn't she. Well, I must get on. I'm running late as it is.' Owen picked up the camera bag with his free hand and slung it over his shoulder.

The agent moved towards him. 'Let me help you.'

Owen smiled. 'Thanks, but I think I can manage. You might get the door, if you would.' He picked up the suitcase. 'Thank you again, Mrs Wainwright,' he added.

'We enjoyed having you.'

'I enjoyed it, too. Goodbye now.'

Owen's car was waiting outside. He dropped his bags in the trunk and pushed the panda bear on to the back seat. Then, with a final wave, he got in behind the wheel and drove out through the gate.

A phone rang in the guest cottage behind the Wainwright house – the direct line from Washington. The agent-in-charge picked it up, listened a moment, then took off towards the house at a run.

'Where's Drake?' he demanded as he burst through the front door.

Mrs Wainwright looked up, startled. 'Why, he just left. Is something wrong?'

The agent brushed past her to the stairs, taking them two at a time. He pushed open the door to Anne's room and stopped suddenly, feeling a moment's relief as he saw the form of her small body under the bed covers. Then a new fear gripped him when he realized there was no movement. Anne wasn't breathing.

He crossed the room in three strides and yanked back the covers. Then a cold wave of fear swept over him as he recognized a truth more horrible than anything he'd confronted before.

It wasn't Anne, but the panda! The President's daughter was gone!

ten

The impostor had a ten-minute head start, but the Secret Service car roared powerfully along the only road that gave access to the Wainwright house, in the direction the impostor had taken. There were two agents in front – one driving, one on the radio and watching the road ahead. Two more sat behind, keeping an eye on the trees growing thick on both sides.

Six miles ahead lay the town of Indian Springs and the first intersection offering a choice of direction, but police roadblocks were already being set up to stop all traffic moving in either direction.

It was a sandwich manoeuvre. The impostor couldn't get away.

Then one of the agents in back gave a shout and pointed towards the sky, where a small airplane was just clearing the tops of the trees – a Piper Cherokee, dark against a dark sky.

The agent behind the wheel slammed on the brakes and the other three jumped out. In a moment, they were back. The impostor's car was there, all right, abandoned in the open meadow from where the plane had taken off. The agent next to the driver grabbed up the radio and was already issuing orders to track the plane as the driver swung the car into a wide u-turn and headed back towards the house.

From the trees by the side of the road, Owen watched the Secret Service car turn around.

He knew they would be back with reinforcements. Later, these woods would be swarming with federal agents of one kind or another, from Detroit, from Chicago, from Washington. But that would take time, an hour or two at least.

Meantime, the crew at the house were on his trail; that much was clear. But the ruse of the plane apparently had worked.

The plane was gone, heading west over Lake Michigan. Now it was time to activate the plan for his own escape.

He switched on the small radio transmitter left for him in the woods and spoke into it briefly: 'This is Sunflower. Make the phone call now.'

Somewhere in the distance, a man – placed there by Simon – received the message. 'Roger, Sunflower.'

Owen switched the transmitter off. Radio contact was too easily picked up, too easily traced.

He stood there a moment watching the dark road. Then he

moved away through the trees. Half a mile back towards the Wainwright house, he found the car. And in it, a change of identity.

The housekeeper sat rubbing Mrs Haskins' hands. They had found her in her own room on the bed, unconscious. She was breathing, alive. She was going to be all right.

Father Healy promised to come at once.

He left his office, jumped into his black Dodge Dart and turned north, heading for Indian Springs.

The Wainwrights weren't members of his parish – they were part of the summer people – but they did attend Mass from time to time and always remembered the church with a cheque at the end of the year.

And now they needed him. Some kind of big trouble out there. Someone sick. Someone dying. The man on the phone hadn't been clear. He pushed on through the darkness, rounding a curve in the road. Then suddenly he stepped down on the brakes.

A roadblock. Two state police cars parked at the berm on each side, their front beams crisscrossed, forming an arc of light and outlining the figures of three uniformed men.

Father Healy stopped the car and wound down his window. One of the men came forward. A state trooper, no one local, no one the priest recognized.

'Where are you going, Father?'

'Out to the Wainwright place. I've had a call asking me to come.'

The policeman glanced back at the other men, but Father Healy couldn't guess the meaning of the look that passed between them.

'Do you have some identification'

'Yes, of course.' He produced his driver's licence and a clerical identification card.

The policeman took them and moved back to one of the parked cars, where he lifted the radio mouthpiece away from the dashboard and talked into it. Father Healy couldn't hear what he was saying, but the other two men, he noticed, stayed where they were, blocking his passage.

In a moment, the policeman was back. 'It's all right, Father, you can go on.' He handed back the cards and signalled his colleague to move aside.

'Thank you,' the priest said. 'May I ask what this is about?'

'I'm sorry, I can't tell you. But I suspect you'll know soon enough.'

Twenty minutes later, Owen pulled the car out of the trees and turned south. He passed through Indian Springs without attracting attention. His car was familiar to the people there, a black Dodge Dart identical to Healy's even to the licence plates. Virtually the only difference was that Owen's Dodge had a roomy, ventilated trunk – with a toy panda inside it.

Ten miles on the other side of town, he slowed the car to a stop just short of the wide circle of light. Two cars, three cops, all state police.

One of the cops came forward. 'Oh, it's you again, Father,' he said. 'How are they doing out there?'

'About as you'd expect,' Owen replied sadly. 'Is there any news?'

'Not that we've heard, but the feds don't tell us much. They haven't called us off yet, that's all I know.'

Owen shook his head grimly. 'Well, I'd better be getting home.'

'Sure, Father, go ahead. Maybe we'll see you later.'

'I hope not,' Owen replied. 'I hope you won't have to be here that long. Goodnight.'

He rolled up the window as he passed between the two parked cars. There was a curve in the road ahead. Once he was past it and out of view from behind, he pulled off the grey wig and the clerical collar.

Then he stepped down on the gas, moving fast through the night. He knew when the priest had been summoned to the Wainwright house, had seen the car pass by as he waited in the woods. But he couldn't control the other man's departure. The real Father Healy might not be far behind.

The man behind the controls of the Piper Cherokee maintained a steady course, due west. He was somewhere over Wisconsin and bored. A clear sky, little wind, and a simple piece of machinery –

73

child's play for an old stunt pilot, hardly fair for the five hundred dollars he was going to be paid.

On the other hand, for five hundred bucks in one night, he didn't have to ask questions.

Ahead of him now the terrain steepened. He brought the nose up smoothly, pulling up and levelling off at an even 6,000 feet.

The SAC bomber diverted from routine NORAD patrol duty along the Canadian border was cruising at 10,000 feet. A small blip on its radar screen showed the Piper Cherokee heading west, five miles ahead and 4,000 feet below.

The US Air Force pilot glanced across at the man on the other side of the cabin. 'He's making no effort to lose us, is he?'

The copilot, a Canadian, shook his head. 'Steady on course, routine as can be.' Then, suddenly, he sat forward in his seat, staring at the radar screen. 'He's gone!'

'*Gone?*'

'Completely. Damn! He couldn't have landed that fast.'

'No,' the American agreed. 'Not, at least, as a matter of choice.'

The agent-in-charge picked up the phone in the guest cottage behind the Wainwright house.

'Bad news,' said the voice at the other end. 'That Piper you had us tracking. It crashed in northern Wisconsin.'

The agent gripped the telephone hard as he asked the inevitable question. 'Were there any survivors?'

'Hard to say,' the voice replied. 'You see the plane crashed, but there wasn't anyone in it.'

The sign was impressive: *Kalkaska Aviation Incorporated: Flight Instruction, GAT Simulator, ATP Specialist, Hangers, Tiedowns, Aircraft for Rent or Lease.* But the building looked like a temporary barracks, and the boy behind the counter was not yet of drinking age.

He'd only had a few beers, and why not! Someone had left a six-pack of Bud in the office. What was he supposed to do, throw it out!

He stared at the customer on the other side of the counter. No one from these parts. A fancy dude, probably up from Detroit.

'All we got that size is a Lear jet,' he said. 'And they cost plenty.'

The customer reached into his pocket and brought out a money clip. 'How much?'

The boy's eyes slowly widened as he looked at the size of the bills. Nothing smaller than a fifty . . . No black man he'd ever met made that kind of dough. No white man, for that matter. What the hell, black money bought the same as white.

'Just you?' he said.

'And my daughter,' the black man replied. 'She's asleep outside in the car.'

The boy looked up sharply. He'd had a call from the state cops less than an hour ago. Be on the lookout for a man with a little girl. Descriptions and all that. But this dude was making no effort to *hide* his daughter. And besides, the man the cops wanted was white.

The boy relaxed and brought out a triplicate form. 'How long do you need it?' he said.

'A week ought to do.'

'Where are you going?'

'The northern peninsula. I'll file a plan for Marquette.'

The boy nodded. 'Okay, if you've got three kinds of identification, including your pilot's ID, I think we can do business.'

Twenty minutes later, the Lear jet was off the ground, clearing the trees, heading north until it was out of sight from the airfield below. Then it banked steeply to the east. Away from Kalkaska, away from Petoskey.

Towards Washington, DC.

eleven

At 8.45, Ed Nichols was still at his desk on the seventh floor of the massive CIA headquarters building at Langley, Virginia, twenty minutes across and up the Potomac from downtown Washington. A buzzer sounded. He flicked on his intercom.

'Excuse me, sir,' said Nichols' staff assistant, who manned the office outside. 'I know you said not to disturb you, but it's the Secret Service director on the phone.'

Nichols glanced up impatiently. 'Wycoff? What does he want?'

'I don't know, but he says it's urgent.'

Nichols hesitated a moment. Then he switched off the intercom and picked up the phone.

'Yes, Sam.'

In an instant, his impatience was gone. His attention was riveted to the words he was hearing even as his mind rejected them as impossible. He sat frozen in his chair, his astonishment total. He listened in stunned silence.

When Wycoff was finished, Nichols asked one question: 'Does the President know?'

'Yes. He's on his way back from Mexico right now. He wants to see you as soon as he arrives.'

No doubt.

'I'll be there,' Nichols said.

He hung up the phone and sat there without moving, staring into the empty space on the other side of his desk.

The President's daughter kidnapped?

Kidnapped?

By whom? For what? He wasn't sure he really wanted to know.

The President brought his fist down hard on the desk.

'Damn it, Ed! The Secret Service had me wrapped in cotton down there. They imagined terrorists under every bed. *What* were they doing in Michigan? *How did they let this happen?*'

Nichols didn't reply for a moment. He waited for the outburst to run its course, like the others interspersed between moments of great calm – controlled, unnatural, forcefully self-imposed. He had known Matt Easton for more than twenty-five years, since their college days together, through all the years of campaigning, in Congress, right up to the Oval Office.

Here, now, in this historic moment.

Historic, yes, but the crisis of the President's daughter was not a thing of the past. If only it were . . . Just an interesting footnote to ancient history. Agamemnon offering Iphigenia to the gods. It would be, some day, after they got Anne back. If they got her back in time to prevent the threat that loomed ahead, undefined, and all the more frightening for it.

Nichols looked at his friend, a young President, not yet fifty years old. A man who thrived on conflict, the tougher the better. 'Impossible' was a verdict Matt Easton refused to accept. Problems existed for the challenge of finding solutions.

He wasn't a fighter like Nichols, who relished the blood of the battle. He was far too elegant for that. Elegant and austere like the office, with its white walls set off by thick carpet and heavy brocade drapes. Matt *fitted* here, as well as any man ever had.

But the man Nichols saw at the moment was full of anger, torn between lashing out and concealing intense personal fear.

Deep anguish, boiling beneath the surface. Nichols knew it was there. And frustration beyond any political crisis. A man who was used to solving the problems of the world, now – like the father of any kidnapped child – had to rely on others. With all of his power, he could not go find her himself.

And something else, Nichols thought. He frowned. There was something in Matt's face that caused a flash of memory. A nuance of expression that made him think of something grossly inconsequential – *a campaign poster pose*.

Nichols pulled off his glasses and passed a weary hand across his eyes. It was three a.m. and he hadn't slept. He didn't know when he would sleep again.

'Nobody *let* this happen,' he said. 'This was no crackpot scheme that might have been prevented with tighter security. The man who did this was a professional, a highly skilled professional.'

'And the Secret Service?' the President demanded. 'They're *not* professionals?'

Nichols sighed heavily. 'There are professionals and professionals,' he said. 'I'm not talking about trained bodyguards. I'm talking about skilled intelligence agents. You can't blame the Secret Service.'

'I can blame anyone I damn well feel like blaming!'

The President stared back at him. Then he leaned back in his chair and closed his eyes as the anger began to drain away. He raised his hand in a gesture. 'I know,' he said quietly. 'Placing blame is counter-productive.' He opened his eyes again. They were troubled, but calm. 'Is that what you think, Ed? A foreign intelligence agency?'

Nichols pulled himself up straight in the chair. 'If I had to bet, that's where I'd put my money. It had to be someone with a sophisticated understanding of our security systems. The impersonation was flawless, the timing perfect. That takes skill, but skill backed up by knowledge.' He leaned forward against the desk. 'But that kind of judgement is premature for now. It would be a mistake to eliminate anyone. Foreign enemies. Domestic enemies. Even political enemies.'

'*Political* enemies?'

Nichols caught the President's eyes in a direct gaze. 'Anyone, Matt. *Anyone* who might benefit from having you over a barrel.'

The President laughed, but there was no humour in it. 'That certainly narrows the field,' he said dryly. 'Is there anyone who wouldn't benefit from having me over a barrel?'

He pushed himself up out of the chair and began to pace the room – to the fireplace, with its carved antique mantel under a portrait of George Washington by Charles Willson Peale. Back again, to the broad sweep of windows behind his desk. His hand touched the thick partition of green-tinted bulletproof glass.

'Foreign intelligence,' he said more to himself than Nichols. Then he turned. 'What do you think, Ed? The Russians?'

Nichols shrugged. 'The most and the least obvious.'

'The least? How?'

'Because it's a hell of a risk, and they've got a lot to lose if we catch them.'

'*If* we catch them? This is *Anne* we're talking about! We're talking about her life – and God knows what else!'

No pose, Nichols decided. This was a man brought face to face with the high cost of power, and feeling guilty about it.

'They won't kill her,' he said with more conviction than he felt. 'Whoever has her won't kill her. They are professionals; we know that. That's the best guarantee we've got.'

'How can you be so sure?'

'Because she's not worth a damn cent dead.'

The President stared back at him. 'You can't think they're going to want *money* . . .'

'A figure of speech.' Nichols shook his head. 'Not money, no. What's money to a man who sits on top of the US Treasury.'

'And a lot of other things more valuable.' The President looked down at his own hands, then thrust them deep into his pockets. 'Well, they're going to want something. Something big – and probably something I won't be able to give them.'

Nichols nodded silently to himself. Matt Easton, the father, would do anything to get his daughter back. But Matt Easton, the President, had more than two hundred million people to worry about. If the kidnappers' demands ran contrary to the national interest – and it was hard to think they wouldn't – the responsibilities of father and President would meet on collision course.

Both men knew who would die. In a democracy, the majority always rules.

The President stood by the window a moment longer. Then he moved back to his chair. 'We've got to find her and fast,' he said, '*before* they make their demands. That's why you're here. I don't trust anyone as much as I trust you.' He sat down. 'The new FBI chief, for instance. I chose him, but hell, he's been here less than six months. I don't know *what* he can do.'

Nichols leaned forward in his chair. 'I'll do what I can, Matt, but you know the law says it's the FBI—'

'Because it's domestic? I don't know that at all. If it's a foreign intelligence agency, you've got authority there.'

Nichols nodded. 'As long as it's your decision.'

'It is. Besides, I'm not talking about the FBI or the CIA. I'm talking about you, Ed, you personally. I want *you* to find my daughter.'

Years of trust looked at Nichols across the desk. Years of deference looked back. Deference to Matt's needs, to Matt's goals. Years of handling the touchy stuff to keep Matt's political friendships intact, to keep his image pure.

'You'll have the CIA *and* the FBI,' the President went on. 'The Secret Service, if you want it. Treasury. Defense. The military. All the resources this government has to offer. I'm putting them all in your hands.'

Nichols nodded slowly. He'd expected a major role in the search for Anne. Even *the* major role. But *this*? He rubbed his hands together; they were damp with perspiration. Enormous power. Enormous responsibility. Enormous risk.

And no choice. 'I'll do my best,' he said.

Elizabeth Easton's press secretary felt sick, but she knew what she had to do.

She sat down at the typewriter, inserted a piece of paper, and pounded out the statement as quickly, as professionally, as if it dealt with nothing more dramatic than the acquisition of a new antique for the White House.

Anne Easton has been confined to bed with a virus while visiting her aunt and uncle in Indian Springs, Mich. Doctors describe her virus as mild, but the President's daughter will not return to Washington for at least another week.

The statement would be released from the East Wing tomorrow, routinely, in a kit with several others dealing with domestic issues of little importance. The White House press corps would not give it much attention.

Nichols flipped over the last page of the thick report. He took off his glasses and sat there a moment, rubbing his eyes. Then, decisively, he leaned forward and pressed a button in the brass panel on his desk.

'Yes, sir?'

'Tell Fleming I'm ready to see him now.'

'Yes, sir.'

Paul Fleming was Nichols' deputy director, a small man, thin and agile, with greying brown hair falling loose across his forehead and a face that seemed somehow unfinished. He was a former field agent who had made it his business to stay in good condition. He was in his forties but looked younger, and he was still known in official Washington circles as the boy genius who worked in the woods at Langley.

Nichols looked up as Fleming entered the office. Young and eager, he thought. Fleming would still be young and eager when he was eighty-five.

'I've read the speculations, Paul,' he said. 'They're all right as far as they go. Sit down.'

Fleming dropped into a chair and stretched his legs out in front of him. Like Nichols, he was in shirt sleeves and looked like he hadn't slept for a week.

'What do you mean, as far as they go?'

Nichols rested a hand on top of the report, two hundred and fifty-odd pages of conjecture and suggestion culled from CIA's computers and human information bank.

'There's got to be something more we can do, something more *immediately productive*.'

It was the standard conflict between them – the agency chief, who established policy, and the first lieutenant, who had to deal with the limitations of reality.

'I don't know what it is,' Fleming replied. 'I've got the War Room on red alert, coordinating with the Pentagon and the National Security Council. I've alerted our station chiefs here and abroad. I've been in contact with every friendly foreign agency. I've got the military playing bloodhound. Pretty general stuff, but that's about all we can do until we have a direction. More specifically, we're tracing the leads – the panda bear, the getaway car. We're trying to find out who placed the call to the priest. We're tracking everyone who knew Edward Drake was coming to the US. We've got the FBI lab studying every piece of that plane—'

'That's just what I mean,' Nichols broke in. 'We won't learn a damn thing from that airplane. The kidnapper was never in it.' He shook his head. 'That plane was a diversionary tactic, and it worked. Bunch of damn fools working for the Secret Service!'

Fleming nodded sympathetically. 'I know. It's frustrating, and you're the one who has to deal with the President. But frankly, unless we get a break on one of these things, we're going to be stuck waiting. First move, theirs.'

Nichols sighed. 'Like a game of chess where we can't see the board. No, Paul, I want action . . . I want utter thoroughness!' His hand dropped back to the report. 'This thing, for instance – it only surveys hot spots for the last six months. I want to go back at least two years. Tell the analysts to look for any kind of activity that might provide a motive for this. Any kind, any time, anywhere.'

Fleming pulled an index card from his shirt pocket and made a note. He looked up again.

'You say you've alerted our station chiefs,' Nichols went on. 'What about our key field agents?'

'I assumed the station chiefs would—'

'No assuming, Paul! I want *you* to decide who our top agents are, and I want *you* to free them up from whatever else they're doing. We've got to focus all our assets on this.' He pounded his fist against the report. 'Damn! I wish we still had Richard Owen.'

Fleming nodded. 'We could certainly use him.'

'And ten others like him.'

'There are no others like Owen.'

'I know that. Hell, I've known that every day since he was killed.'

Then, abruptly, Nichols dismissed the thought. Wishing for a dead man was only a waste of energy. 'You should also alert the political officers in our embassies,' he said. 'Tell them to keep their eyes open for anything brewing with the foreign intelligence agencies or the super-terrorist organizations.'

Fleming made another note.

'Maybe for once,' Nichols added, 'the political officers will turn up something we don't already know. By the way, we'll take no crap from military intelligence. If they get something, I want to see it now. Don't give me any of this end-run-to-the-President business. And Paul, keep an eye on that greenhorn who thinks he's running the FBI. He doesn't understand who's got access to the Oval Office around here.'

Fleming grinned. 'Give him time. He'll learn. Anyway, I never deal with the director. I've got my own man at the FBI. He's been playing ball for years.'

Nichols nodded. Count on Fleming to have his own personal lackey, even at the FBI. 'Good,' he said. He pushed himself up out of the chair and moved across to the windows. Bright lights outlined the parking lot below, and darkness still covered the thick forest that surrounded and screened the building, but grey light was beginning to show over the tops of the trees.

'Just remember one thing, Paul,' he said over his shoulder. 'Every s.o.b. in Washington's going to want to be the hero on this.' He turned. 'But I *intend* to be.'

Dawn was breaking as Owen turned east on Virginia Route 123, passing practically in the shadow of CIA's Langley headquarters on the other side of the trees. But he didn't turn in. Instead, he veered off on the Old Georgetown Pike, which led him around to the turn he was looking for – Turkey Run Road, where the houses were in the luxury class, a paved path winding back into the very woods that shielded the CIA.

He had landed the Lear jet routinely at Washington's National Airport, a computer salesman arriving in town for an eight o'clock breakfast meeting, getting off the plane with an attaché case and a thick garment bag. No one had paid much attention.

If anyone had, his flight plan was retraceable: straight back to Knoxville, Tennessee, where an identical Lear jet had taken off about the same time Owen left Michigan. That plane had landed elsewhere. And that pilot would arrive here at National tomorrow to retrieve the plane Owen no longer needed.

Owen turned right at a fork in the road, moving deeper into the trees. His speedometer had clicked off less than a mile when he spotted the roadside mailbox with its fresh-painted, bright yellow sunflower.

Simon came out of the house and signalled Owen to the back, where a two-car garage was open on one side. Owen pulled in, and Simon lowered the door behind him.

'You made good time,' Simon said.

Owen nodded.

'How's your passenger?'

'Still sleeping.'

Owen unzipped the garment bag – his own design, drawn to precise specifications, the parts custom built, separately, by Technical Services at Langley and assembled later by Owen. It was ordinary vinyl on the outside, a dull shade of brown and thick enough to carry several suits of clothes without crowding. Inside, it was something else – a minor feat of engineering.

Steel stays held the shape of the bag against excess weight; they were padded to prevent injury to the occupant. The back of the bag was stiffened by a thin sheet of steel, as strong as it was light-weight. Next to the steel sheet, a solid cushion of foam; then another layer, thicker, cut out to accommodate Anne. She was strapped to the steel sheet by padded belts around her waist and under her arms. A bar lower down supported the weight of her feet when Owen held the bag upright.

Another cushion lined the front side of the bag. It was made of a different substance – a thick, spongy, plastic mesh developed by NASA as space suit insulation for the Apollo probe. It was flexible, like a suit of chainmail, but more porous, and it weighed no more than the same thickness of cotton. It was through this mesh, and vents built into the vinyl exterior of the bag, that Anne was able to breathe without strain.

She lay there now, surrounded by cushioned comfort, her face as peaceful as if she were asleep in her own bed. Owen checked her pulse and breath rate and gave her another injection. He had switched to Valium, a simple tranquillizer that was slower but safer than sodium pentothal for an extended nap. Again, the dosage was exact, just enough to maintain a shallow level of unconsciousness for the period required.

Then, at a gesture from Simon, he got up and crossed over to the vehicle that occupied the other half of the garage.

'A beauty, isn't it?' Simon said.

Owen studied the long black hearse with the words *United States Army* painted on its side door in small, discreet gold letters. 'A good copy,' he agreed. He pulled open the rear door and glanced inside.

There was a hole in the floor, coffin shaped and dropping down maybe twelve inches to a second floor below.

'Where's the insert?' he said.

'Over here.' Simon led the way to the front of the garage, to a long, flat box that stood a foot off the ground.

Owen examined it carefully, opened the lid, tested the locks. 'Have you checked it for fit?' he asked.

'It's perfect.'

'Good.'

'There's one question,' Simon said.

Owen glanced up.

Simon gestured back towards the hearse. 'Graham wants to know just how you're planning to use this.'

Owen smiled. 'You tell Graham I said not to worry about it. He'll know soon enough.'

twelve

The next night, Saturday, a few minutes past six o'clock, Owen strolled into the wood-panelled lobby of the Hay-Adams Hotel across Lafayette Square from the White House. He asked the man behind the desk for William Hirsh's room number, though he knew it already, then made his way across the lobby to the house phones.

Hirsh answered quickly. 'Yes?' He was a busy man, the vice president of Syntax Corporation, and clearly impatient with un-expected distractions.

'Mr Hirsh, my name is Chandler,' Owen began. 'I'm with the State Department.'

'Yes?'

'I'd like to come up if you have a moment.'

'Now?'

'Yes. It's rather important.'

Hirsh hesitated at the other end of the phone. Then he said, 'All right, but be quick about it. I'm going out soon.'

'Yes sir, I know. I'll be right up.'

Owen took the elevator to the fifth floor, made a left turn into a carpeted corridor, and found William Hirsh standing in the open doorway of his room. He was wearing tuxedo pants and a formal shirt, with a bow tie hanging loose at the collar. His grey hair was combed neatly back from his forehead, and on his face was a look of mild annoyance.

'What's important enough to bring the State Department out on a Saturday night?' he wanted to know as Owen crossed into the room.

'A rather embarrassing problem, I'm afraid,' Owen replied. He closed the door behind him, then turned to look at the other man. He did not sit down, nor was he invited to. 'We have received a formal protest from the Austrian government,' he began.

'A *protest*?' Hirsh's voice was indignant, but his face was puzzled. 'What sort of protest?'

'Regarding payments to certain Austrian officials. By your corporation.'

Hirsh's mouth dropped open and he stared at Owen in apparent disbelief. 'What kind of nonsense is this? We've had our head-quarters in Vienna for over thirty years. Our relations with the Austrian government are excellent.'

'That may be, sir, but as we understand it, legal action is already underway.'

'Is this a joke, young man?' Hirsh demanded suddenly. 'Who *are* you?'

'My name is Phillip Chandler. I'm a protocol officer with the State Department.' Owen produced his wallet and handed Hirsh a government ID with his picture on it. He was watching Hirsh's face, admiring its obvious control over inner feelings. There was nothing there to indicate that Hirsh knew what Owen knew, but Owen knew he did. Syntax Corporation had indeed been bribing Austrian officials for favourable decisions on export quotas, tax matters, shipping problems. They'd been doing it for years.

Of course, the Austrian government had not yet caught on, but that didn't matter. Knowledge of guilt was enough to make Hirsh move cautiously. It would be Monday, at least, before he discovered the hoax. And then there would be nothing he could do about it, not unless he was willing to draw closer scrutiny to the truth.

'In light of this,' Owen added, returning the card to his wallet and the wallet to his pocket, 'the Protocol Office feels it would be inappropriate for the corporation to be represented tonight at the White House.'

'I see. So, I'm to be officially ostracized on the basis of some vague charge, as yet unsubstantiated. What charge, Chandler? Who made it?'

Owen shook his head. 'I'm sorry. We're operating on a report from a foreign government. I can't tell you more.'

'But I'm no longer welcome at the White House.'

'I wouldn't put it quite that way, Mr Hirsh,' Owen replied. 'It's nothing personal. But I think you can understand, it would be rather—'

Hirsh finished the sentence for him. '*Inappropriate*.' He yanked the tie out from under his shirt collar and flung it across the room. 'Get out of here, Chandler,' he said. 'I've got some phone calls to make.'

Owen nodded, then turned and left the room unobtrusively. Let Hirsh try calling the State Department or the White House. He would only run into some Saturday night duty officer who would claim, honestly, no knowledge of the affair. And given time to think, Hirsh probably wouldn't try. More likely, he would be on the next plane back to Vienna.

More than an hour later, a grey-haired, formally dressed Richard

Owen presented himself at the East Gate of the White House, timing his arrival after the crowd but not yet conspicuously late. He handed the engraved card to the gate guard, who checked Hirsh's name off his list and handed the card back. Owen moved ahead, into the East Wing, where a woman in formal military dress took the card and kept it.

'Have a nice evening, Mr Hirsh,' she said with a warm smile.

'Thank you, I'm sure I will.'

He followed a broad hallway past the Jacqueline Kennedy Garden on the other side of large windows, past the cloakroom and into the main part of the mansion, into a dimly lit, red-carpeted corridor with portraits of the recent First Ladies lining the walls on both sides. There were people here, but not many – a few guests, more uniformed social aides, two men in dark suits and Secret Service lapel pins.

Owen had never been inside the White House. He knew it only by reputation and floor plan. He stopped beside one of the uniformed men and said, 'Where's the men's room, please?'

'Through the library, on your right.'

Owen followed the gesture into a room lined with books on four sides, with a fire blazing in the hearth, a room made for historic fireside chats, or – if only the furnishings had been a little less valuable – for settling down with a good book. Owen was alone in the library. The entrance to the men's room was set into the east wall, past the portraits of four Indian chiefs, through a green door with a brass marker – *Gentlemen*.

He emerged again after a few minutes, nodded to the uniformed aide, and followed the red carpet up a brass-banistered stairway to the state level of the mansion.

There he turned into the glittering gold and white East Room, where equally glittering guests drank and danced and chattered under the stern faces of George Washington and John Quincy Adams. There were a few hundred of them, men done up in black tie and women in fluttering gowns – members of Congress and cabinet officers, foreign diplomats, famous journalists and high-level White House staff. Owen glanced up at a Stuart painting of Martha Washington, no less severe than her husband on the other side of the mantel. Crashing the White House, he decided, was a time for sheer bravado, and for an old rule of thumb – the less said, the better.

He took a scotch from a passing waiter and wandered through the crowd, stopping to chat where good manners required him to, then moving quickly on. Washington was a city not particularly kind to outsiders. It was easy enough playing the odd man out, one of a handful of guests who didn't work for the company in a one-company town. Once it became clear he didn't understand the local brand of shop talk, where agencies were identified by initials and prominent officials by nicknames, he was left alone. He had only to avoid the notice of the social aides, who were there precisely to make sure no one felt left out.

He wandered through the Green Room, the Blue Room, the Red Room, admiring the period antiques and the paintings, the priceless curios public guests were never allowed to touch. And he wound up in the State Dining Room, where a crowd of people clustered around a long buffet table. Others were hovering near the bar. Still others waited to pass through the receiving line in the Cross Hall that led back to the East Room.

Owen stopped at the bar for a refill. Then he too took his place in line, waiting to shake hands with the President.

And his guest of honour.

Elizabeth Easton stood in the receiving line for ten minutes before she knew she couldn't stand it ten minutes more. She hated receiving lines under any circumstances. Two seconds per person was hardly time to smile. But tonight even that was too much human contact. She made her escape, and went back upstairs, shielded by the relative privacy of the family quarters.

Vanessa Nichols found her in Anne's bedroom, dry eyed, motionless, staring down at the smooth surface of a bed last made when Anne left for Michigan.

Vanessa paused in the doorway. 'Elizabeth?'

The First Lady looked up. Her voice was as numb as her eyes. 'Hi, Vanessa. Come in.'

'What are you doing here?' Vanessa crossed the room and put

89

an arm around Elizabeth's shoulders. 'This is the last place you should be.'

'I keep thinking she'll be here.'

Vanessa smiled sympathetically but remained firm. 'Come away with me. You're torturing yourself.'

'I know.' Elizabeth glanced at the closed door to the adjacent room. 'Even Mrs Haskins asked to be moved down the hall. She said she couldn't stand it here.'

'How is Mrs Haskins?'

'All right physically. But she's blaming herself. *That's* torture.' Elizabeth closed her eyes. 'Oh, Vanessa, I blame myself, too!'

'That's nonsense! How could it be your fault?'

'If I hadn't gone to Mexico, if we hadn't sent Anne to Michigan—'

'They'd have done it another way.'

'They might not have.'

Vanessa shook her head. 'Professionals make opportunities if they have to. I know that much about Ed's work.'

Elizabeth wasn't convinced. She leaned forward and picked up a doll resting against the pillow, smoothing the yarn hair back from the painted face. 'What am I going to do?' she said softly. 'I can't paint, I can't do my mail—'

Vanessa's arm tightened around her shoulder. 'I know what you're going through. Dear God, I can't think of anything worse! But they're going to find her. There are thousands of people looking for her right now. Why, I've hardly seen Ed since—'

'I know. But it's been *two days*! And they haven't found *anything*!'

Elizabeth's eyes were no longer just numb. They were dark and tormented. She sank back on the bed.

'I'd give anything, *anything*—'

She stopped, unable to speak the words. Then, suddenly, she clutched the doll to her breast and burst into tears.

Owen was one of a few hundred people in the receiving line. The President shook his hand without hearing anything more than his name. Possibly not even that.

'I'm glad you could come,' he said. 'And have you met the Maestro?'

Owen's eyes shifted to the small, white-haired violinist as the President turned to greet the next person in line.

'This is a very great pleasure, Herr Heinemann. I've enjoyed your music for years.'

Franz Heinemann smiled. 'Thank you. I'm pleased to hear it.'

'I believe we have a mutual friend,' Owen added then.

'Oh?'

'Anna Schurz.'

For a moment, Heinemann only looked back at him. Then his eyes showed an emotion very close to fear. Perspiration broke out on his forehead. He produced a handkerchief and wiped it away.

'Perhaps we should talk later,' Owen said.

'Yes, I think we should.'

Owen nodded. Then he turned and disappeared into the crowd in the East Room.

Heinemann stood quite still – erect as always, his eyes cold, his face a mask of arrogance. He looked at Owen as he might have looked at an insect, or a crippled child – or a Jew.

'Anna Schurz,' Owen said. 'Your conduit to the SS.'

There was no one else in the room. They were in calling distance of the security agents and military aides outside in the red-carpeted corridor, but here in the White House library, they were alone.

'Who are you?' Heinemann said.

Owen didn't reply.

'Israeli?'

Owen laughed. 'No, but I suspect they'd like to know about you in Tel Aviv. They've scoured the world for lesser men.'

Heinemann smiled, but his eyes remained cold. 'If you're not Israeli, who are you? Who else could *care*?'

'There are one or two people outside Israel who disapprove of mass slaughter,' Owen replied. 'But don't worry, your secret is safe with me. I'm not going to tell a soul.'

A flicker of suspicion passed across Heinemann's face. As quickly, it was gone. 'Do you think I'm frightened of *you*?'

Owen shrugged.

'Who would believe you against me?'

'I don't think it will come to that.'

'But Anna died in Berlin. Everyone else is dead, too.'

'I wouldn't count on it.' Owen smiled. 'There are always survivors. Even in the Nazi death camps, some people survived.'

Heinemann turned away; it was a gesture not of remorse, but dismissal. He sat down in a chair by the fireplace and looked up at Owen with eyes that were coldly impassive. Auschwitz and Dachau meant less to him now than they had forty years ago. Their only purpose, their function; that gone, they mattered no more.

Nothing had changed.

'Perhaps you should tell me what you think you know,' Heinemann said.

Owen remained standing. He lit a cigarette without taking his eyes off Heinemann. '1938,' he said. 'You were a young violinist with a growing international reputation and a friend named Anna Schurz. *Anschluss*. The Nazis annexed Austria, and suddenly passports could be revoked at a whim.'

Heinemann glared at him scornfully. 'History. My own and the Third Reich. Both are well known.'

'Quite so,' Owen replied. 'But history never recorded a meeting between you and Anna in the fall of 'thirty-nine. *Who's Who* doesn't tell us how willingly you paid the price for preserving your own passport – how quickly you agreed to inform on your own friends in Vienna's artistic community.'

'Not friends,' Heinemann broke in. 'Jews.' His voice was calm, his words the more cutting for their lack of fervour. He might have been arguing the authorship of an obscure violin concerto. Infallibility wasn't a question; this was a matter of fact.

Nothing had changed.

'Jews in hiding,' Owen said. 'Whole families of them. Names and addresses. How many, do you remember?'

'What difference does it make?'

'Very little at this point.'

'Nor then.'

'Nor then,' Owen agreed. 'Who was to notice a few among so many? Who could have picked out whole groups betrayed by you? Who could have known it *was* you, a young violinist – arrogant, perhaps, but no Nazi. You kept your true feelings a secret. But you *welcomed* the Anschluss. You *believed* in the Nazis—'

'I supported the Nazi *cause*,' Heinemann said as he might have corrected a pupil. 'The Nazis were inferior creatures themselves. They lacked distinction. Better men could have made it work.' Then he dismissed the point with a gesture. 'None of this matters today. They are gone; the cause is not. What matters is how you know this. Who could have told you? Anna died more than thirty years ago.'

Owen drew on his cigarette. 'Anna died *two* years ago,' he said. 'She took her own life. In Brazil. *After* she had signed this.'

He reached into the jacket of his tuxedo and brought out a thickness of paper, several sheets folded together. Heinemann took them, glanced through them. Then he looked up at Owen. His eyes were no longer cold; they were burning with hatred. Anna's confession told it all.

'What do you want?' he demanded.

'The same thing the Nazis wanted. Your cooperation.'

Owen glanced at the door as a swell of voices arose outside in the hall. They came and went, some of the President's guests making an early departure. He turned back to Heinemann.

'You can call for help if you like. Or you can come with me.'

Heinemann hesitated a moment. He glanced at the papers in his hand. Then, reluctantly, he got up and followed Owen through the green door with the brass marker. They passed through a sitting room, where more bookshelves shared the walls with a large mirror, and made their way into the bathroom itself.

Heinemann seemed suddenly smaller under the bright light reflecting off porcelain tile. There was no time to waste now. The guest of honour was bound to be missed eventually, even in the crowd upstairs.

Owen reached into his pocket and brought out the fountain pen. He pulled off the cap and the pen point.

Heinemann saw the sharp needle inside. He looked at Owen,

and his mouth twisted into a kind of smile. 'My cooperation?' he said. Then the smile vanished, was replaced by a look of utter contempt. The voice dropped to a whisper, derisive, mocking: 'Swine! My life will speak for itself!'

'I daresay,' Owen replied. Then he plunged the needle into Heinemann's arm, through the cloth of jacket and shirt, straight into the flesh. The old man did not resist, as Owen knew he would not. Franz Heinemann would not demean himself with a futile physical struggle.

He died as he lived. Proud. Arrogant. And without a trace of remorse.

thirteen

Simon rounded the curve on to Memorial Bridge, leaving the Lincoln Memorial behind, eerie and white, only half-visible through the breaking darkness and a cover of morning fog. He switched to his lower beams as he crossed the bridge and turned south on the George Washington Parkway. There were few other cars on the road. It was not yet five a.m.

A mile or two down the parkway, his lights caught the small brown and white sign and he made a sharp right turn. A drive wound back through the trees to a paved parking lot, where he brought the car to a stop, shut off the engine, and got out.

There were no other cars in the lot, only silence and fog all around. Simon followed a pebbled path into the rows of evenly spaced pine trees set in azalea-edged patches of bark mulch. Ahead, through a clearing in the trees, a huge slab of rock rose up out of the mist like an ancient monolith. The LBJ Memorial Grove.

Graham was waiting on one of the stone benches. Simon dropped down beside him.

'I want you to contact Owen immediately,' Graham said. 'Tell him I want to know exactly what he's doing and when he's doing it.'

'I don't think he'll like that,' Simon said.

'I'm quite sure he won't, but that's neither here nor there. Tell him he can go right on making his own plans. He just has to let me know what they are ahead of time. Through you, of course.'

'Of course.' Simon lit a cigarette. 'It may be too late for that,' he said.

A look of concern crossed Graham's face.

Simon tossed his match into the bark mulch. 'I've just left Owen,' he said. 'Did you know he was at the White House last night?'

'Owen was?'

Simon nodded.

'How did he manage that?'

Simon shrugged. 'How does Owen manage half the things he does I suppose he took someone's place. He'd requested a copy of the guest list, and I got it for him. In any case, there was a bit of excitement. Franz Heinemann is dead.'

Graham's face tensed as he waited for Simon to go on.

'Heart attack,' Simon added, and Graham relaxed a bit. 'Or should I say *apparent* heart attack.'

Graham looked back at him with cold, unmoving eyes. 'Are you telling me Richard Owen *killed* Franz Heinemann?'

'That's right.'

'In the *White House*?'

'Right under the President's nose.'

For once Graham was speechless. He sat there, staring at Simon, horrified. Then he exploded. 'Christ almighty, I've got a madman on my hands!'

'I don't think so.' Simon smiled. 'Wait till you've heard the rest.'

The fog had lifted by the time Owen left Washington on a morning shuttle bound for New York City. The papers he was carrying identified him as a French antique dealer. In New York, he would

95

change identity once more, to become an Austrian businessman on his way home to Vienna.

The morning papers carried the story of Heinemann's death. The *Times* gave it a properly serious tone, but the *News* did it up right, full of melodrama, an old man alone with his failing heart, in the men's room – at the White House, for God's sake.

If only they'd known the truth, Owen thought, the tabloids would have gone berserk.

In any case, the White House had issued a statement expressing regret over the loss of a great artist and dismay that it happened there. The President had ordered a military transport to take the maestro home. The military jet, in fact, was taking off from Andrews Air Force Base shortly after Owen's commercial flight departed from JFK.

The President had appointed an official party to escort Heinemann home – a former ambassador to Austria, a prominent American pianist, and no less a presidential emissary than the Secretary of State.

And one other distinguished passenger, Owen thought with a smile – small, but distinguished – and of far greater interest to the newspapers, had they known, than anyone else on that plane.

Ed Nichols had been thinking about Franz Heinemann all day. Officially, it wasn't his concern. Unofficially, it interested him greatly. He wasn't sure why. Instinct, perhaps. Or the timing . . .

The *timing*. My God!

He leaned forward and pressed the button on his desk.

'Yes, sir?'

Nichols almost shouted into the intercom. 'Get the White House physician for me,' he said, 'and tell Fleming to get in here on the double.'

Nichols was on the phone when Fleming came through the door, breathing heavily. He had been down in the War Room, and had taken the stairs rather than wait for an elevator. He dropped into a chair and waited for Nichols to finish.

'Then it's possible,' Nichols said. He nodded. 'Thank you, doctor. That's what I wanted to know.'

He replaced the receiver and looked across at Fleming, eyes bright behind the wire-frame glasses. 'Here's a theory for you, Paul. I think Franz Heinemann was murdered.'

'*Murdered?*' Fleming stared back, astonished. 'But why?'

'For a US military transport and no customs search.'

'But that's all standard procedure—'

'Not when someone's got the President's daughter and may be trying to smuggle her out of the country.'

Nichols didn't wait for Fleming's mouth to close. 'Get on the horn to our station chief in Vienna,' he said. 'Tell him to get on this right now. Also alert the proper officials in Austria and adjacent countries. I want everything covered – airports, railroad stations, border crossings, *everything*.'

Fleming nodded and got quickly to his feet. Then at the door he stopped.

'Ed, let *me* go.'

'To Vienna I can't. I need you here.'

'More than you need me there. This may be the break we've *needed*. We can't trust this to a station chief alone. I don't care how good he is.'

Nichols hesitated. Then, decisively, he pressed the button on his desk.

'Call Andrews,' he said into the intercom. 'Tell them to have a plane ready to leave for Vienna in thirty minutes. And get a helicopter warmed up.'

'For you, sir?'

'No, for Paul Fleming.'

Traffic was heavy around Vienna's Schwechat Airport as evening settled over the city. Simon made his way slowly through the maze of cars, then veered off suddenly towards a drive where public cars were banned. He flashed his pass at the guard and was let through.

The American jet was sitting on the concrete apron, about two hundred yards beyond the terminal. Simon pulled up near a cluster of people on the ground, got out, and opened the rear door of the hearse.

Then he stood back and waited while a baggage lift was rolled into place alongside the plane. The passengers began to disembark while four men in coveralls positioned the coffin on the lift. They rode down with it and carried it to the waiting hearse.

Pallbearing was no regular chore for the baggage men. If any of them had ever seen the inside of a hearse, they wouldn't remember the details. The cavity in the floor was there, obviously, to prevent the weight of the coffin from shifting during the ride.

Simon closed the rear door and climbed back in behind the wheel. He started the engine and pulled up behind the police escort. Then he pressed a lever under the dashboard. Behind him, locks disengaged. The coffin and the separate compartment beneath it were no longer fastened together.

He followed the escort car in through the streets of Vienna to a mortuary in the inner city, near the banks of the Danube and St Stephen's Cathedral. When the coffin was lifted out, no one but Simon noticed that the cavity was no longer there. Now, the floor of the hearse was perfectly flat.

He watched the coffin being carried up the steps, then started the engine again and slipped away unnoticed. After a while, he made a left turn into a drab industrial section of the city. The garage was on his right. As he swung into it, the door lowered behind him and an overhead light came on.

A woman came forward, young and blonde. She smiled prettily. 'Any problems?'

'None.' Simon got out and handed over the keys. 'She's all yours from here,' he said. 'I've got a plane to catch.'

Owen's plane touched down at Schwechat an hour after the American jet. As he left the terminal, he opened his wallet for the parking stub that had come with his Austrian passport. The stub belonged to a blue Volkswagen, and the keys were under the floormat.

He bypassed Vienna, skirted the village of Grinzing at the northwest edge of the city, and turned west, into the Vienna Woods.

The directions that came with the passport were explicit, and he had no trouble finding the small road that led off the autobahn into the thick forest, where the cottage was hidden from view. He drove past the place about fifty yards, then – with no other cars in sight – made an abrupt u-turn and nosed the Volkswagen into the wooded lane. From there he set off on foot.

The path was lined with trees and shrubbery, thick on both sides. After several feet it turned sharply into the woods, and Owen could just see the cottage through the thickness of green. A quaint little scene, like something from *Hansel and Gretel* – a gingerbread house surrounded by deep, dense forest.

The door swung open as Owen approached, but the woman who stood there was not the witch of the fairy tale. She was big boned but slender, with delicate colouring and blonde hair pulled back in a neat little knot at her neck. The chic black dress was gone, replaced by more practical slacks and a heavy sweater. She was herself now, not the American beauty who had so effectively captivated the German back in Athens. But it *was* the same woman.

Blondie!

fourteen

Blondie led Owen upstairs to a loft with an eiderdown mattress on the floor and a lamp beside it. On the mattress lay a small, pyjama-clad figure. In her arm was a needle, attached by tube to a bottle hanging overhead. Glucose water with vitamins and minerals added. Even unconscious, Anne Easton had to eat.

Owen nodded his approval. This was not the dark curly-top he had stolen out of the house at Indian Springs. Her hair was straight now, and cut in a boyish style, with long bangs across the forehead.

Blondie came up behind him. 'Well?'

'Excellent,' Owen replied. Once they got her into the right clothes, she could easily pass for his son. He leaned down to check her pulse and breath rate. Then he said, 'She'll be needing another injection.'

Blondie pointed to a hypodermic kit on a table nearby. 'How long can you keep her drugged?' she asked.

'A few more days won't hurt.'

He got up and looked at Blondie. She wasn't American, as Owen had learned back in Athens, but her American English was excellent. Her eyes were grey, big under finely shaped eyebrows, soft against a face as pink as any of the plump *madchen* working the wine houses back in Grinzing.

'What do I call you?' he said.

'Erica.' She flashed her familiar sweet smile. That, at least, hadn't been part of the act at the Grande Bretagne. 'Erica Foley, of course,' she added in the same nearly flawless English.

Owen nodded. 'The passports are ready?'

'Downstairs. Would you like to see them?'

'Yes.'

He followed Erica down the steps to the main room of the cottage, with its stone fireplace and open, beamed ceiling. Erica picked up a manila envelope and handed it to him.

Inside, he found three US passports, one for the father, one for the mother, and one for the four-year-old child. The Foleys of St Louis, Missouri – a happy family threesome on holiday in Europe.

Owen probed deeper into the envelope and found more papers, including the rental forms for the blue Volkswagen he had left outside. He examined them all and dropped them back inside.

'What about my things?' he said.

'You'll find everything you need in the bedroom.' Erica gestured towards a closed door.

'And the rendezvous?'

'Day after tomorrow, near the Semmering Pass.'

'Good.' Owen smiled. 'We have nothing to do, then, until it's time to cross the border.'

'I don't think I'll mind waiting,' Erica replied. She smiled again – not the sweet smile, now. It was more like the smile that had captivated the German back in Athens.

*

The mortuary director bowed deferentially and closed the door behind him, wondering if the American and the maestro had been personal friends. He didn't know who the American was. The man from the foreign ministry had told him only that the visitor was an important official of the US government and to give him fullest cooperation.

He shook his head and turned down the hall towards his office. Why an important US official would go through the foreign minister's office for the simple business of a private viewing was beyond him. But then, perhaps, it was just bureaucratic habit. Government officials, once accustomed to working through channels, soon forgot there was any other way.

Inside the candle-lit chapel, Paul Fleming switched on the overhead lights and moved quickly to one side of the casket, a superbly crafted box of walnut and bronze that had been America's contribution to Franz Heinemann's final rest. He looked down at the face of the old violinist, eyes closed against pale cheeks, body rigid against a cushion of white satin. Only the Stradivarius looked real, carefully arranged in a pair of lifeless hands.

Fleming felt like a grave robber, like a man intruding on a privacy more intimate than any moment of life. He shrugged it off. There had to be something here.

He bent down to examine the surface of the coffin, running his fingers along the polished wood, rapping occasionally with his knuckles. Nothing. Nothing to suggest Anne Easton had been here once.

She had been. He knew it. Attached to this casket somehow. But he had to have concrete evidence, something Nichols could carry into the Oval Office. Proof.

He shook his head and stepped back to study the casket from a different angle. And then it caught his eye: a tiny scratch in the bronze trim that edged the bottom of the casket. Not just a scratch, but several, all with one thing in common. Their spacing. Fleming measured them off with his hands. Yes, they were perfectly spaced at exact intervals, about eighteen inches apart.

His eyes brightened and a smile crossed his face. He reached into his pocket for the camera and began to record the evidence on film.

Ed Nichols leaned forward, excited. 'Good work, Paul!' he said into the phone. 'Get those photos to me as fast as you can.'

'It's not as good as it might be,' Fleming replied from Vienna. 'There's no trace of the man who drove the hearse.'

'You're convinced she was transferred inside the hearse?'

'Had to be. Nothing came off that plane but the coffin and the official party with their hand luggage. The mortuary director supervised the arrival at the other end, along with about thirty other people. No one was alone with that coffin until I got here. It had to be inside the hearse, Ed, but the driver has simply vanished.'

'As long as Anne doesn't vanish,' Nichols said. 'I want that country blanketed with people who know what to look for.'

'It is. I'm using all our people and half the military intelligence agents in Europe.'

'The Austrians?'

'Full cooperation.'

'You've alerted the borders?'

'Before I left Washington.'

'Well, do it again. I don't want any chance for a slip-up. Airports and railroads?'

'They're covered.'

'Good.' Nichols nodded and leaned back in his chair. 'They may have smuggled her into Austria,' he said, 'but by God, they won't get her out!'

Nichols watched the last part of the welcoming ceremony from the inside of the hedge.

The speeches were over, and the Marine Band was playing, one national anthem followed by the other. A colour guard presented the flags of both countries, and the President stepped down from the platform, escorting the Belgian Prime Minister around the small circle of guests and towards a black limousine waiting near the Diplomatic Entrance.

The President smiled cordially as he shook the other man's hand. Later, there would be talks, but now the Prime Minister was on his way to Blair House. The President stepped back, still smiling, as the limousine pulled away to a flourish of trumpets, following the circular drive back towards the outer gates. The ceremony was over. The President turned towards the break in the hedge.

Inside, his smile vanished. The public man was gone.

'Ed, you're here. Good.'

Nichols smiled as he fell into step along the covered colonnade that skirted the Rose Garden and led to the Oval Office. 'I was already on my way when I got your message to come,' he said. 'I've got some good news, I think.'

The President looked up sharply.

'We know Anne is in Austria.'

The President stopped. 'What makes you think so?'

Quickly, Nichols explained. He was watching Matt, watching for a change in the eyes – for a new look of hope, even gratitude. Instead, he saw only confusion.

'The point is,' Nichols finished, 'now we know where to look. Now we know where to concentrate our resources.'

The President looked back at him for a moment. 'I'm not sure we do,' he said, and resumed his pace along the passageway. 'I called you here because we've had contact.'

'From the *kidnappers*?'

'Yes.'

'What? Where? From Vienna?'

'From Berlin.'

'*Berlin?*'

The President cut across the Rose Garden and pushed open the glass-paned doors that led directly into his office. Another man was waiting inside. He got to his feet. Sam Wycoff, the Secret Service director.

'Show him,' the President said.

Wycoff picked something up from the President's desk and held it out to Nichols. A locket, small and gold, attached to a delicate chain and engraved with the single initial *A*. Nichols let out a slow whistle. He recognized the locket instantly. He and Vanessa had given it to Anne on her third birthday.

He looked up at Wycoff. 'She was wearing it—?'

Wycoff nodded.

'How did it get back here?'

'Through the mail, addressed to the President. The mailroom sent it to me. The package was mailed air special, two days ago from West Berlin.'

'This is all that was in it? Just the locket?'

'No, this too.'

Nichols put the locket back on the President's desk and took the piece of paper Wycoff held out to him. He read it, and his face went pale. He dropped into a chair.

Four words: *Cannon the Racy Bar.*

'I don't know what it means,' Wycoff said. 'Apparently you do.'

Nichols nodded slowly. Then he glanced up at the President. 'Could I see you alone?' he said. 'I'm sorry, Sam, it's a matter of national security.'

The President nodded, and Wycoff left the room. Then the President moved around his desk and sat down, obviously exhausted.

'Where is she?' he asked. 'In Austria or Germany?'

Nichols didn't say anything, just shook his head.

'But you do know what that means?' He nodded at the paper in Nichols' hand.

'Yes, I'm afraid I do.' Nichols pulled himself up straight in the chair. 'The Racy Bar is a nightclub in West Berlin,' he began. 'It's called the Resi, actually. American GIs renamed it after the war.'

'Who would know that, besides a GI?'

'Anyone who knows Berlin.'

The President nodded. 'And Cannon?'

'Cannon's one of my agents in the Soviet sector. I assume the message means we should send him into the Resi and wait for a move from them.'

The President leaned forward. 'For God's sake, what's all the mystery then? *Send him!*'

'It's not that simple. Cannon's a code name. He's under deepest cover. He's a high-ranking military official in the Soviet's East German Command.'

'Christ, Ed! A *Russian*?'

'More or less. He was born in Omaha, but the CIA sent him into the USSR years ago, created a background, let him sit there – doing nothing, attracting no suspicion. For all purposes, he *is* Russian. He *worked* his way up through their military. He worked for them, straight, doing a damn good job – until he got near the top. That's when we started cashing in. Hell, Matt, he's our primary source of intelligence on Soviet activities in East Germany. We *can't* risk his cover!'

The President leaned back. 'It seems to me his cover is already blown.'

'Not necessarily,' Nichols said. 'Someone may know about Cannon; that's the code name *we* use. But they may not know who he is.'

'And they will if he goes to the Resi.'

'Yes.'

Silence fell over the room as the two men looked at each other across the desk, silence broken only by the rhythmic ticking of an antique clock against one curved wall.

Finally the President said, 'We *have* to risk his cover.'

Nichols nodded.

Cannon be damned! They didn't have any choice.

Fleming entered the lounge on the top floor of the old Reichstag building in West Berlin. The door he closed was marked *Private*. He crossed the room to the window.

The building sat close in to an angle formed by the river Spree and the Berlin Wall. The window gave a view of the Soviet sector, with the Wall below and – discomforting yards away – a guard tower manned by East German *Vopos* armed with submachine guns.

Fleming lowered the shade.

Cannon would see the signal and make contact as soon as he could.

The door locked behind Fleming as he turned and left the room.

*

The Resi was a cavern of a place with just two hundred intimate tables connected by telephones and pneumatic message tubes. It was jammed.

Hell of a spot for a secret meeting, Cannon thought, knowing, in fact, that it was. If only he weren't quite so conspicuous here, a Russian colonel sampling a taste of western decadence.

Yet he didn't dare break cover. There was still a chance his cover might be preserved.

He found an empty table and ordered a glass of vodka.

The tables were arranged in a huge semi-circle around a large dance floor, where the orchestra was holding forth with Broadway show tunes. Behind it, fountains danced to the music. The crowd was a mixture of young and old, natives and tourists – all involved in a lively conspiracy to keep the pneumatic circuit, as well as the bartenders, in business.

Cannon spotted the agent called Zebra at a table on the other side of the dance floor. He knew there were a dozen CIA agents posted around the room, but he made no effort to find them.

Now, he could only wait.

For what? For whom?

He took a deep breath and leaned back in his chair, wishing he'd skipped dinner tonight. It felt like a piece of lead in his stomach.

The waiter returned with his drink, and Cannon paid the tab. He wanted no delay if he had to leave the place in a hurry. Then he tasted his vodka and let his eyes scan the room.

He'd spent an hour talking possibilities with Fleming. West German intelligence? No. Both sides of Berlin were constantly whispering about secret manoeuvres in Bonn – neo-Nazism, communist infiltration, one thing or another. But the fact remained, West Germany was America's strongest ally, economically if not culturally. West Germany would not kidnap Anne Easton.

Cannon felt a dull ache forming at the back of his head. Not really pain, just pressure. Tension, he decided, and took another drink of vodka.

One of the super-terrorist organizations? They wouldn't mind the risk, and the audacity of it was perfect. But there was nothing subtle about the German terrorist groups. If they were going to kidnap Anne Easton, they would move in with a commando squad and probably kill everyone in sight. Nothing as cunning as a single man, taking the place of another and walking out through the front door with the President's daughter tucked under his arm.

The terrorists, furthermore, would have made their demands clear by now. They weren't a patient lot – nor did they like to keep their successes secret. If they had been behind this, the whole world would know.

Not the terrorists, no.

That left the East Germans, acting alone (not likely) or with the advice of Mother Russia. But if that were the case, he would have known about it – *unless* his colleagues on the other side of the wall had kept him in the dark on purpose.

Good God! Cannon's mind veered away from the thought. No wonder he had a headache!

The headache was getting worse, spreading across his temples and around behind his eyes. Pounding, true pain now, making it hard to think. He looked around for his waiter. A couple of aspirin might help. This was no time to be sick.

He winced as the pain sharpened. Damn! Where had the bastard gone?

A man made his way through the kitchen to the back door that opened on to an alley behind the Resi. His car was waiting there. Inside, he pulled a coat on over his waiter's costume, started the ignition, and drove off through the night.

Something was terribly wrong.

Cannon's vision was starting to blur. He looked for Zebra on the other side of the room but could no longer see her. He couldn't see anyone, just a splash of colour and light. The music from the orchestra pounded painfully in his head. Not music. An aching crash of sound.

He had to make contact. He had to let Zebra know. To hell with breaking cover! Something was *wrong*!

The telephone on his table moved into focus, then blurred away again. He reached for it, fumbling, upsetting his glass. Then he found it, grabbed the receiver, tried to raise it to his ear.

Where was Zebra? What was her table number?

Cannon tried to remember, but the pain was too much. It was agony! He couldn't think, didn't want to think. He wanted to sleep. If only he could put his head down on the table. And sleep. Sleep . . .

On the other side of the room, Zebra saw Cannon collapse against the table, like a man who'd had too much to drink. She waited a moment or two, but Cannon didn't move. Then she got up and moved casually through the room, smiling here, fluttering an eyelash there. She was a young woman, attractive, looking over the crowd.

She approached Cannon's table and started to move on past it. Then, curiously, she turned back.

'Hello there, honey.' Brightly. 'What's the matter with you?'

Cannon didn't move.

'Are you sick?' She bent over him, placed a hand against his neck. Then, suddenly, she stood up and summoned a waiter. 'This man needs an ambulance!'

The woman stepped back as the waiter bent over Cannon, and she raised her hand to her neck. It was the signal they used. The others would know what it meant.

Cannon was dead.

fifteen

They approached the Austrian border. Erica nosed the blue Volkswagen into the line of cars waiting to cross into Italy. The US passports that belonged to the Richard Foleys of St Louis were in the glove compartment, with the papers for the car. Their story was set. It was time to make it work.

'Wake up,' she said urgently. 'We're at the border.'

The man in the seat beside her stirred and opened his eyes. He was about thirty-five, with a fresh American face; unsophisticated, though well dressed in casual warm-weather clothes. A tourist on vacation with his family in Europe.

He was instantly alert.

He turned to look at the child sleeping across the back seat. Johnny Foley didn't move; he wasn't well. Chicken pox – it had to happen now!

Richard Foley nodded to his wife as a customs inspector approached them on her side.

'*Buon giorno.*'

'*Buon giorno,*' Erica replied in her best imitation of an American who had learned the travel basics of the Italian language.

'Your passports, *per favore.*'

Erica smiled as she handed them through the window.

The inspector glanced at them, then sharply back at Erica behind the wheel. He bent over, glanced at the man. Then his eyes shifted to the back seat.

'What is the purpose of your visit to Italy, Madame Foley?' he said tightly.

Erica looked back at the stern dark eyes in a face that was full of suspicion, and suddenly her mind went blank! She remembered nothing, none of the questions and answers she and Owen had practised. No destination. No purpose.

But the inspector didn't notice. His attention had been diverted by the clatter of an old pick-up truck that rolled into place in the adjacent line. With it came squeals and grunts – and an unmistakable odour. The truck was full of pigs.

Erica took a deep breath and relaxed against the seat.

The inspector studied the truck for a moment, sniffing the air with obvious distaste. Then he turned back to the passports in his hands.

'Yes, Madame Foley, the purpose of your visit.'

'We're on vacation,' Erica replied evenly, even smiling. 'We're driving south to Venice, Florence, and Rome.'

A swell of voices rose from the area of the truck. Questions. Impatient, Italian. Vaccinations and quarantine papers.

The inspector shook his head impatiently. 'And the car?' he said. 'Is it yours?'

'We rented it in Vienna.'

'May I see the papers?'

Another clattering as the driver of the truck climbed down from the cab. He was an Italian peasant, small and stooped, with wisps of grey hair showing under the edge of an ancient cap. He hobbled towards the back of the truck on uneven legs. Three customs agents clustered around him as he grabbed one of the pigs and showed them a metal tag wired to its leg.

The inspector sighed heavily and forced his concentration back to the passports. Behind him, the squeals and grunts grew louder as the agents moved in to check the rest of the truckload.

Finally, he could stand it no more. He turned. 'What's the delay there?' he demanded.

An agent explained in a stream of rapid Italian.

The inspector cut him off with a gesture. 'Are the papers in order?'

'Yes, sir.'

'And the pigs are tagged?'

'Yes.'

'Then get them out of here.'

The agent motioned to the driver, who shrugged and hobbled to the front of the truck. The inspector turned back to Erica.

'*Please*, your car papers.'

Erica unlatched the glove compartment and produced the car-rental forms. 'I believe they're in order,' she said, smiling.

But the inspector was in no mood for pleasantries now. 'We shall see.'

He examined the papers while, behind him, the truck pulled away. Suddenly, it was very quiet. The inspector bent over again, letting his eyes probe deeper into the car. This time they lingered on the sleeping child. T-shirt and jeans. American tennis shoes. And red spots on the face.

'Your son has a rash, Madame Foley.'

'Yes, chicken pox.'

'Chicken pox?' The inspector was clearly doubtful. He opened

110

the rear door of the car and bent in for a closer look. Gently he touched the child's face.

Suddenly, he straightened up. His face was no longer stern, but grim. 'I'm sorry, Madame, but you'll have to come with me.'

Erica's eyes shifted to the customs building, then back to the man standing at stiff attention on the other side of the window. 'Is something wrong?' she said.

'These are *not* chicken pox. Come with me. You too, sir. And please, bring the child.'

Nichols' fist turned white as he gripped the telephone harder. 'What do you mean, *Cannon is dead*?'

'He's *dead*,' Fleming repeated. 'I'm telling you, Ed, it's as if someone set this up to flush Cannon out and kill him.'

'But who? The Russians wouldn't kill him without knowing exactly what information he had passed on to us. They'd never kill him without finding that out first.'

'They wouldn't do it in public, either.'

'Then who? Who else would *want* Cannon dead?'

The answer was simple. No one.

Nichols brought his fist down on the desk. Damn! Even brought home with his cover blown, Cannon would have been a valuable resource. An *invaluable* resource. But now he was dead, murdered for no apparent reason, in plain view of CIA's deputy director and a dozen crack agents.

And what had they learned about the President's daughter? *Nothing!*

Nichols sighed heavily. 'Are you sure no one made contact with him before he died?'

'I'm positive,' Fleming replied. 'I was there the whole time. No one got near him but the waiter.'

'The waiter! For God's sake, Paul, if the poison was in the vodka' —

'That didn't escape me,' Fleming broke in dryly. 'The waiter has disappeared.'

Nichols nodded. 'Like the driver of the hearse in Vienna.'

'Exactly. We don't even have a name.'

'Someone at the Resi must know him—'

'Sorry, he was a temporary. He showed up in the kitchen and said he was filling in for a buddy who was sick.'

'And the buddy?'

'Gone, too.'

Nichols nodded grimly. 'I wouldn't want to hold my breath until he shows up alive.'

'No, neither would I.'

'Look, Paul, use the whole damn army if you have to. I want that waiter found. And stay in touch with the West Germans. If the kidnappers are in Berlin, Anne may be there, too. It's possible they've slipped her over the border, in spite of our precautions. And if they have –' he paused '– it must not happen again.'

'Not *real* chicken pox,' Erica said. She glanced nervously at her husband, then down at the child between them. Johnny Foley, still dazed by the abrupt interruption of his nap.

The inspector raised an eyebrow. 'What other kind of chicken pox are there?'

'It was a *joke*,' Erica explained. 'Johnny drew them on himself. It's indelible ink. It won't wash off. Believe me, we tried everything.'

'Why didn't you tell me the truth when I asked you about the rash?'

'You didn't give me a chance. I was going to tell you—'

'Madame Foley,' the inspector said, 'we do not have time here for jokes. We have a border alert to watch for a missing child about the age of your son. We've been told to detain anyone with a child if the circumstances are at all suspicious. And false chicken pox are suspicious.'

Erica's eyes widened as she stared at the inspector without saying anything.

Then Richard Foley leaned forward across the desk. 'What are you suggesting, Inspector? That we've kidnapped our own son?'

'I'm suggesting nothing, sir. I am only saying you can't leave until we've verified your identity.'

Foley was quiet for a moment. Then he said, 'At home we have the right to make a phone call.'

'You have the same privilege here.'

'Then I must insist on placing a call to the nearest American Embassy.'

Owen had grown used to the odour of pigs and hardly noticed it now. He was driving south through Italy, keeping an eye on the rearview mirror, watching for Erica on the road behind him. An hour had passed since he crossed the border with his truckload of pigs, but still no blue Volkswagen. He wasn't moving fast; she should have caught up by now.

Obviously, they had stopped her at the border, just as they had planned.

Owen smiled, remembering the sleek blonde of the Grande Bretagne, passing a message skilfully over the table, in plain view, yet unnoticed by anyone but him. Erica, walking away on the arm of the unknown German, and his own thoughts as he left the G.B. alone. Two days in Vienna had been better than two minutes in Athens, but once again he wished their meeting had been a little less brief.

His smile broadened. He wasn't worried about Erica; she could take care of herself. And, of course, the American Embassy would make the identification. The man in the car *was* Richard Foley of St Louis, Missouri. He worked for the CIA. And the boy in the back was his son. Only Erica had a part to play, and Owen had no doubt she could do it.

He drove on, picking up speed. The truck looked like a wreck, but its engine was a custom job, powerful and finely tuned. He would make good time from here.

North of Venice he turned off the main highway and followed a winding road back through the countryside, counting the kilometres as the speedometer ticked them off. The farm lay just ahead, nestled against the gentle slope of a hill, newly ploughed fields marked off by fresh-painted fences. A farm well tended and, for the moment, unoccupied.

Owen pulled off the cap and grey wig as he drove into the barn.

Then he began to peel away the thin layers of rubber that had added forty years to his age. A pad of cotton and a bottle of alcohol removed the stubborn adhesive. He looked at himself in the mirror, saw a new version of the man he had been – an Italian peasant, but younger, his back straight, his hair still black like Edward Drake's.

Then he climbed down from the seat and pressed a hidden button. The seat opened up like a coffin, revealing the child inside. Not the dark curly-top, no. The President's daughter was a boy now, in peasant clothes like Owen's, with straight dark hair not unlike his own.

Owen nodded. It wasn't enough to fool anyone who knew her, but it would avoid a chance sighting if he had to take her out of the truck.

He checked her pulse and breath rate, then closed the compartment. Fifteen minutes later, he drove out of the barn with new licence plates and papers, but leaving the pigs behind.

The President's eyes turned progressively colder as Nichols described what had happened in Berlin. He sat behind his desk without moving, shoulders square, jaw tight, mouth a firm line. When Nichols finished, he pushed himself up out of the chair and began to pace off the anger he was feeling inside.

'Damn it!' he exploded finally. 'What kind of operation are you running? My daughter's been missing for *six days*. I've given you every power of this office, and what do you have to show for it? Nothing!' He swung around. 'Nothing, that is, except one top-secret, deep-cover agent murdered under the nose of your own top man.' He raised his hands in a gesture of futility. 'My God, I'm surrounded by bunglers. First the Secret Service, now you. You, Ed, of all people! I thought I could surely trust you!'

Nichols looked back without flinching. 'You know you can trust me.'

The President stood there, glaring at Nichols. Then, slowly, his eyes softened, his face sagged, his arms fell wearily to his sides. He moved back to his desk and dropped down into the chair. '*Why* don't they say what they *want*? Cannon? Okay, they got him.'

Nichols shook his head. 'Cannon as motive doesn't make any sense.'

'Why not? You said he was vital—'

'And he was. Oh yes, if the Russians knew about Cannon but didn't know who he was, they might well kidnap Anne to force him into an open move. But if it were the Russians, they'd have done nothing but identify him at the Resi. They'd have let him walk out of there, go home. Then they'd have rushed him off to one of their horror chambers at Lubyanka, and we'd never have seen him again. No, it's not the Russians, but I can't figure out who else would want Cannon dead. Or why they would go to such elaborate lengths to accomplish something that could have been done a hundred easier ways. It makes no sense at all.'

A buzzer sounded softly on the President's desk. He leaned forward. 'Yes?'

'The Secret Service director is here to see you, Mr President.'

He glanced up, exchanging a look with Nichols.

'Send him in.'

Sam Wycoff closed the door behind him and stood still a moment. His shoulders were stooped with a kind of weariness that went far beyond fatigue. In his eyes, a look of defeat. He was holding a box in his hand.

'This arrived in today's mail,' he said. 'From Johannesburg, South Africa.' He crossed the room and put the box down in front of the President.

Matt Easton lifted the lid. A pair of pyjamas. A *child's* pyjamas.

'Mrs Haskins has identified them,' Wycoff said. 'They're the pyjamas Anne was wearing the night she disappeared.'

The President nodded without looking up. He lifted the pyjamas out of the box, held them in his hands. A sharp look of pain crossed his face.

Nichols leaned forward and pulled out a piece of paper that was protruding from the box. He read it and leaned back again.

Sherman Old South Church.

The same thing, all over again.

sixteen

Paul Fleming saw the black man standing in the shadow of a tree across from the church, his dark skin and clothing hardly separate from the darkness of shadow and night. He was standing alone, watching the church.

Fleming raised his binoculars, focused them in on the man. It was Sherman.

Frankie Sherman. Baseball superstar, retired. An American in South Africa on a State Department exchange, setting up Little League ball teams among the local blacks. It was a programme designed to create goodwill with the blacks while not offending the whites who were in power. Obvious. Simple. Non-controversial.

Only Frankie Sherman was also on assignment for the CIA. His job, to act as contact with a local black activist leader who had been banned by the Apartheid government. Banning was the same thing as isolation; the man was cut off from his colleagues, from his work – until Frankie Sherman became his legs and his voice.

More goodwill: Sherman was an American, and the local activists loved him. More important, the intelligence flowing into the CIA from the black South African underground had doubled with Sherman in place. He was important; he was doing an excellent job. But the President's daughter was more important. In spite of Berlin, they had to take the risk. Again.

As Fleming watched, Sherman moved away from the tree. Then, looking right and left to make sure no one was coming, he hurried across the street and tried the church door. It was unlocked.

Inside the church, there was darkness and total silence. Sherman stood still, trying to get his bearings and let his eyes adjust. Slowly a dim light began to give shape to the entrance hall where he stood. He moved forward, towards the source of the light, into the sanctuary.

Old South was a Methodist church, and John Wesley would have been proud of it. There were no frills here, just a bare wooden floor under rows of uncushioned pews. A simple altar. On it, a plain gold cross, a Bible, a pair of candlesticks. Walls plain, painted white. No stained glass in the tall windows on both sides.

And, Sherman thought, no sign of a back-up team. Fleming had promised he had the place covered. Six CIA agents who attended evening services didn't leave when the service was over. Six, as many as they dared, still here now – Fleming said so. In the balcony, perhaps. Or maybe the choir loft up front.

They'd better be here, Sherman thought. After Berlin, they'd better be!

Still, he wasn't planning on sitting down for a drink.

He moved along the back wall and down the side aisle, ducking low under the windows. He wasn't interested in being spotted by a passing police patrol, a black man out after curfew in a place where he shouldn't be. He wasn't interested in testing the strength of his diplomatic passport. He had no immunity. Only the big shots got that.

At the front, some low shelves stacked with hymnals and offering plates. Steps leading up to the altar. Like the floor, bare wood.

And on the steps, an envelope. White, letter sized. Not dropped by accident. Balanced, in plain view.

Sherman moved towards the steps and bent down to pick up the envelope. Then as he straightened up, he heard a sound. High and to his right. A window. A sharp crack. A whining through the air.

In that instant he knew what the sound was, but his reflexes weren't that fast. A millisecond elapsed between sound and impact.

Sherman's head exploded as the bullet penetrated his brain. His body reeled sideways and crashed into a pew. Then he dropped to the floor. Bare wood, now thick with blood.

Inside the church, footsteps ran down wooden stairs, too late. In front, Fleming heard a motor start up, a car driving away. He glanced at his watch. It was midnight. Then the door of the church burst open and someone was running his way. Not Sherman, but Zebra.

Fleming knew before she told him. Frankie Sherman was dead.

*

The ferry from Brindisi was twenty hours at sea. Owen booked the cheapest passage, no bed or food. He brought his own food. Peasant fare – bread and cheese, a hunk of salami and a litre of Italian wine. Like his passenger under the seat, he would sleep in the truck – if he slept at all.

He lit a cigarette and glanced out the window at the rows of assorted vehicles lined up under the deck of the ferry. He had plenty of company here, poor Italians and Greeks who made the trip out of need, not for pleasure like the tourists in the state rooms upstairs. It was after midnight. From somewhere came the sound of snoring. But for Owen, sleep wouldn't come. He drew on the cigarette, thinking about what lay ahead.

The ferry would dock at Patras on the northern coast of the Peloponnesus. From there he would drive east, across the Corinth Canal. To Piraeus, the port of Athens. Another change of identity and transportation. Another car ferry. South this time. To Heraklion, on the island of Crete.

Crete, a parched and rugged island where people valued their independence above all else. And gave it in return. Owen smiled. As long as he kept to the countryside and away from the tourist resorts, no one would bother him or the peasant boy who was really the President's daughter.

He stubbed out his cigarette in the ashtray on the dash board and took a drink of wine. Sleep would come later, at the house in the countryside. There, he could relax. But here, he decided, it was better to stay awake.

It was a warm spring day in Washington, sun bright, trees budding, banks of red azaleas in bloom around the White House pool.

The President climbed out of the pool, dripping water across the concrete apron, and pulled on a terry cloth robe. A poolside table was set for coffee. He gestured for Nichols to join him.

It was hot in the sun, too hot for a shirt and tie. Nichols ran a finger under his damp collar. He remembered other times when he had joined Matt at the pool – a quick swim, a bite of lunch, and back to work. Moments of shared relaxation that rested and sharpened the mind.

Today would not be like that. It was hot in the sun, but the President's face was like ice. Rage under icy control.

'You've read my report,' Nichols said.

'Yes, I've read your report,' the President replied calmly. Too calmly. 'I've also been unavailable to the Secretary of State all morning.'

Nichols nodded. He knew why.

'Tell me, Ed, when we send people like Frankie Sherman into foreign countries on a State Department exchange, do we or do we not guarantee their political neutrality?'

'State does. I don't.'

'Obviously!' The President turned to him, glaring. 'Where do you get off countermanding State Department procedure without even asking me?'

Nichols looked back at him evenly. 'And if I had asked you?'

'I'd have said no, it's illegal.'

'Exactly.' Nichols nodded, like a prosecutor who had just proved his case. 'I didn't see it as a question of permission but expedience. Intelligence out of South Africa is critical right now.'

'I know that. But there's also the matter of you and me both being accountable to the law. Or had you forgotten?'

Nichols didn't reply.

'You've put me in a hell of a spot,' the President added angrily. 'If this thing blows open, I'll have not only the State Department and the South Africans to answer to, I'll have a credibility crisis that could affect our relations with every country in the world. And Congress! Christ! If they find out about this they'll crucify both of us! And for what?' His jaw tightened and his eyes turned a shade colder as he fired off the questions. 'Who kidnapped my daughter? Why? What do they want? And –' he leaned forward across the table '– *where is she?*'

Nichols felt a new, uneasy tightening in his chest. He and Matt had had their disagreements over the years, there had been plenty of those, but never anything like this. This wasn't Matt, but the President. He was furious. And, Nichols knew, he had good reason to be.

Nichols' hand moved to his pocket, produced a ballpoint pen, fingered it nervously. He looked at the man on the other side of the table. 'I don't know,' he said quietly. 'But,' he added before the President could explode, 'I'm beginning to get some ideas.'

'Ideas? Goddamn it! You sit on top of a multibillion-dollar intelligence operation. I don't want ideas – I want *facts*!'

Nichols didn't reply. He knew the spot he was in, knew it all too well. With all the resources of the federal government under his temporary control, he *had* no facts – except the one that refused to change. The President's daughter was missing, and all of Nichols' efforts had failed to produce the intelligence they needed to find her.

None of it made any sense. Except that. His own utter failure.

The President stared back at him. Then finally he leaned back in his chair. 'All right, let's hear your ideas.'

Nichols nodded. The mood was no warmer, but it was, perhaps, more receptive. In the absence of facts, ideas would have to do.

'Two things,' he began. 'First, the motive. We've lost two extremely valuable agents, but if the kidnappers were after Cannon and Sherman, them *alone*, I still say there would be other, easier ways to get them.'

The President shrugged, without committing himself.

'So there's more,' Nichols said. 'Cannon and Sherman are part of it, but there's something bigger they're after. Something or someone. And Matt, I think it's me.'

'You!' The President's forehead creased into a frown.

'Not me, personally,' Nichols added quickly. 'Me as CIA director. Or maybe it's bigger than that. Maybe it's you they're after.'

The ice melted. The President was fully interested now.

'I feel as if I'm being manipulated,' Nichols explained, 'and through me, you are, too. We've been forced to act without the usual caution. We pushed Cannon and Sherman out front. We had to; the kidnappers left us no choice. Now they're both dead, as easily and openly as if I'd offered them up for sacrifice. They're dead without a clue to who killed them. More important, without a clue about Anne. *That's* what doesn't make sense. I should have learned *something* by now. I haven't exactly been sitting on my hands.'

120

The President looked back at him thoughtfully and Nichols knew that for the moment, at least, he had won. He'd bought time. Time for another try.

'So that first,' he said. 'The motive. Not a specific ransom demand, but something far more complex. Me, you, the CIA. Maybe the whole damn government. There can be little doubt of it. The kidnappers have an informant. *Someone on our side.*'

The President looked up sharply. 'Good God!'

'It seemed positive to me after Cannon,' Nichols explained. 'Then it happened again. You see, the kidnappers couldn't have known how long it would take us to make the arrangements with Cannon and Sherman. Cannon, especially. In his case, we signalled and he made contact as soon as he could. We never knew how long that would be. A couple of hours? A couple of days? *We* didn't know when he would go to the Resi until he contacted us. And yet the waiter was there on the right day, at the right time, and not before.

'Sherman, too,' he went on. 'Sherman was killed from a tree outside the church. I suppose it's possible someone sat in that tree for two days, waiting for him to show up, but I doubt it. Once again, the killer was there at the precise right time.'

Nichols leaned back. 'Coincidence? Once, yes, but not twice.'

The President was still stunned. 'I don't believe it.'

'I know. It's hard to believe.'

'Do you have any idea *who it is*?'

Nichols shook his head. 'No idea at all. It could be any number of people. But,' he added, 'next time I'm going to find out.'

The President looked at him for a long moment. Then his face changed. He turned and nodded to a Secret Service agent who was standing out of earshot, back near a West Wing door. The agent raised his hand in a signal to someone else.

The President turned back to Nichols. 'You may be glad to know, then, that the next time is here.'

An aide appeared through the West Wing door, handed an envelope to the President, and disappeared back the way he had come. The President handed the envelope to Nichols without saying anything to explain it.

Nichols glanced at the postmark: Washington, DC. Then he tore it open.

A sheet of paper. On it, a small footprint. And four words.

He glanced up. 'The footprint is Anne's?'

The President nodded. 'It matches the footprint the hospital made when she was born.'

Four words: *Shelley Curtis the Rotunda*.

This time, there was no surprise, no shock. Nichols was beyond reaction. Another key agent who worked under deep cover for the CIA.

The President's eyes asked the question.

'Shelley Curtis,' Nichols said, as much to himself as to Matt. 'Shelley Curtis. My agent-in-place inside the US Congress.'

seventeen

Shelley Curtis watched the vote totals as they added up, scoreboard style, on the lightboard built into the gallery rail over the House floor. She smiled. They were winning by a large margin.

She was sitting on the aisle in the last row of seats before the rear wall of the chamber. Before her, her colleagues in Congress, weary from a long night's debate, seemed anxious to go home. She sought out the chairman of the Intelligence Oversight Subcommittee and gave him a victory sign.

An agriculture bill. Appropriations. Routine. And in it, secretly – unknown even to most of the voting members – money that had nothing to do with agriculture. Money to buy training planes, to build airfields, to pay the secret soldiers who worked for the CIA.

The chairman returned her sign. Intelligence work did not always accommodate democracy. Congressional appropriations were a matter of public record, available to anyone from Des

Moines to Havana or Peking. Some things had to be kept entirely off the record if the enemy wasn't to know.

Shelley asked with a gesture: did he want her to stay. The chairman shook his head. She had already cast her vote, a yea, recorded by a green light next to her name in the computerized blue silk wall above the press gallery. Final passage was moments away. There was no longer any chance she might be needed to influence some well-intentioned member bent on amending the wrong part of the bill.

Congresswoman Curtis – not yet forty, one of the new young breed in the House – was free to go home. But Paul Fleming wouldn't like it much if she did. One job was done for the day; another one now began.

She stopped in the cloakroom for her coat, then left the chamber by the east exit. There were no metal detectors here, as there were at the gallery doors upstairs. One piece of security was missing from this Capitol fortress – protection against a congressman gone berserk. So far it hadn't happened; the occasional lunatic ravings had been confined to debate.

Shelley smiled at the guards, made her way through the swarm of lobbyists at the door, and headed for the elevators before the crush that would come with the close of the session. It was nearly eleven p.m., a good night's work in Congress. But for Shelley, the night had just started. She had a late date of sorts at the club they still called the Rotunda.

She was no longer smiling as she waited for the elevator alone. The Rotunda could mean one of two places – the great domed hall of the Capitol, or the private political club on Ivy Street. Fleming had opted for the latter, and Shelley agreed. She worked in the Capitol, was there every day. She also belonged to the club, but she didn't go there often. It seemed the better choice.

In the meantime, Fleming warned her to be careful.

Shelley didn't need the warning. She was a graduate of CIA's training school and had spent five years in the field before she retired to a desk job at Langley. There she became dissatisfied with certain CIA methods. She took her complaints to the Federal Intelligence Board and eventually to public hearings in Congress.

Her testimony before the intelligence subcommittee caused a minor sensation and made Shelley into an overnight celebrity. Two years later, she ran for Congress herself. She won. And with her obvious credentials, she had no trouble acquiring a seat on Intelligence Oversight.

It was an ideal spot for a loyal former agent who claimed no fundamental objection to the CIA, only to its excesses. It was also an ideal spot for an agent who never did object to the way things were run at Langley.

Shelley's complaints had been handed to her along with supportive evidence. She was set up for her testimony on the Hill. Her election had been financed in part by covert government funds, like the money approved tonight. In truth, she never had *stopped* working for the CIA.

An elevator door opened. She stepped through and it started to close again, but a hand reached forward to block it. A man entered the elevator. He was tall and blond, with blue eyes and a scar at the side of his head.

'Simon! What are *you* doing here?'

'We've got to talk,' Simon replied quietly. He pushed the button for the first floor. 'Follow me, but remember, we're not together.'

Shelley nodded and asked no more questions. She knew Simon, knew he worked for the CIA. Something must have gone wrong.

The door opened again; Simon got off first. He flashed a card at a guard and moved off down the hall.

The guard recognized Shelley. 'Late night,' he observed.

'Aren't they all?' she replied with a smile and headed down the hall, keeping distance between herself and Simon ahead.

She wondered what kind of card Simon had shown. A congressional ID? Press credentials? Either one was readily available at Langley. Either one gave access to the Capital, even now that it was closed for the night.

Simon turned right into a wide corridor that ran the full length of the building. Shelley followed, her footsteps echoing against the old tile floor. They were one floor down from the House chamber. Here, there were no people, only the giant figures carved out of marble, and in bronze, overflow from Statuary Hall upstairs.

Shelley knew where Simon was going – to the Crypt, a tiny chamber in the lower depths of the building that was designed to be George Washington's tomb. There would be no guards at the Crypt at this hour of the night.

She nodded to herself as Simon turned into a door at the flight of circular stairs that led down through a narrow shaft to the cellar below. She'd had meetings at the Crypt before; she even carried a key to the iron gate.

Shelley followed the circular stairs down to a corridor that wound its way between thick stone walls, under open pipes and grating, into the heart of the building.

The corridor came to an end at the iron gate, where Simon was waiting for her. On the other side of the gate, white walls moulded into cathedral-like arches, and a long box draped in fringed black velvet. The Lincoln Catafalque, unused between state funerals, stored here in this appropriate place.

Shelley looked up at Simon and said, 'What's wrong?'

Simon smiled. 'Nothing.'

'Nothing?' Shelley frowned.

But Simon didn't reply. He dropped his hands into his jacket pockets and turned away. His steps were slow and easy, back the way they had come. Then, abruptly, he stopped and turned back to her.

The smile spread across his face but didn't touch the ice blue of his eyes. The scar showed up clearly under a harsh overhead light. So did the small automatic he was holding in his hand.

Shelley froze in a moment of panic and disbelief. '*Simon!* What *is* this? What are you *doing*?'

The voice was calm; the smile remained in place. 'I'm going to kill you,' he said.

Shelley stared back at him. She knew this wasn't a joke. But *Simon*? They were on the same side!

Her hands pushed deeper into her coat pockets. 'Fleming *didn't* send you,' she said.

'It doesn't matter who sent me.' Simon pulled back the safety with a click that echoed through the long, empty hallway behind him.

125

Shelley remembered a man called Cannon, dead at the Resi in Berlin. Another named Sherman at an old church in Johannesburg. And now here she was, at the Crypt, two floors down – straight down – from the Capitol Rotunda.

She smiled uneasily and tried to sound reassuring. 'Look, Simon, put the gun away. If you don't I'm going to scream so they'll hear me from here to the White House.'

Simon laughed out loud. The sound echoed harshly down the hall and faded into the distance. 'A lot of good that will do,' he said, and tipped the automatic towards the thick stone walls that hemmed them in on both sides. For an instant, his eyes turned away.

Shelley fired.

The bullet exploded out of her coat pocket and straight into Simon's chest. His hand lost its grip on the automatic, and his face froze in a final expression of shock. The automatic fell to the floor with a clatter much louder than the soft spat that had killed him, and blood began to spread across the front of his shirt. Then his knees gave way to his own dead weight.

Shelley's hand released the gun still in her coat pocket. She looked up into the loneliness of the long corridor. No footsteps rushing towards them. No one had heard. Then her eyes shifted down to Simon sprawled against the stone floor.

Good God! She had to find Fleming, and fast.

Paul Fleming was waiting in a car in the parking lot on Ivy Street. He saw Shelley approaching the door of the club, saw the look on her face, rolled down the window, and softly called her name.

She turned, saw him, and came running to the car. There was a hole in the pocket of her coat, a hole surrounded by a dark powder burn. Her eyes were wide and dark with something closer to panic than fear, and her hands were shaking as she pulled the door open and jumped in beside him.

'What's the matter?' Fleming asked urgently.

'Simon, my God! I just *killed* him!'

Fleming stared back, astonished. '*Simon?*'

'*Our* Simon,' Shelley confirmed. Then the rest came out in a rush: Simon finding her at the Capitol, leading her down to the Crypt. Simon pulling a gun, and Simon dead on the floor.

Fleming listened in stunned silence. '*Simon*,' he said when she finished. 'What in the world?' He looked at Shelley. 'Did he tell you *why*?'

Shelley shook her head quickly. 'I'm sorry, I know I should have tried to find out. I was so stunned, I couldn't *think*—'

'It's all right,' Fleming assured her. 'Take it easy. I'm just glad you're alive. What did you do with him, leave him there?'

'I hid him under the catafalque.'

Fleming gave a dry little laugh. 'Handy,' he said. 'What about his gun?'

'I have it.' Shelley produced the automatic from her coat pocket.

'Yours, too,' Fleming said. 'It could be traceable if someone else gets to Simon before we do. We'll issue you a new one.'

Shelley passed it across. She never carried a gun, anyway, except on special assignments. Like tonight in the Rotunda.

'Do you still want me to go in there?' she said.

Fleming hesitated a moment. Then he said, 'I don't think it will come to anything, but let's find out. I'll talk to Nichols in the meantime and get back to you here.'

Shelley nodded as she reached for the door handle.

'Be careful,' Fleming added.

Shelley looked back at him. Then she turned and got out of the car.

Technically, the Rotunda was no longer the Rotunda. The name belonged to a private restaurant that had occupied the building before the club took it over. But to the people who worked on Capitol Hill, the old name died hard. The club was still the Rotunda to the people who'd known it before.

The interior hadn't changed either – a baronial hall scaled down to size. A wide staircase with heavily carved wooden banisters branched off at the entrance, climbing two ways to the balcony that served as a gallery for presidential portraits. Kennedy, Johnson, Truman – a show of partisanship undisguised.

A third branch of the stairway led down from the entrance. Below there were linen-clad tables clustered under dim lights. Dinner was over; this was the drinking crowd, mostly congressional staff unwinding after a long day on the Hill.

The bartender recognized Shelley. 'Hi, Miss Curtis. What can I get you?'

Shelley folded her coat with the bullet hole inside and climbed up on one of the bar stools. 'Brandy, please.'

'Sure thing.'

Shelley smiled as she remembered a story she'd heard the Speaker tell. A presidential candidate working the crowd in a workingman's bar in Pittsburgh – steelworkers, most of them. The candidate, an elegant man of education and breeding, ordered drinks all round. The beer flowed; maybe a little whisky. Then the bartender turned to the candidate and asked what *he* would have. *Courvoisier*, the candidate replied. No wonder he lost the election!

Shelley picked up her glass and took a drink. She could feel herself starting to relax. The scene with Simon seemed far away, nothing that had happened to her. Then she realized she was not relaxed but numb. It was a long time since she'd been involved in anything like this. Old reflexes weren't that quick to reactivate. Like the Speaker's friend, she was too much accustomed to another style of life.

But nothing would happen here.

She glanced up as a man detached himself from a group at the other end of the bar. He was coming towards her; he was smiling. She recognized him – a lobbyist who would not be content to let a long day be done.

Shelley lifted her glass and steeled herself for a different kind of attack.

There was no one stationed at the Rotunda's front door. Proof of membership was required only to buy food or drink. Graham pushed open the door and stepped in.

He glanced down the stairs to the bar, then turned to the steps on his left and made his way up to the balcony. He was wearing a bulky raincoat to disguise his own shape, the collar turned up, almost meeting the brim of his hat.

He located the door to the men's room, preparing to move towards it if he needed an ostensible purpose for being here on the balcony. He didn't. No one came through the front door; no one appeared on the stairs.

He stood there alone, listening for the sound of the telephone.

'Phone call for you, Miss Curtis,' the bartender said. 'You can take it by the coatroom.'

Shelley nodded. It was probably Paul Fleming telling her to go home. She had been here for thirty minutes, and no one seemed to care, no one but the lobbyist whose interest in legislative affairs seemed to have no limit.

She made her excuses gratefully and crossed the room to the phone at the bottom of the stairs.

'Hello?'

'Miss Curtis?'

A man. Not Fleming.

'Yes?'

The answer came from above, a sharp whine through the air. The bullet hit at the back of her head and escaped again through her mouth. Her face fell away; blood splattered the wall and the telephone.

A waitress screamed. Faces at the bar turned around, following the horrified gaze. Incredulity gave way to shock, to frozen silence. No one moved.

And in that instant of horrified inaction, a man raced down the stairs from the balcony level above. A man in a shapeless raincoat with a hat pulled low on his head. He burst through the door and into the darkness outside.

The lobbyist leaped from his stool and raced up the steps, with the bartender close behind. They reached the door and pulled it open. But the killer was gone.

Graham had made his escape.

eighteen

Owen felt an enormous sense of relief. There had been no alert from Simon or, through Simon, from Graham. No one on his trail. He had successfully eluded the searchers and was here now, on the island of Crete – a grain of sand among billions, the fox leaving the hounds with no scent to follow and a whole world to search.

The sun was bright on the dark Cretan sea and turned the leaves of the olive grove a shimmering silver. Through gnarled tree trunks he could see the rocky coastline, awash with foam as the treacherous waves rolled and broke against the shore. Except for the waves there was no sound, nothing to shatter the silence of morning. The air was cool, full of the scent of mint and lemon, but morning had barely started. Owen knew the lush growth of the island would be short lived, would soon give way to brown under the parching heat of Greek summer.

He hoped he wouldn't be here when it happened.

He turned and walked back into the house, a small two-storey bungalow with whitewashed walls and wide windows, along a path that led through the olive grove to the sea. Later, at harvest time, men and women would be coming to work here. But now the house was surrounded by solitude, set back from the coast road that ran east from Heraklion, and protected from its nearest neighbour by distance and the wild growth of the island.

Owen climbed the stairs to the second floor and unlocked a door. The room inside was spotless, painted white and sparsely furnished in a strictly utilitarian style. He looked down at the child on the bed. Anne Easton lay motionless under the white covers, dark eyelashes resting lightly against her cheeks. The lashes fluttered; the eyes moved under closed lids. Owen pulled up a chair and sat down.

It was another five or ten minutes before she opened her eyes and lay there without moving, staring vaguely at the unfamiliar room. Then she rolled over slowly. Her eyes brightened as her gaze fell on one thing she recognized.

The face of Edward Drake.

Owen smiled. 'Take it easy,' he said. 'Just lie still for a while.'

'Where's Haskie?'

'She had to go away for a few days. She asked me to keep you until she gets back.'

'Is this your house?'

'For now, yes.'

It was explanation enough. No distrust showed in the big dark eyes. She was used to strange places and people, this cosmopolitan child who had travelled more in four years than most people did in a lifetime. And in any case, Edward Drake was no stranger; he was Mrs Haskins' friend.

Anne looked at him and smiled. Owen smiled back. Then he glanced down at his watch.

It was still night in Washington. He wondered briefly how the President was sleeping these days.

Matt Easton lay quietly on his back, eyes open, staring up into the darkness over the bed. Beside him Elizabeth, asleep at last, her breath soft against the starched case of the pillow. Matt listened to her breathing, then raised himself up on one elbow to look at her face. Not even sleep smoothed the deep lines of tension he saw there.

Dear God, what had he done to her? And what had he done to *Anne*?

He got up quietly and made his way across the thick carpet to the bathroom door. Inside, he switched on the light, flinching against sudden brightness. Then he sat down on the wide edge of the tub, elbows on knees, face in hands.

The bathroom – one of the only places in the White House where he ever felt truly alone. It was almost comical. But take one step outside a door and two Secret Service men would close in behind him, like a couple of leeches hanging on wherever he went in the house.

He needed to be alone now, and not in the darkness of the bedroom where problems always seemed much worse than they really were. Not there, no. Reality was bad enough.

He closed his eyes, thinking back to the first campaign for Congress, a shoestring affair run out of a rented room by a handful of volunteers, primarily Elizabeth. And Ed and Vanessa Nichols. Good friends. Election night. Victory. Total joy.

If he'd known then where he was heading, he might not have considered that night an occasion to celebrate. What began in that rented room had come to this. His wife distraught with fear. His daughter the victim of power out of control. His best friend a stranger.

And himself?

He smiled wryly. The President of the United States, perched on the edge of a bathtub, alone with his thoughts, with his fears and guilt, wishing he'd never been caught by the lure of the White House or the terrible price it had cost.

'Matt—' A voice through the door.

He glanced up. Elizabeth was awake.

'Are you all right?' she said.

'I'm fine.'

He got up and opened the door. A path of light fell across the bed, on Elizabeth sitting up, her expression concerned.

'No,' he said. Then, 'I'm not all right.'

He moved back to the bed and put his arms around her shoulders, pulling her close, seeking comfort as much as he sought to give it.

'Matt—'

He placed his fingers lightly against her lips. 'Please don't talk, just listen.'

Elizabeth looked back at him. She nodded.

'This whole thing is my fault,' he said quietly and raised the hand again to silence her protest. 'I've been thinking about it all week, trying to make up my mind. And now I've made a decision.' He looked down at the tense face, at the dark eyes staring back at him. 'I have something to tell you,' he said.

Paul Fleming drove straight to Langley, only to learn that Nichols had left for home. A call to the house got Vanessa. Ed wasn't there yet; he must be still on his way.

132

'Have him call me *the minute* he gets in,' Fleming said and hung up.

He kept a nervous eye on the time as he turned to the other matter. Simon, *dead* in the Capitol Crypt, his body stashed under the Lincoln Catafalque. There was irony in that. CIA heroes rarely got their just honours when they died. Neither did CIA traitors.

Irony and outrage. Simon, dead, was worth precisely nothing.

Fleming reached for the phone again, placed two inside calls. Renovation of a building as old as the Capitol was an ongoing thing. No one would notice an extra crew of painters with an official job order and their equipment loaded into a rolling cart. No one would know Simon had ever been there. That much was under control.

By the time those arrangements were finished, Simon's file had arrived. Fleming read through it carefully. There was nothing there, nothing to connect him with Shelley or Anne Easton. He shoved it aside, pushed himself up out of the chair, and began to pace the room.

The phone still didn't ring. *Where* the hell was *Ed*?

Then a knock came at the door.

Fleming swung around. 'Come in.'

A messenger from Communications downstairs. He handed Fleming a sealed envelope and left the way he had come.

Fleming looked at the envelope. It was inter-office, red for ultra-urgent, and marked 'Eyes Only' for him. He tore it open and read the telex inside. Then he grabbed up the phone and dialled Nichols again.

'I'm sorry,' Vanessa Nichols said. 'He's *still* not back. I don't know where he is.'

Fleming was silent for a moment. He glanced down at the message in his hands. Then he switched on the scrambler attached to his telephone.

'Look, Vanessa, tell him I can't wait. We've had a telex from Athens. An agent there says she's *seen* Anne Easton.'

'She saw *Anne*? Where? When?'

'I can't explain it now. Tell Ed I'll leave the telex in my safe. He can read it for himself. And tell him I'm leaving for Athens right away.'

133

'Tonight?'

'As soon as I hang up. If Ed gets back in the next thirty minutes, he can probably reach me at Andrews. Otherwise, I'll call him from Greece.'

'All right.'

Fleming leaned forward, his finger hovering over the disconnect button. 'One more thing – tell him I left Shelley Curtis down at the old Rotunda. She's got a hell of a story. I don't want to repeat it here, even with the scrambler. Just make sure Ed calls her as soon as you hear from him. And tell him there's a file he'll want. I'll leave it in my safe with the telex.'

'I will.'

'Thanks.' Fleming disconnected the line without saying goodbye.

Nichols didn't have to be told about Shelley Curtis. He knew more already than Fleming had told Vanessa. He knew Shelley Curtis was dead.

He was sitting in his car four blocks from the old Rotunda, where the police were at work in swarms. The police and, no doubt, the press. It was a hell of a story – a member of Congress shot to death at a posh political club, her unknown assailant escaping through the front door. That was dramatic enough.

But there was more. A bullet hole in the congresswoman's coat, and a fresh powder burn that proved a shot had been fired from *inside* the coat pocket. Tonight. Yet, there was no gun. And the coat had been folded on a bar stool across the room when the attack occurred.

Where was Shelley Curtis *before* she came to the club? The police would want to know that.

So did Ed Nichols.

He glanced at the man on the other side of the car. The lobbyist who had talked to Shelley at the club, a man with a wife and four kids – and a boyfriend on the side. The CIA kept track of these things; they came in handy sometimes, like tonight, when Nichols had needed someone at the Rotunda who would report to him, alone. Honey might attract more flies than vinegar, but nothing beat blackmail at securing the absolute allegiance of a man with a lot to lose.

'Did she say where she'd been tonight?' Nichols asked.

The lobbyist shook his head nervously. 'On the floor, I expect. The session went till eleven.'

'Till just *after* eleven,' Nichols said. He had checked that already. 'You said she arrived at the club about midnight. Where was she in between?'

'I don't know. Her office, maybe? She didn't say.'

Nichols nodded. The man was terrified; he wouldn't lie. 'All right, you can go now,' he said.

The lobbyist looked relieved.

'But don't forget our agreement.'

'I'm not likely to.'

'See that you don't. One hint of my interest in this and a duplicate of your file will be mailed to your wife.' Nichols smiled. 'And I'll make sure you never work again.'

The lobbyist looked back at him for a long moment. Then he turned quickly and got out of the car.

Nichols switched on the ignition as the other man disappeared into the darkness of Capitol Hill. He drove aimlessly, not caring where he went, wanting only this time, alone, to think.

Like Cannon and Sherman before her, Shelley Curtis was dead. The killer had been there at the precise right time. He *had* to have been tipped off. Again. By someone on the inside.

But who had known when Shelley was going to go to the club? Nichols did. He and Fleming had set this up, which meant that Fleming knew, too. And one other person whom Nichols reported to. Matt Easton.

Beyond that, Nichols' directions were clear: Tell no one. Limit knowledge this time to three people who are above suspicion. Eliminate any chance of a setup like the ones that trapped Cannon and Sherman.

And yet, the killer was there. Not too soon or too late. He was there when he had to be.

The passing lights on the other side of the windscreen suddenly paled, and Nichols' mind reeled against a blow more stunning than any physical force. The informant! The insider who had tipped off a killer in Berlin and Johannesburg, in Washington, DC. Informant was hardly the word! *It had to be Paul or Matt!*

Nichols had thought he couldn't be shocked any more. And he wasn't shocked. It was something far worse than that. The President of the United States *permitting* his daughter's abduction? *Helping* the abductors? Impossible! But Paul? That was almost as bad. The deputy director of the CIA involved in a plot to kidnap the President's daughter? Why would he do it? What would he have to gain? What would *either* of them have to gain?

Nichols brought the car to a stop at a red light. His mind was a jumble, his heart pounding inside his chest. Adrenalin surged through his body, energy without direction, energy spawned by shock. He took a deep breath and forced himself to relax against the seat. He had never had to deal with anything like this before. A problem of staggering proportions, beyond precedent – but one he had to handle like any other. Logically. One step at a time. Another deep breath.

Matt.

Nichols' mind veered away again. It *couldn't* be Matt. It was out of the question, defied everything sane. It *had* to be Paul.

The light changed, and Nichols stepped down on the gas, moving ahead with the traffic. His hands were tight on the wheel, but his mind was beginning to clear. He was starting to see himself from an entirely new perspective – and he wondered, for the first time, how much he really controlled the CIA.

He was the director, yes, but an outsider brought in at the top by the President. He owed his allegiance to the White House, to the man who was his best friend. Because of that, he had never fully subscribed to the unwritten motto at Langley: what's good for the CIA is probably good for the country. Because of that, he could never really belong.

But Fleming was not an outsider. He was a CIA professional who had come up through the ranks. He knew the agency as Nichols never could. Presidents came and went; so, too, their appointed directors. But professionals like Fleming stayed on through political change. Among the other professionals, it was

136

Fleming who had the standing, Fleming who had earned their loyalty, *Fleming* who controlled the CIA.

Nichols turned the car into the Southwest Freeway and stayed in the right-hand lane. There were other cars on the road and the lights of the city all around. Even a few tourists paying a late visit to the Jefferson Memorial. But Nichols felt stranded, isolated – cut off from both sources of what was supposed to be his own far-reaching power. The White House and the CIA. He had to find out what Paul Fleming was doing, but he couldn't go to Matt. Not yet, not until he was *sure* Matt wasn't involved. And he couldn't go to the people who worked for him, either.

That left one choice: he had to get *outside* help.

He had crossed the Potomac and was heading north on the parkway along the Virginia side of the river. Without thinking about it, he had turned the car towards Langley, the last place he wanted to be.

But he did want to talk to Fleming.

He turned off the parkway and wound his way into the cluster of buildings that was known as Crystal City. There he found a filling station that was closed for the night. Floodlights lit the pavement around it, but the phone booth stood in a corner of darkness just beyond the lights.

He dialled the Agency switchboard.

'I'm sorry, sir,' the night duty officer said. 'The deputy director left here forty-five minutes ago. He said if you called in to tell you to call your wife.'

Vanessa? Nichols hung up and dialled his home.

'Ed, where are you?' Vanessa said when she picked up the phone.

'Never mind that. Did Paul leave a message for me?'

'Is the line safe?'

'Yes, I'm in a phone booth. But switch on the scrambler there.'

There was a moment of silence as Vanessa found the switch. When she spoke again, her voice had a hollow sound. The scrambler was working.

But there was no disguising the excitement in her voice. 'Someone in Athens saw Anne!' she said. 'Paul's on his way there now.'

'*Paul* is?'

'He tried to reach you twice and said he couldn't wait any longer. There was a telex from Athens. He said to tell you he would leave it in his safe.'

Nichols was silent for a moment. Where did *this* fit in?

'Is something wrong?' Vanessa asked.

Nichols ignored the question. 'What else did Paul say?'

'He said you're supposed to call Congresswoman Shelley Curtis. Immediately. She's down at the old Rotunda. Do you want me to look up the number?'

'That won't be necessary,' Nichols replied dryly.

'Something *is* wrong,' Vanessa said. Worry was clear in her voice.

'Not something, everything,' Nichols replied. 'I don't know when I'll be home.'

'*Ed—?*'

But Nichols didn't hear her. He had disconnected the line.

He replaced the receiver and sat there for a long time, thinking over his plan. A *dangerous* plan. But unless Paul Fleming was cleared of suspicion, he couldn't trust anyone Fleming might control. And there was no one else on this side. Nowhere else to turn.

A dangerous plan, a huge risk. But Nichols felt he had no choice. He reached for the phone again and dialled another number.

The man who answered at the other end was named Kolonov. He was Special Assistant to the Vice Consul at the Soviet Embassy in Washington. And something more than that. He was also the Senior KGB Resident in the United States.

nineteen

Fleming flashed his official passport at the customs agent in Athens and was passed through airport security without delay. A driver was waiting for him on the other side. It was not the CIA station chief, who would not care to be seen meeting a high-ranking Langley official. Nor, for the same reasons, would it be the woman who had reported seeing Anne Easton.

This was a driver from the American Embassy on Queen Sophia Street, a man whose job was completely overt, who needed to feign nothing more than a courteous welcome for another visiting VIP from back home.

'I have a car outside,' the man said pleasantly.

Fleming nodded and followed him through the crowd. They passed through the outside doors and into the bright sunshine, where a black Pontiac was waiting by the kerb. The Pontiac and a few dozen other cars, some buses, a limousine or two. A throng of people streamed out through the doors, meeting and mingling with another throng coming the other way.

And one face Fleming recognized!

His step didn't falter; his eyes showed no sign of surprise. He climbed through the door the driver was holding open, into the back seat of the big American car.

The driver moved around to the other side, got in behind the wheel, and pulled away from the kerb and into the flow of traffic. Fleming did not look around. He merely glanced to his right, back towards the terminal building, but he caught the grey Mercedes in his peripheral view.

It, too, was pulling away from the kerb.

A grey Mercedes, a common sight in Athens, an ordinary taxi-cab. Hardly unusual in front of the airport building. But there was no mistaking the wide face, the broad Slavic features of the driver.

Svitsky!

Fleming leaned forward and spoke to the driver. 'Do you see the taxi behind us?'

The driver's eyes shifted to his rearview mirror, then back to the road. His head gave a slight nod.

'Can you lose it?' Fleming asked.

The driver grinned. 'You bet I can.'

'Then do it.'

Spring in Washington had taken a sudden backslide, giving way to a grey sky and a wet, chilling mist. It was darker than usual for this time of year, for this time of day.

Nichols glanced at his watch – it was five p.m. – and quickened his pace across the natural footbridge of earth and stone that connected the Virginia shore with the peninsula called Teddy Roosevelt Island. He knew the park closed at sundown, by the combined orders of the US Parks Service and the rising Potomac tide. He didn't care to be stranded here overnight; the meeting would have to be short.

On the other side, the bridge gave way to a path that cut through tall trees and rugged natural growth to a clearing, where a bronze figure of the Old Rough Rider stood tall against the grey sky, over a wide circle of terraced stone. The statue was enormous, its patina darkly ominous in the fading light. Nichols moved quickly past it, across the terrace, into the woods on the other side.

He had encountered no one – in this weather, it wasn't likely he would – but he kept an eye on the path in both directions as he stood there, in the deepening shadows of the trees. Then, from behind, came the snapping of a twig.

Nichols turned. It was Kolonov, dressed for business at the embassy and not for a walk in the woods. The collar of his overcoat was turned up against the damp chill of the air. His eyes were without expression, revealing nothing of the thoughts behind them, but his mouth was set in a firm, tense line.

Nichols moved towards him. 'Well?'

'I did my best,' the Russian replied. 'I put Boris Svitsky on Fleming. He's the best we've got in Europe.'

'And?'

The Russian hesitated for a moment. Then he said, 'Your Paul Fleming's no fool. He spotted Svitsky and lost him.'

'Lost him.'

The Russian shrugged. 'It's not so surprising. Two good field agents, pretty evenly matched.'

'Except for the fact that Fleming's a *retired* agent.' Nichols glared back at him angrily. 'I won't accept that, damn you! I want Fleming found.'

The Russian laughed uneasily. 'Isn't that a little unreasonable at this point?'

'Not half as unreasonable as I'm going to be,' Nichols replied. He turned away in frustration. If Svitsky was the best they had, it was a wonder there was any conflict at all. Boris Svitsky, of all people! Fleming would recognize him in an instant.

No, Svitsky was good; Nichols knew that. He turned back to the Russian. Then suddenly a new thought struck him. One thought and another, they all fell into place. He stood there, looking past the Russian, through mist and shadow as storm clouds darkened overhead.

He knew, now, who had ordered the kidnapping of Anne Easton. He also thought he knew why.

Furthermore, he had a pretty good idea where she was.

Owen watched Anne's face as he opened the brown paper package from the market. Her curiosity gave way to open disgust.

'What's *that*?'

Owen laughed. 'It's octopus. Want a bite?'

Anne shook her head decisively. 'Peanut butter, please.'

'Yes, I thought you'd say that. Sit down. I'll fix you a sandwich.'

She did as she was told, and Owen was grateful for that. If he had to play Mary Poppins, he'd just as soon do it opposite a well-behaved child. A *bright* well-behaved child. He fixed the sandwich and put the plate down on the table in front of her, then poured her a glass of milk. It had been a week since she left the United States, drugged, in the false compartment under Franz Heinemann's coffin, two days since they'd arrived here on Crete. Good food and fresh air had done their work. Anne's dark eyes were shining out of a pink face as she looked up at him and smiled.

'Are you really going to *eat* that octopus?'

'I don't plan to make a pet of it,' Owen replied. 'Now be quiet and eat your lunch. I want to read the paper.'

He sat down and picked up the *Herald Tribune*. A labour dispute in Britain. Inflation rampant in Germany. A congresswoman murdered near the Capitol in Washington, DC. But nothing about the President's kidnapped daughter. Owen turned inside.

The phone rang.

He looked up, startled. Then, with a gesture for silence, he crossed into the next room and picked it up.

'Hello?'

A woman's voice: '*The promised hour is come at last.*'

Dryden. The signal from Graham.

'*The present age of wit obscures the past*,' Owen replied. He smiled. 'How are you?'

He had recognized the voice as the words came out of her mouth.

'Busy,' Erica said. 'I have a message from Graham.'

'I know. *The promised hour is come*. When is it?'

'Midnight tonight. At Knossos. Sunflower is going home.'

'Tonight! Graham said I'd be here two weeks or more. What's gone wrong?'

'Nothing I know of.'

Owen was silent a moment. Then he said, 'All right, what's the plan?'

'Simple. You'll turn Sunflower over to Graham, and he'll take her home.'

'What happens then?'

'I don't know. You'll have to ask Graham.'

Yes, Owen thought, there were several things he would have to ask Graham. But that would come later. 'There are night guards at Knossos,' he said.

'Two men – one at the gate, one inside the grounds. Graham wants you to see to them before he arrives.'

'Is there more than one shift?'

'Just one. The night guards come on at nine p.m. and stay until the day shift arrives at seven.'

A rather sloppy arrangement, Owen guessed. Except for the palace itself, there wasn't much of value inside the gates at

Knossos. Most of the treasures had been removed to the museum at Heraklion. The guards were probably more concerned about vandalism than theft, and there wasn't much of that in Greece.

'Will you be there?' Owen asked.

'I doubt it.'

'Too bad.'

'I could be available after this is over.'

Owen could feel the familiar smile at the other end of the line. 'I'll keep that in mind,' he said.

'Good. Midnight, then.'

Owen hung up and stood a moment staring through the window at the olive grove and the dark sea beyond. He knew he should be relieved. The danger was almost over; he would turn Anne over to Graham and be done with it. But he wasn't relieved. He felt a vague sense of concern. The signal had come too soon; they'd been two days on Crete, not two weeks. Had something gone wrong? And how was Graham planning to take Anne home?

He turned back to the kitchen.

'Who was that?' Anne asked.

Owen picked up his paper and sat down. 'It's not polite to pry.'

Anne looked down at her plate. 'I hoped it was Haskie.'

'It wasn't Mrs Haskins.' Owen looked back at the small, un-happy face. 'But you'll be seeing her soon,' he said. 'Your parents, too.'

Unhappiness faded to a look of total joy. '*When?*'

'I don't know yet. Soon. Now please be quiet and let me read.' Owen folded the paper to an inside page and started to read again.

But Anne could not remain silent. 'Look, it's Uncle Ed!'

Owen turned the paper around. It was a picture of Ed Nichols, flanked by a couple of diplomats at some embassy affair in Washington. *Uncle* Ed, was it? He nodded and turned the page.

Anne took a drink of her milk, then cocked her head to one side. 'When is Uncle Ed going to be Vice President?' she asked.

Owen let out a deep sigh. Reading, obviously, was out of the question for now. He folded the paper, dropped it on to a chair and looked up at Anne. 'What makes you think he's going to be Vice President?'

'Daddy said so.'

Owen raised an eyebrow.

'He told Mommy. I heard him.' She turned to the window and looked out at the sunny day. 'Can we go swimming now?'

'After your nap,' Owen said. He was studying Anne with mild interest. 'Did your father say when Uncle Ed was going to be Vice President?'

Anne shrugged. She didn't remember, or she didn't care. Perhaps she never knew. 'Why can't we go swimming *now*?'

'Because you haven't finished your lunch or had your nap. And anyway, it's too hot. We'll go swimming later.' Owen reached for his newspaper again.

'After the next election.'

He glanced up. 'What?'

'That's what Daddy said. Uncle Ed will be Vice President after the next election.' Anne's face creased into an earnest frown. 'What's the next election?'

Owen ignored the question, but he *was* interested now. 'Your father said that? You're sure he said that?'

'I heard him.'

'*When?*'

'I told you.'

'No, when did he *say* it?'

'I don't know.'

Owen dropped the paper and leaned forward across the table. He kept his voice calm, not wanting to startle away whatever memory she had. 'This is very important,' he said. 'Think hard. What were you doing when your father and mother were talking?'

Anne closed her eyes tightly. Then they popped open again. 'I was opening a present.'

'What kind of present?'

'A book. It was for my trip.'

'To Michigan?'

Anne nodded.

'When was that?'

Anne stared back at him. Then suddenly her face broke into a grin. 'The day we *went* to Michigan!'

144

'You're sure of that?' Owen said, more urgently now. 'You're sure it was then? Not before?'

'I *remember*, Mr Drake. I put my book by my suitcase, and we went on the plane the same day.'

The day Anne left for Michigan. A full week *after* Owen's meeting with Graham in New York.

He sat quite still, staring at the child on the other side of the table. She was without guile, totally innocent, totally lacking self-interest in the matter of Uncle Ed. She had no idea of the *significance* of what she had said.

If the President thought Ed Nichols might be guilty of treason, he would hardly be thinking of making Nichols his running mate!

And that meant Graham had *lied*! The President had authorized *nothing*!

Owen leaned back in the chair without taking his eyes off Anne. She stared back, frightened by the intensity of his gaze. But he paid no attention.

He was thinking about her father – the President, the American commander-in-chief – a man whose power was limited by little more than his own ability to use it. Owen had kidnapped Anne *with* her father's permission. So he thought. Now, in a flash of memory, that sanction was gone. It had never existed!

If the President hadn't authorized the kidnapping, then he couldn't have *known* about it, not until after it happened. He could not be working with Graham. He must be distraught with fear for his daughter's safety. President and father, a man of enormous power and extraordinary motivation – all of it aimed now at Owen.

A tightness gripped Owen inside and was spreading across his chest. For a moment, he couldn't breathe. Fear, a new sensation. A threat more dangerous than a gun at the side of his head. A threat, not to life, but to freedom. Freedom *was* life. Without it, he would rather be dead.

'*Mr Drake!*'

Anne was at his side, tugging at his sleeve for attention. Owen glanced down, startled. 'What?'

She looked terrified. 'What's the *matter*?'

Owen's hand moved, and he touched her cheek. 'I'm sorry,' he said. 'Nothing's wrong. I was thinking of something.'

Anne was not convinced. But then a smile spread slowly across her face. And dimples, at least as famous as Shirley Temple's curls.

'Up to bed with you now,' Owen said. 'We've got a swim on for later.'

The smile changed to a grin of pure delight as Anne turned away and scampered out of the room.

Owen watched her go. Then he pushed himself up out of the chair and began to pace the room. The fear was gone; he felt anger. For Graham, for the lie. Alone, that was bad enough. But Graham had used him, had led him into the worst kind of danger – without warning, with a *lie*. Graham had given his word, falsely, and that Owen couldn't forgive.

Then, in an instant, the anger disappeared, too. There was no time now for emotion. This was a time for careful analysis, for thinking and planning. Graham had lied about the President, that much at least, maybe more. Had he lied about Nichols, too? If so, why the kidnapping? *Why* the kidnapping?

Owen was sure of one thing, that Graham had a lot of explaining to do before the night was over. And he'd better be convincing. Otherwise, there wasn't a chance that Owen would relinquish Anne.

He glanced at the door through which Anne had disappeared. The rendezvous was set, midnight tonight at Knossos. Sunflower was going home.

Or was she?

twenty

Nichols made good time moving against the traffic, disregarding the speed limits and prepared to use maximum threats against any policeman who tried to impede his progress. He didn't have to. No one stopped him.

146

He drove straight to the White House, passed through the gate with a wave and brought the car to a halt in front of the West Wing entrance. Inside, he bypassed the aide on duty without a word and pushed open a door that led to the staff offices.

'Mr Director?'

The aide ran after him.

But Nichols paid no attention. He hurried on to an anteroom that bordered the Oval Office.

Matt's secretary, red eyed and worried, was sitting behind her desk. A man was pacing the floor in obvious, extreme agitation.

The man was the appointments secretary, gatekeeper to the President. He looked up sharply as Nichols strode into the room. 'Where in the hell have you been?' he demanded. 'We've been trying to find you for over an hour!'

Nichols ignored the question. 'I've got to see the President,' he said, and moved towards the heavy carved door.

The other man moved to block him. 'You can't see him now. He's on his way over to the E.O.B. He's called a press conference.'

'A press conference?'

'Damn it, Nichols! He's going to *resign*!'

Nichols stared back at him, stunned. 'But *why*?'

The appointments secretary was no longer just agitated; he was on the verge of hysteria. 'God only knows! He's got some crazy notion that this whole thing with Anne is his fault. And that if he resigns, they won't *want* her any more.'

Nichols' eyes narrowed. 'You've got to stop him.'

The other man raised his arms in a gesture of total frustration. 'I've tried. We all tried.'

'I didn't say try, I said *stop him*! Listen, you bastard, he's making a huge mistake. You get him back here right now. Tell him his wife died, *anything*, but get him back here. And don't let him talk to anyone on the way.'

The appointments secretary stared at him for a moment before he turned and left the room in a hurry.

Nichols glanced down at the red-eyed woman behind the desk. 'Pull yourself together,' he said. 'It's going to be a long night.'

Then he opened the door and disappeared, alone, into the Oval Office.

There were two cars in the paved lot cut out of the trees that lined the approach to Knossos. A modern chain-link fence enclosed the ancient ruins. It was nearly ten p.m. Daylight was gone, and so were the tourists who came here in droves at this time of year.

Owen could not see the ruins from where he stood, surrounded by the shadow of trees, only the bright glow of floodlights from the top of the hill. But he could see the gatehouse, the souvenir shop and the ticket counter, both closed for the night, and the small adjacent room that gave overnight shelter to the guard on duty at the gate.

The smell of coffee and the sound of *bouzouki* music floated across to Owen. He moved quietly out of the trees, keeping to the soft earth that bordered the gravel path. The music stopped as he approached the gatehouse from behind, was replaced by the voice of a radio announcer who gave the time in Greek. Then he launched into the news.

Owen heard the scraping of a chair, a footstep on the concrete floor inside. The announcer's voice was cut off mid-sentence; the radio dial was spun, more music located. The guard settled down again.

Owen edged his way along the side wall of the building, moving up to the corner that turned on to the door of the guardroom, just inches away. He stood there a moment, listening. Then he bent down and picked up a handful of gravel. He threw it against the fence.

There was a soft staccato of sound, a spray of stone against metal. The guard heard it, shut the radio off, listened. But he did not get up from the chair.

Owen picked up more gravel.

This time the chair moved. Footsteps came across concrete towards the door. Owen stood flush with the wall, taking air in silently through his mouth. His hand moved to his waist and checked the position of the revolver in his belt. Then the guard stepped through the door and out into the night.

Owen gave him no time to turn around. The edge of one hand struck the man's neck sharply as the other hand clamped across his mouth; then both arms dropped to catch the unconscious body before it fell to the ground.

He dragged the guard back into the gatehouse and laid him out on the floor. Then he produced a plastic syringe; in it, enough Valium to keep a grown man sleeping through the night.

Next, he turned his attention to the room itself, letting his eyes scan the walls. The fuse box was behind the door. He yanked it open, studied the wiring inside, located what he wanted. He pulled the master switch. The guardroom fell dark as the overhead light went out, and with it the glow of floodlights at the top of the hill outside.

Owen stepped behind the door and waited.

In less than five minutes, the other guard came to investigate. Owen saw the beam of his flashlight cutting through the moonlight outside. He heard footsteps approaching on the other side of the gate.

Finally, the voice. 'Niko?'

The guard on the floor didn't stir.

'*Niko?*'

Still no movement.

The flashlight turned away briefly as the second guard unlocked the gate from inside. The gate swung open; there were footsteps on the gravel path outside. Then the beam of the flash moved into the guardroom.

The man came just behind it. '*Niko!*' He dropped to his knees beside the prone body.

Owen sprang forward, his hand slicing the air in a single, swift movement, coming down hard against the man's neck. The second guard collapsed beside the first. Owen produced the syringe and plunged it into the arm. Then, as an extra precaution, he taped the mouths of both men, tied their arms behind their backs, lashed their legs together. He stood back to study his work. For the first time in four millennia, Knossos had been secured.

Owen left the guardroom and made his way through the gate and up the hill to the place where the Palace of Minos once stood above the banks of the river Kairatos. A palace that was immense by ancient or modern standards – a vast, sprawling, multi-levelled structure that covered more than five square acres and housed as many as eighty thousand people in its day. An architectural miracle built in the days of prehistory, when even ancient Greece was yet to come.

Death had come to Knossos without warning. The river was still there, but the palace had been levelled to a shambles of rock-strewn rubble by a sudden catastrophe – a massive earthquake, probably, that obliterated this and every other trace of Minoan civilization for nearly four thousand years.

Now it had been laid bare by the archaeologist's spade. The structure of the ground floor was like an architect's plan done in stone – a large central courtyard surrounded by the foundations of what had been hundreds of rooms. It was a forlorn shadow of history, with weeds sprouting unchecked between ancient paving stones.

Now there were only patches of restoration to whet the imagination. A few reconstructed walls, some small buildings rebuilt of old stone, two restored columned porches. Modern copies of painted wooden pillars, tapering down to the base. Giant storage urns had been patiently pieced back together. And bulls' horns everywhere – the stylized stone bulls' horns, as tall as a man, that once edged the palace walls like turrets on a mediaeval castle.

Owen listened to the crickets in the trees at the base of the hill, to the flow of the river nearby. In the distance lay the lights of a city, Heraklion. Otherwise, there was no man-made light to counteract nature's own. Knossos remained as it had been through the millennia. Isolated. Inviolate. A place of brooding mystery that only sharpened as Owen surveyed the ruins, alone, under the black night sky.

The moon threw its pale light across ancient paving stones once stained by blood. It raised distortions of shadow behind raw-edged foundations of rock. It edged across pits once used for storage of oil and wine and turned them into gaping holes of darkness.

Knossos was a place where history merged with myth and dark

visions lingered on beyond the passage of time. The legendary home of Minos, King of the Aegean, son of the mighty Zeus. And Androgeus, prince of Knossos, whose murder by the King of Athens sent Minos into a rage of blood and lust. Minos demanded his price, the finest youth of Athens, for sacrifice to the Minotaur – a fearsome beast, half-man half-bull, who dwelled in the fabled Labyrinth beneath the Minoan palace.

The retribution continued for twenty-seven years, until the Athenian king sent his son, Theseus, to slay the monster of Minos. Theseus succeeded and escaped, with the help of Ariadne, who led him through the twisting Labyrinth with her ball of fine-spun thread.

All legend, without support in history, until the excavations at Knossos gave the myth a home. A prehistoric civilization beyond anything dreamed of on Crete. A king of enormous wealth and power. A culture where the bull was revered above all other creatures. Artistic renderings of a ritual called the Bull Dance, pitting unarmed youth against a massive beast, and a paved arena where the dancing had been held.

All of this and the ruins of a structure so vast, so complex, so intricate in design, that one conclusion was clear. Whatever its history, Knossos didn't house a Labyrinth. It *was* one.

And it still was today. Owen's gaze swept the ruined remains of the upper levels of the palace. Beneath all this rock, beneath the earth where he stood, he knew that underground passageways still wound their way in a maze among the restored chambers. He knew that even today, a visitor could lose his way, without a guide, without Ariadne's thread.

Then, abruptly, he turned away. There was work to be done, and the night was wearing on.

Nichols sat in the President's chair, looking at the President's phone. It was the most secure phone in the world, debugged daily, sometimes twice a day. That was why Nichols had come here.

And thank God he had come! Matt Easton could not be allowed to resign.

Nichols looked up as the President entered the room and closed the door behind him. Matt's face was pale and haggard, his skin drawn tight across his cheeks. His eyes were dark and burning with a quiet intensity.

Anger? Nichols wondered. Despair?

'What is it, Ed?' the President asked in a voice that was tight with emotion.

Nichols didn't move from the chair. He looked at his longtime friend across the length of the room.

'I've figured it out,' he said then. 'And we've got a hell of a problem.'

The British ambassador to Washington hung up the phone and sat at his desk, staring into space. It was the strangest request he had ever received from the White House, the strangest and perhaps the most urgent.

Then he leaned forward quickly and pressed down his intercom.

'Yes, sir?'

'Get me a scrambled line to the Foreign Office,' the ambassador said. 'Right now.'

Within the hour, the same request had been posed to four other parties. International operators stayed busy through the night as calls flew back and forth across the ocean – from Washington to London and back again, to Paris and Bonn, to Athens, to and from Tel Aviv.

Nichols had pulled out the stops, wherever they were worth pulling. Everywhere except Langley. The one agency he didn't press into service was the CIA.

A lone man dressed like Owen, in black, appeared through the restored South Gate of the palace, where the tours of Knossos began. He paused there a moment, then quickly moved forwards and up the open steps that led to the central courtyard. As he cleared the steps, his face passed out of the shadows and into the light of the moon.

It was Graham.

Owen stepped forward to meet him. 'It's not like you to be late,' he said. It was twenty minutes past midnight.

'Christ, Owen! What kind of game are you playing?'

'Game?'

'I didn't expect you to make me search the damn ruins! I expected you to meet me at the gate.'

Owen shrugged and turned away. 'This seemed more historically pure.' His gaze swept the broad view that made Knossos an ideal site for the seat of Minoan power. Ancient hills sloping to flat plains, olive groves and cypress trees, all cast into dark relief by the moon. Except for the sound of the river, and the crickets below in the trees, the night was completely silent.

'Besides, we need to talk,' Owen said over his shoulder.

'Talk? There's no time for talking! Where's the girl?'

'She's here,' Owen said.

'*Where*, damn it?'

'Down there.' Owen gestured towards a flat-roofed structure that covered the Grand Staircase, five flights of steps descending into the underground levels of the palace. 'She's down there somewhere. I daresay you could find her on your own. You might get lucky and do it inside of a week.'

Graham glared back at him. 'What *is* this, Owen? What do you think you're *doing*?'

'Just this: I've got the girl. You want her. And you can have her. But first I want to know something. Why have you cut this short? What's the rush? What's going on?'

'*Owen!*'

'The *real* story,' Owen said.

Graham stared back at him, eyes furious. 'All right, you want to know I'll tell you. Fast. Sit down.'

Owen preferred to stand. But he leaned back, letting a shoulder rest against one of the sculptured bull's horns.

'I am in a hurry,' Graham said, 'and with good reason, I think. For one thing, Simon is no longer available to plant the false clues.'

'He's dead?'

'Yes.'

'Pity.'

'Not just dead, he was *killed* – by one of Nichols' agents.

There's no more doubt about Nichols. He's done everything I expected him to and more. He's turned the whole thing around to his own advantage. Three of our key agents are dead because of Nichols. Dead, that's bad enough. They were all extremely important. But in each case there's also a scandal brewing. If even one of them blows, we've got the kind of trouble that could destroy the CIA. At *least* the CIA!' Graham shook his head angrily. 'I don't know how he did it, but I can guess. I think Simon was working for Nichols all along.'

Owen's mouth dropped open as he stared at Graham without trying to conceal his astonishment. 'Simon working for *Nichols*? Then Nichols knows—'

'Yes, Nichols has to know about you. And where you are. Is that rush enough to suit you?'

Owen was still too stunned to reply.

'There's more,' Graham said. 'Nichols *did* go to the Russians. God knows how many Soviet agents are on your trail right now. We've proved our case. Enough! We've got to get that girl back to the White House before—'

Graham didn't finish the sentence. He swung around, horrified. In that instant, the lights had come on at Knossos.

Floodlights, everywhere. Then the sharp crack of a pistol and a whining through the air. The tip of one of the bull's horns burst away in an explosion of dust, and the bullet smashed into the courtyard behind them.

Graham dove for cover behind the low edge of a nearby foundation. Owen grabbed his revolver and ducked behind the base of the bull's horns.

Then a voice came to them from the south end of the courtyard. A voice. A thick voice. Russian.

'*That was a warning shot, Fleming. You know we can do better. Come out with your hands in the air.*'

Graham turned his face back to Owen, his eyes wide with shock.

'*Here's another warning, Fleming.*'

A second bullet, fired from a different position, smashed into a wall on the opposite side of the courtyard.

Owen flattened himself against the ground and pulled himself across to the place where Graham was crouched behind the low edge of wall. Graham had produced a pistol. He drew himself up and peered cautiously over the wall. No gunfire, no voice. He dropped back down again.

'I can't figure out where they are,' he said, his voice barely more than a whisper. 'Or what the hell they're doing.'

Owen shrugged. 'I thought you said the Russians were after *me*.'

'Don't split hairs with me, Owen. They've got us *cornered* here!' He peered up over the wall again. Still nothing happened.

'*Us ?*' Owen said. He smiled. 'I believe the man said *Fleming*.'

For a moment, Graham didn't move. He turned slowly back to Owen. Then his face went pale. He was staring into the barrel of Owen's revolver, inches in front of his face.

Graham, the code name Fleming had used when he worked in the field, a name he retained at Langley for the key agents he supervised directly. Owen was one of the few who had known Fleming in the field. He had always known both names, and that they were one person, but he never before referred to Fleming as Fleming.

Nor had he ever held Fleming at the end of a pistol.

Fleming's hand released the pistol he was holding; it dropped to the ground. His face was contorted by a mixture of rage and fear. His eyes were furious, yet uncertain. He still didn't understand.

'*Come out now, Fleming. We don't want to kill you. We want to take you home.*'

Fleming's eyes remained on Owen. 'What *is* this ?'

'Why don't you do what they say,' Owen said. 'They're *your* colleagues, not mine.'

'That's insane! What are you talking about ?'

'You, Mr Deputy Director.' Owen smiled. 'There was only one thing wrong with your story. It wasn't Nichols, it was you. From the beginning. *You're* the leak to the Russians. *You're* the traitor. And now you've dragged me in with you.'

Fleming started to protest, then changed his mind. He stared at Owen in silence, his eyes appraising, his face cold, hardly admitting defeat. Then he laughed wryly. 'I knew I should never have trusted you with this.'

'But you did.'

'I had to. Who else could have done it?'

Owen shrugged.

'I never used you before,' Fleming said. 'Every assignment I ever gave you was strictly legitimate.'

'Legitimate from whose point of view?'

'They *were* CIA jobs. Until now. I never used you for anything else because, frankly, I was afraid to. You're too damn smart.'

Owen did not acknowledge the compliment. 'It's a tough game you play,' he said. 'An agent-in-place, especially at your level. Pressure from Moscow, pressure in Washington, having to please both sides. How long has it been going on?'

'For years.'

Owen nodded. He wasn't surprised. Fleming was good, always had been. He admired the man for a difficult job well done. But admiration was irrelevant to the job Owen had to do.

'Why did you do it?' he said.

'You said it – pressure from Moscow. They couldn't be content to have me where I was. I had to move a notch higher. I had to get Nichols' job.'

So that was it. Nichols' *job*. Suddenly it all made sense. Kidnap the President's daughter, and count on the President to rely on his best friend. Then lead Nichols on a goose-chase halfway around the world. Dangle a clue in his face, then snatch it back just as he starts to pounce. Do that a few times, and make Nichols look like a bungler – on an issue the President could hardly fail to notice. Or care about.

'And you, I suppose,' Owen said, 'would have rescued the victim and taken her home in triumph.'

Fleming looked back at him without saying anything. He didn't have to reply.

'Brilliant,' Owen said. 'It might have worked.'

'It still might.'

'I don't think so.'

'Why? Are you going to kill me?'

'Of course not.'

A look passed between them, like the silent exchange of two doctors who agree on a simple diagnosis without having to put it in words. Fleming was a Soviet agent of considerable rank. The knowledge he carried in his head was far too valuable to lose. No fellow agent who was loyal to the CIA, for whatever reasons, would willingly let that die. Owen could not kill Fleming as long as he had a choice.

And he did have a choice at this point.

Another bullet hit the pavement on the other side of the wall. This one came from behind them. They were exposed on both sides, clear targets in the Soviets' crossfire.

Owen didn't move.

Fleming stared at him, incredulous. 'What the hell? You're going to let *them* kill me?'

'Hardly. Just stay where you are.' Owen started to get to his feet.

'*That was our last warning, Fleming. Come out now, or . . .*'

The Russian voice suddenly lost its power, thickened, ground to a halt. Silence. Then darkness. The lights went out overhead.

Owen jumped to his feet, his astonishment genuine, his hand tightening on the grip of the revolver. He kept the gun pointed at Fleming as his eyes swept the ruins.

Fleming's gaze shifted, too. He could see what Owen could not, and his face showed enormous relief.

Owen looked at Fleming and started to turn, but a voice from behind cut him off.

'Drop the gun, Owen.'

He stood there a moment. Then he slowly opened his hand and the revolver fell to the ground.

Erica was standing by the bull's horns, her face a pattern of light and shadow under the pale moon. She was holding an automatic in one hand. In the other, a small electronic device – the master switch from which Owen had controlled the lights, the tape deck and amplifier, the guns he had positioned precisely to avoid their line of fire.

Fleming glanced at the switch, and now he understood. He turned on Owen, glaring. '*Tapes!* You bastard! I should have known!'

Owen shrugged. 'I found out what I had to.'

'You were *guessing*!'

Owen nodded. 'But now I know. You're a Soviet agent. So's she.'

Erica smiled sweetly. 'You're surprised?' she said.

'No. It happens.'

The smile faded. There was some satisfaction to Owen in that. He turned back to Fleming, who had retrieved his pistol, who was aiming it now at him. Owen would not kill Fleming, but he knew the same restriction did not work in reverse.

'We're wasting time,' Fleming said. 'Where's the girl?'

Owen's eyes shifted from one gun to the other. He stood there for a long moment, saying nothing. Then his shoulders sagged, his eyes went flat, his expression admitted defeat.

'Follow me,' he said. 'I'll show you.'

twenty-one

'I *blackmailed* Kolonov,' Nichols said.

The President looked up sharply. 'You *what*?'

'That's what I said. Kolonov made a mistake once, an affair with a woman. That's nothing, but the woman in this case was a Red Chinese agent.' Nichols smiled. 'Kolonov didn't know it, and by the time he found out the affair was a *fait accompli*. I knew they didn't know it in Moscow, or Kolonov would have been recalled. So when Fleming took off for Athens, I went to him for help.'

'You went to the *Russians* for help?' The President passed a hand across his eyes. 'I'm glad I didn't know it at the time.'

'I told you why I couldn't come to you.'

'Yes, I know. You thought *I'd* kidnapped Anne.'

'I never believed it, but I had to find out.'

'Under the circumstances, I won't argue the point. But never mind that. Go on with Kolonov.'

'I told him to put the best agent he had on Paul Fleming and report every move to me. He could hardly say no. He did it, an agent by the name of Svitsky, and Fleming did make a move. He *spotted* Svitsky. And *lost* him. And that, I knew, was impossible.'

'Why?'

'Because Svitsky's too good to let himself be seen – unless he *wanted* to be, unless he'd been *ordered* to let Fleming see him. And that could mean only one thing: Kolonov, a high-ranking KGB officer, *didn't want Fleming tailed.*'

Nichols smiled at the irony of what had happened. In his haste to avoid the people who were loyal to Fleming, he had stumbled straight into the source of loyalty itself!

'I asked myself why,' he went on, 'and suddenly it all made sense. Who would want Cannon dead? The Russians. *Only* the Russians. We were right about that all along. But the Russians wouldn't kill Cannon without grilling him first to find out what he knew. Unless they *already* knew, through their own agent inside the hierarchy of the CIA!'

'Fleming.'

'Yes, Paul Fleming. A traitor of the worst kind. I *trusted* him.'

'Could you be wrong?'

'I could be. I don't think so.'

'But why would he kidnap Anne? Assuming he does work for the Russians, what are they after? They haven't sent me anything vaguely resembling a ransom note. What do they want?'

'Three of my key agents, obviously.'

'You said it yourself. They could have done that without Anne.'

'Diversion,' Nichols said. 'It's an eye for an eye in this business. They kill one of ours, we return the favour. And vice versa. As a result, we have a kind of agreement that saves a lot of recruiting on both sides.' He shrugged. 'With Anne, perhaps they hoped to make us think someone else was behind this. The killing of Cannon. Frankie Sherman. Shelley Curtis. Perhaps they hoped to avoid retaliation.'

The President looked back at him coldly. 'I wonder, sometimes, if we're any better than they are.'

'We fight for the better cause,' Nichols replied matter-of-factly.

'And God's on our side.' The President smiled. A buzzer

sounded on his desk. He picked up the phone, listened a moment, hung up. 'The French have agreed,' he said.

Nichols nodded. 'Good. The French, the British, the West Germans, and the Greeks. That leaves the Israelis yet to hear from.'

'They'll cooperate,' the President replied with a grim uncertainty. 'If they don't, they'll never get another cent from this government, not while I'm minding the purse.'

Nichols smiled. This was the Matt Easton he knew and admired. 'Still sorry you didn't resign?' he said.

'I don't know. I may do it yet.' He raised a hand to fend off Nichols' protest. 'Nothing's changed because we now suspect Paul Fleming,' he said. 'That only explains why we've been so deceived, and to some extent why this happened. Otherwise, it's still the same. If I weren't President, Anne would not have been kidnapped. And Elizabeth wouldn't be suffering this ordeal. They're paying the price for my ambition. So am I. And it's far too much to pay.' He turned away. 'I don't know the answer. Maybe I will after this is over.'

Nichols nodded. He understood. 'It will be,' he said, 'and soon. Fleming can't get away from us now, not with half the world's intelligence agents on his tail.'

Fleming stayed above as Owen began to descend the Grand Staircase with Erica close behind. She switched on a flashlight and pointed its beam into the darkness below.

The staircase had been rebuilt, with huge wooden beams and inverted Minoan-style columns supporting its weight and the rooms at the lower level. There was still some moonlight here, filtering down through the columns, enough to give shadow and shape to the space beyond the beam of the flashlight. They reached a landing, turned, and began to descend yet another flight of stairs.

Owen had learned to sense danger from a far greater distance than this. Erica's automatic was not touching his back, but he felt its pressure as clearly as if it were. He moved on to the bottom of the stairs.

They were in the east wing of the palace, the area of the restored royal apartments, the highlight of the guided tour. Large geometric patterns in the shape of figure eights lined the ochre-toned walls. A doorway led to a corridor on the right. Somewhere beyond it, the rooms where the monarch had lived. Owen led the way through the door but did not stop to point out the historic features. He turned left into a long passageway that led to a different set of rooms.

There was no moonlight here, utter blackness beyond the light in Erica's hand. The walls, where Owen could see them, were no longer painted; they were rough stone. This was the palace workshop, where the suddenness of the final destruction was made vivid by work left in progress, unfinished, by tools cast aside in their users' haste to flee.

Owen moved on, turning right, turning left, winding his way through the maze, away from the part of the palace that the tourists got to see. The air turned steadily damper; the darkness remained intense.

Erica spoke only once, from anger more than concern. 'What are you doing?' she demanded. 'There must be a shorter route.'

'Sorry,' Owen replied. 'There is no such thing down here.'

Erica looked at him through the dim outer edges of the flashlight beam, then nodded for him to go on.

After that, there was nothing to say.

They had moved around to the opposite side of the palace, the west wing – a working area full of long, narrow storage rooms, some not entirely cleared. There were mounds of earth, modern tools – not cast aside but left here by archaeologists who continued to sift the earth. Gradually, Owen began to pick up his pace. Erica stayed close behind. They passed through a door, made a turn to the left. Another door lay just ahead.

'Watch it here,' Owen warned. 'There's scaffolding overhead.'

He ducked as he crossed the threshold.

Erica swung the light up, keeping Owen in view under the crisscrossed beams of modern metal and wood. Scaffolding. More digging out. More history to be revealed.

Owen grabbed a bar overhead as his feet found another below. And Erica stepped through the door.

Into nothing!

An open shaft of stone. A pit rising to a ceiling above and a floor thirty feet below. There was no natural light here, but Owen had seen it before. A large slab of stone below suggested the pit's ancient purpose. A temple, for sacrifice.

A gasp of fear escaped from Erica's mouth as she teetered at the edge of the door. The gun and the flashlight flew from her hands and her arms flailed the air, struggling to maintain balance. The beam of the light swung around in a graceful curve. Owen stood on the scaffolding that rose up from below. His eyes met hers – full of terror, an instant of recognition, a futile moment of hope.

Erica's arms reached out to him as her body weight shifted forwards, balance gone. Then the light turned down, dropping fast like the gun, its beam towards the stone floor below.

A scream began in near darkness. Owen felt a rush of air as the shadow of Erica fell past him and became a free-floating silhouette against the dim light further down. A metallic crash echoed back up through the pit as the gun hit the floor below. A second crash brought total darkness. Then came the crush of bones and flesh against rock. The screaming ceased. There was silence, and fresh blood on ancient stone.

Owen jumped back through the door. He retrieved the extra revolver and flashlight he had hidden behind a loose piece of rock and ran.

Fleming stiffened at the muffled sound of a scream from deep inside the ruins. He stood quite still, trying to pin down its direction. Then he raised his pistol and moved to the top of the staircase where Owen and Erica had descended.

A woman's scream? A man's? Impossible to tell. And either way, it could be one of Owen's tricks, designed to draw Fleming away from this open space and into the darkness below.

Fleming was sure of two things: Anne Easton and Richard Owen were both essential to his plan. Anne was his trump card, to be played at the end of the game. Rescue. The triumphant return, just as Owen had guessed. A personal success in contrast to Nichols' bungling. A simple request, the directorship. And why not? Nichols would be finished.

But without Anne, Fleming's whole plan caved in. He would be a bungler *with* Nichols, a victim of his own scheme to discredit and destroy. Failure in Washington. Worse than that, failure in Moscow.

Yes, he had to get Anne – that first. And he had to get Owen, too. But Owen would not go home. He would not leave Knossos. He was too great a threat; he had to die.

Fleming crossed the courtyard and jumped up on the edge of a wall that gave a clear view of the ruins from one end to the other. There were several points of exit from the underground part of the palace. Most were simply openings in the ground, easy enough for Owen alone – he could pull himself up and out – but not with the girl in his arms. He would have to use the stairs, one of two – the Grand Staircase or the others near the restored North Porch. Wherever Owen emerged, with or without Erica, with or without Anne Easton, Fleming would see him first. And he had to come up. There was no other way out.

But there *were* footsteps at the far end of the courtyard!

Someone moving in stealth, trying not to be heard. Someone moving up the open steps from the South Gate, where Fleming himself had entered the ruins over an hour ago.

Owen? Impossible! But still, one of Owen's tricks?

Fleming dropped to a crouch, raised the pistol, and held it firmly in front of him with both hands.

A whistle, the sound of a bird formed by human lips. A signal. A switch pulled at the bottom of the hills. The lights flared on overhead.

Fleming's eyes darted to the top of the Grand Staircase, across the North Porch, back to the steps at the south end of the courtyard. Then a voice broke over the silence of the night.

'*Police! Drop your weapon and come out. We have all exits covered.*'

Greek, this time. Through a bullhorn!

Fleming shouted across the courtyard. 'Forget it, Owen!'

The voice switched to English. '*Heraklion Police! Come out with your hands in the air!*'

Fleming remained silent. He waited.

'*I warn you, Kyrie, we are prepared to fire.*'

Then a face appeared over the top of the steps, head, and shoulders. White shirt, gold and black epaulets. A black cap with a sharp, shining bill. Two hands aiming a police revolver.

Fleming waited no longer. He fired.

The policeman's body rose up in the air, hung there suspended, then toppled backwards out of sight down the stairs. Suddenly there were two more figures in white shirts and black hats. Crouching, running, ducking behind cover. Three, four, a whole damn battalion of cops! *Real* cops!

Fleming jumped, landing on his feet on the far side of the wall. A volley of gunfire followed him. Bullets whined through the air, ricocheted off the rock foundations, gouged holes in ancient stone. Fleming ran to his left, back to the right, zigzagging across open pavement, leaping foundations, taking cover where it appeared. There was no time for strategy now, no odds for fighting back. There was only speed, and escape. He couldn't think of Anne Easton, or Owen, of the fact he was leaving them there. He could only hope that the scream had come from Owen, not Erica, that she had the girl; that she, too, would find a way to escape.

Fleming ran for the fence at the north end of the grounds, scrambled up the side, and threw himself over into the grassy meadow on the other side. He landed with a sharp jolt of pain, but he pushed himself up and ran on. There were shouts from behind. Bullets sprayed the meadow, but Fleming was just out of range. Then suddenly a policeman appeared before him, raising his gun, taking aim . . .

Fleming fired. The policeman spun around and fell on his face in the grass. Fleming leaped over him and ran to the car he'd left parked down the road. He got there first and jumped in, then got the ignition going. A new volley of bullets missed his tyres as he swung out into the road and took off at high speed, back towards Heraklion.

A mile or so down the road, he made a sudden sharp turn, into a drive that wound back to a farmhouse. The barn door was standing open. Fleming drove in, cut the engine, and slammed the barn door shut. He ducked beneath a window, then raised his head and peered out as two police cars roared by and out of sight.

Fleming dropped to the floor, breathing hard, his whole body trembling with exhaustion. Erica had secured this place beforehand, thank God she had! He had left his clothes here, his papers, his official passport. Here was a second car, a telephone.

Fleming's head ached. His back was throbbing with pain, his lungs burned for air. A moment more to catch his breath, and he would make a phone call – the call to bring reinforcements who were standing by on alert.

If Erica had the girl, she would find her way here. But now, with a moment to think, Fleming had to be realistic. He knew inside that the scream had not been Owen's.

Owen would escape from Knossos. One way or another, Fleming knew he would escape. But with a four-year-old child, he could not go far on foot. That meant a car, and the road – this one north-south road that was the only link between Knossos and the modern world.

Fleming pushed himself up and was heading for the door, when a sound came from behind. He drew the pistol as he swung around.

'Don't fire!'

A man moved out of the shadows at the rear of the barn. A wide face. Broad, Slavic features.

'Svitsky?'

The Russian gave a slight nod.

'What are you doing here?'

'I'm making contact with you.'

'I might have killed you.'

'I had to be sure it was you.'

'What's this about? I don't have time—'

'You'll *make* time, Comrade.'

Fleming's eyes narrowed angrily. '*What?*'

Svitsky moved forward into the path of the moonlight coming through the window. 'We've got a big problem,' he said. 'Nichols is on to you.'

Fleming's anger vanished, and he stared at the Russian with open-mouthed astonishment. Questions raced through his mind.

How? Why? What had happened? He slowed them down. The answers were vital, but he had to postpone them.

'All right,' Fleming said, 'that's a change in plans. Owen's got the girl in Knossos. And I've got to get Owen.'

Owen had almost reached the foot of the Grand Staircase when the lights came on and shouting broke out overhead.

Police! Where had *they* come from?

He ducked into a storage room, where a narrow shaft of stone opened on to the sky. He jumped, reached the top with his hands and held on. Then slowly he pulled himself up with his arms and peered cautiously over the edge.

He watched the whole scene from ground level. Fleming had escaped over the fence, with the police behind him. But other police had remained behind and were starting to search the ruins...

Owen dropped back to the floor and cut across the corridor into the royal apartments. From behind came the murmur of voices and footsteps pounding on stone. The police were descending the stairs now. Orders were shouted in Greek. Men fanning out. Footsteps running this way.

Owen's eyes scanned the room where he stood, a private sanctuary with four walls and ceiling and no place to hide. He moved quickly, quietly, across the floor, through a door in the far wall, into an L-shaped corridor that led to another chamber. This one was smaller, with blue dolphins painted in fresco along the upper walls. A gay room, designed for the Queen of Knossos – and, in this maze, a dead end.

One other door was set into the walls of the Queen's Room. Beyond it, a short corridor and one last refuge – the tiny chamber that had been the Queen's bath. There was no light here, just a deep stone tub, once complete with running water and still intact four thousand years after the last royal soaking. Owen dropped to his knees behind the tub and flattened himself on the floor.

He listened in silence as footsteps echoed along his own path, coming closer, from the sanctuary into the L-shaped hall, into the Queen's Room on the other side of this wall. They stopped there a moment, then came on.

166

Not one man, but two.

Owen lay where he was, not moving, hardly daring to risk the sound of a breath. The footsteps entered the corridor to the bath, one set behind the other. They approached the doorway. They stopped. There was silence, and two policemen were standing in the door, less than five feet from the place where Owen lay.

A flashlight flicked on. Its beam probed the corners of the tiny room, passing over the rim of the tub. Owen lay quite still. Then the hand with the light swung back sharply and aimed the beam at a spot on the floor.

'What's that?'

A moment of silence. Then one of the men came forwards into the room. His hand brushed the floor at the lower edge of the tub.

'A coin. American.'

Silence again.

Then the other man gave a small laugh. 'So what? There were hundreds of tourists here today. Anyway, there's no one here now. Let's go.'

The light flicked off. The footsteps moved away.

Owen took a deep breath, but he waited several minutes before he moved again. Then he sat up on his knees and looked down into the tub. A dark blanket covered the bottom. Owen pulled it back.

Anne Easton lay where he'd left her, in the deep curve of the tub, her eyes closed against a peaceful face. She was unconscious again, oblivious to danger, and Owen was glad for that. The drug, in a way, was her protection – as her life was his.

He checked her pulse, strong and steady. Then he pulled the blanket around her, lifted her up, and carried her out of the room.

A single policeman stood guard in the corridor outside the sanctuary. Owen pulled back and studied the room once again. Solid walls. The ceiling intact overhead. Behind him, the dead end of the Queen's Room. There was only this one way out.

He put Anne down on the floor and peeked out into the hall-way. The policeman was standing near the foot of the stairs. His arms were relaxed at his sides, but his face was alert, his gun in his hand. Owen drew his own revolver. He moved across to the other side of the door and raised the revolver, taking careful aim. He fired.

The policeman swung around, startled, and his gun arm tensed for action. He had turned, not towards the shot, but its target – an overhead light that went out as the bulb shattered with a sharp ping of sound. Then slowly he turned back, holding the gun in front of him with both hands, peering into the dim far end of the corridor. Doors opened to the royal apartments on the right, to the workrooms on the left, to any number of small storage rooms on both sides. At the end of the hall was a small, arching doorway, a wooden door, a heavy lock.

The policeman took a step forwards.

Owen measured the sound of each step. He had moved back across the doorway and stood with his back to the wall, the revolver in his belt, his hands flattened against the stone behind him. The policeman came slowly forwards, approaching the door. He stopped.

Owen gave no warning. He swung into the doorway. One hand came down on the gun, which clattered across the floor. The other spun the man around, pinned him against Owen's chest, and clamped firmly across his mouth to prevent a cry for help. The man struggled, but Owen found the pressure point at the angle of his jaw and pressed a thumb into the soft skin beneath it. A second later, the policeman collapsed, unconscious.

Owen let him fall to the floor. Then he picked up Anne and turned right into the corridor, moving quickly to the far end and the small arching doorway. He had removed the lock earlier and replaced it with one of his own. Now he produced a key, opened the door, and stepped inside.

This wasn't a room, though it had been and would be again. It was an excavation, filled with dirt and digging tools, wheelbarrows, wooden crates brimming with pottery shards. A chamber half-buried and not on the public tour; nor was it on any map.

There was no electricity here, only battery-operated lamps that were strung across the carved-out roof overhead. And the latest 'find' at Knossos: a subterranean tunnel leading down the hill, away from the domestic quarters of the palace.

Owen carried Anne into the mouth of the tunnel, making his way easily along the gently declining stone floor. The tunnel descended in darkness, at an angle to the hill. There was no need to hurry now. He had made his escape. Minutes later, he emerged into open air.

Lights glowed from the top of the hill behind him, but ahead there was only the night – a patchwork of moonlight and shadow. Small mountains of earth and stone removed from the ancient tunnel. More digging tools. Cypress trees lining the riverbank.

And a boat.

A dinghy, a simple rowboat, its oarlocks wrapped for silence. Owen had planned it that way. He lay the girl on the blanket in the grass and pushed the boat quietly into the water. He retrieved the oars from their hiding place in the brush beside the river and slipped them into place. Then he picked up Anne, climbed into the boat, and pushed off from the riverbank.

For a moment, the boat moved out into the current of its own momentum. Then Owen took hold of the oars. They sliced the water, making less sound than the flow of the river. Slow and strong, downstream. Away from Knossos. Away from the lights. Away from the police and Paul Fleming. To a waiting car.

twenty-two

It was dawn. Fleming stood in a window of the farmhouse, watching the sun come up over the mountains of Crete. On a table nearby, the radio set remained silent. No report from the agents he had posted along the road on each side of Knossos. There was nothing *to* report, except for police activity. There hadn't been all night.

It was possible that Owen was still there, hiding out in the ruins, planning escape when the gates were opened to tourists a few hours from now. Possible, but not likely. Owen didn't work that way. He would know the police were there. He would know they would keep watching. He would find a better way.

Had already found it, most likely. Fleming's shoulders sagged. His eyes were flat as he stared at the scenic view. Then behind him a door opened.

Svitsky.

'I take it there's nothing new?'

Fleming nodded and turned away.

'Then you've failed.'

Fleming looked back sharply. 'Failed? Whose judgement is that?'

'Not mine,' Svitsky said. He dropped into a chair. 'I've just been in touch with Moscow.'

Fleming felt a tightening in his chest that he recognized as fear. He felt it and shook it off. 'I'd call that a bit premature.'

'Perhaps.' Svitsky shrugged. 'Nonetheless, they're not very happy with you. You're a liability now. They're cutting the ties while they can.'

'That's it? Just like that?'

Svitsky nodded. 'I agree, it's harsh.'

'Harsh? It's a death sentence! What do they want? I've given them Cannon, Sherman, Shelley Curtis. Probably Owen, too.'

'True,' Svitsky said. 'Moscow is grateful for that. But you've failed the assignment they gave you: a KGB agent in place at the head of the CIA. You've failed the assignment and possibly blown your cover. You've got nothing to bargain with now.'

Fleming glared at the Russian for a long moment. Then abruptly he turned away with a sense of deep frustration beyond any he'd ever known. *It's a tough game you play.* Owen had said. *Trying to please both sides.* This was hardly news to Fleming. Now he had *failed* both sides, not only Moscow, but Langley.

Svitsky had spelled it all out during the night. Fleming had succeeded too well. He *had* forced Nichols to a corner of desperation. Nichols *did* go to the Russians for help, an ironic twist – to Kolonov at the embassy. And Kolonov, of course, had reported the incident to Moscow. Nichols was suspicious; that was enough. Christ! How could he have known this might happen?

There *had* to be a way out.

He stood there, thinking, and an idea came to mind. There *was* a way out, the same plan in variation. He turned to Svitsky.

'Get back to Moscow,' he said. 'Tell them I can salvage this yet.'

'How?'

'Same as before. I rescue the girl and take her home. But I blame the whole thing on *Owen*.'

'Owen! What about Nichols? You've been out of contact too long. That can only confirm what he already suspects. How will you handle him?'

'How will *he* handle *me* when I come home with Anne?' Fleming said. 'Nichols suspects, but he doesn't know a damn thing. I diffuse his suspicions by giving Anne back to her parents. That's got to be worth some confusion, at least. Then I turn his suspicions on Owen.'

'And Owen, of course, will be dead.'

'Precisely. As for my lack of contact, I simply reverse the position Nichols is in. Once I found out who had Anne – Richard Owen – I purposely cut myself off from the CIA. Owen's a CIA agent! I didn't know *what* to think.'

Svitsky smiled. 'It might work.'

'It has to work.'

'Of course, it means you've got to find Owen.'

'I can do that if they'll give me time. Remember, I've still got my contacts inside the CIA. The agents I've turned. They're still loyal to me.'

Svitsky was silent a moment. Then he shrugged. 'All right, I'll see what they say.'

Fleming nodded. He felt enormous relief. Moscow had to go along. He turned back to the window as Svitsky left the room, his mind already churning up thoughts about Owen, about what Owen might do.

He *had* to get Owen. It was vital! He had to get *Anne Easton*. She was more than a trump card now, far more important than that. A four-year-old child, but Fleming's last hope – his only chance for survival.

*

The director of Greek intelligence was in his office as the sun came up over Athens. Another man sat across his desk. A report lay between them.

The director's eyes shifted from the report to the man, a Greek intelligence agent. A quick nod. Then he picked up the phone.

His call had top priority on both sides of the ocean. He reached the White House in minutes; another moment and Nichols was on the line.

'We've located Paul Fleming,' the Greek said, and quickly explained what had happened.

A fisherman setting nets in the river Kairatos, on the island of Crete, had noticed lights going on and off at the nearby ruins of Knossos. Electrical problems, he assumed, and was not unduly concerned. Then he heard angry voices and decided to call the police. A patrol car from Heraklion had been sent to investigate.

When the officers arrived, they found the night guards bound and gagged, unconscious. Later it was learned they had also been drugged, a hint of professionalism. The officers, alert to trouble now, had radioed for help.

The Greek went on, describing the scene at Knossos – one man, alone, an American, escaping over the fence, killing two officers on the way. He had got away in a car and disappeared. A subsequent search of the ruins produced a body, a woman. Her fingerprints were not on record in Athens, were *en route* to Washington now.

'But,' the Greek said, 'the man has been identified by photographs. It *was* Paul Fleming. I'm sorry to say, we don't know where he is now. On Crete somewhere.'

The Greek was silent as Nichols replied from the other end of the line. Then he said, 'There is something else. Another man was seen inside the ruins. Not seen, exactly; he knocked out a police guard. We have no idea who he was. But before Fleming escaped, he called out a name. That name, I am told, was *Owen*.'

Nichols frowned. Owen? Then, suddenly, his face went white. *Owen?*

Of course, *Richard Owen*! A man who could have walked into the house at Indian Springs and back out with the President's daughter. A man who could have and *would* have.

Fleming was Owen's case officer. He had been for years. It was Fleming who went to Oslo, where Richard Owen had died, Fleming who *confirmed* the identification.

But there had been more than that. Dental records. Fingerprints. All in Owen's file. And who had instant access to that file? Who, if anyone, could substitute other records for Owen's own?... *Paul Fleming*.

Richard Owen *wasn't* dead!

Nichols hung up the phone and looked across at the President.

'I hate to say this,' he said, 'but we've got serious trouble. I know who has your daughter – a monster of our own making – and unless he wants us to, we'll have the devil's own time catching up with him.'

Owen pulled into the driveway of the house in Heraklion where Harry Goldman kept his bachelor quarters. Harry had been divorced for nearly a year. Maybe that was why he had left the CIA and returned to the US Air Force.

Or maybe he felt the Air Force was more secure.

Owen hadn't seen Harry since the divorce but knew he was stationed at the US base outside Heraklion. He also knew that Harry would be living off base. Finding his address had been a simple matter. He was in the phone book, under *G*.

It ought to be a happy reunion.

Owen checked the condition of his passenger on the floor in the back seat. Then he got out of the car, locked it, and made his way across the lawn to the front door. He rang the bell once, then after a few moments, again.

Lights came on in the house, charting Harry's progress from his bedroom upstairs. Then a porchlight came on overhead. The door opened.

Harry Goldman stood there, legs bare under an old bathrobe, feet hastily slipped into a pair of sandals. Otherwise, he looked exactly the same. Hair dark and long, but well trimmed. Eyes a little distant. And, yes, the beard was still there, as dark and full as ever.

Harry didn't say anything, just stood there staring at the

apparition on his porch. The distance faded from his eyes, and his jaw dropped open.

'*Richard Owen!*'

Owen smiled. 'You might let me in,' he said. 'Or at least switch off that light.'

Harry's eyes shifted to the street. It was a reflex action. Richard Owen was a sure sign of trouble.

Then he came to life. He grabbed Owen with both arms and pulled him into the house, grinning like the fool he wasn't. 'I can't believe it! My God, they told me you'd been *killed*!'

'They were wrong,' Owen replied.

'Yes, I guess they were! Come on in. What the hell are you doing here at this hour?'

'It's a long story. Do you have a coffee pot?'

'Right next to my fifth of Glenfiddich. Christ, I'm glad to see you!'

They settled themselves in the kitchen over cups of hot coffee and preliminary talk of old times. It was a strange friendship, thought Owen, who rarely allowed himself friends. A friendship where serious questions were asked cautiously, if at all, and where answers were never required. A friendship based on shared experience, shared danger, shared confidence. A friendship that was all the deeper for its limits of privacy.

Owen was glad to see Harry, too, genuinely glad to see him.

'Have you seen Paul Fleming lately?' he asked. Outside the sky was fading from black to grey.

'Fleming? Hell, no! I'm through with all that. I assume he's still chained to a desk back at Langley.'

'Not always. He gets into the field from time to time.'

'That's interesting.'

'He's good.'

'The best, until you came along. But Fleming's getting old now.' Harry suddenly grinned. 'For the field, I mean.' Fleming wasn't much older than Harry.

'Yes.' Owen nodded. 'And I'm not sure I trust him.'

Harry's grin faded, and he stared at Owen, thoughtfully stroking his beard. 'I didn't know trust was ever an issue with you,' he said.

Owen shrugged. 'I trust you.'

The grin returned under a sceptical gaze. 'Sure you do, as long as you can see me. But Christ! Fleming? He's the *Deputy Director!*'

'I know.'

Owen had learned what he wanted to know. Fleming hadn't got to Harry. He dismissed the matter with a gesture and took a drink of his coffee.

'How's Barbara?' he said.

Harry showed no outward signs that he'd noticed the abrupt change of subject. 'Barbara! At the moment I seem to be paying for a world tour.' He leaned forwards, elbows on the table, rubbing his eyes with both hands. Then he got up and started rummaging in the back of a kitchen cabinet. He produced a bottle of aspirin and held a glass under the water tap.

'You mention Barbara, and I get a headache,' he said. 'Last I heard, she was shacked up with some painter in Majorca. Before that it was a skiing instructor at Kitzbuhel. I'll tell you this, I'm never going to get rich unless she gets married again.'

He popped two aspirin into his mouth and washed them down. Then he turned back to the table. He stumbled.

'Hell, what's the matter with me?'

Owen smiled. 'Keeping late hours again?'

Harry managed a sheepish grin but no reply.

'How do you like your job here?' Owen asked as Harry lowered himself carefully into a chair.

'Softest tour I've had. A couple of hours of work on each side of a nice long siesta.' Harry shrugged. 'It's a good break after the mess with Barbara, but not much of a challenge. Frankly, I won't mind when they decide to move me on.'

Owen nodded. 'Enjoy it while it lasts.'

'Yeah.' Harry shook his head. 'Jesus! What's going on?'

Then suddenly he looked up at Owen and knew. He stared across the table without moving, his mind lunging at Owen but his body refusing to budge out of the chair. His eyes were growing distant again, and not as a matter of choice. Distant, and very cold.

'The coffee?' he asked.

Owen nodded.

'What's in it?'

'Nothing permanent.' Owen reached into his pocket and produced a plastic vial of tiny white pills. Diatol, stolen out of a pharmacy on the other side of Heraklion. A routine burglary when discovered – if, in fact, it was discovered at all.

'How much?' Harry wanted to know.

'Enough to make you sleep for a couple of days. You'll feel great when you wake up. And, by the way, you won't have to cover for me. I'll be a long way from here in two days.'

'Thanks.' Harry was slipping fast now, and his head was starting to sag. He was having to make an effort to hold it up. He asked one more question. '*Why?*'

'I'm sorry, Harry, there's not enough time to tell you. Trust me. It's important.'

'It better be,' Harry replied thickly, stumbling now on his words. 'It better be bloody goddamn important . . .'

Then his head dropped and he slumped forwards across the table.

Owen carried him upstairs and laid him out on the bed. Then he found Harry's keys and left the house again. The garage was at the back, hidden from the street by the house, and the car inside was a small white Fiat. Owen backed it out and drove his car in. Then he carried Anne Easton inside through the back door.

Two hours later, he picked up the telephone and dialled a local number. 'This is Captain Goldman. I'm calling to report I won't be in today. I think I've got the 'flu.'

'I'm sorry to hear that, sir,' came the voice at the other end. 'I'll notify your section.'

'Thanks.'

Owen hung up. Then he carried Anne out to Harry's waiting Fiat and drove away.

An agent of Britain's MI6 was sitting on the passenger side of the grey Mercedes that was parked outside the main passenger entrance of the Heraklion airport terminal. Six other British agents were posted near the same door, still more in strategic places around and through the building.

MI6 had the airports here and in Chania down the coast. Other agencies were covering the ports, road traffic, hotels, passport surveillance. Hundreds of eyes were watching the thousands of people who were coming and going from Crete. But no one had spotted Owen.

Richard Owen. The agent wondered what was going on. First Paul Fleming, now Owen. And from what he'd heard, this surveillance didn't end on Crete. Something big was going on, big and very hush-hush. Orders had come straight from the Foreign Office.

And where did the FO get its orders, the agent wondered. From Downing Street? From the White House? The priority this thing had, orders, might have come from Buckingham Palace!

He glanced up as a US Air Force officer passed by the car on his right. He was probably part of the surveillance, too, the agent thought. Everyone else was.

Everyone except Richard Owen. And Paul Fleming. Had the CIA gone mad?

Something big, all right. Something big indeed.

The agent got out of the car as the Air Force man disappeared into the terminal. An airport limousine bus had just pulled up and was letting off its passengers. Another fifty-odd people, another fifty-odd rejects.

Owen could be any of them – hell, even the pregnant woman! But they couldn't round up the people who *might* be Owen. That would take ten years.

Harry Goldman's secretary was a young airman, nineteen years old and a new recruit to the Air Force. He had joined up to see the world, and Heraklion was surely that. Unfortunately, he spent most of his time at this desk.

'I'm sorry, but Captain Goldman is sick today,' he told the woman at the other end of the phone. 'He took the NATO report home last night, and he's not coming in today.'

The woman was also a secretary, but her rank was higher than his. Among other things, she worked for the commanding officer of the base.

'Then someone will have to go get it,' she replied coolly. 'Brussels is expecting an answer. The CO must see the report today.'

Someone. The airman knew who that meant.

'Yes, ma'am,' he said. 'I'll leave right away.'

The woman behind the Olympic Airlines ticket counter smiled at the man on the other side. She'd seen her share of US officers in this job, but never one with a beard like this before.

'Here you are, Captain Goldman,' she said. 'One seat on our flight to Athens, leaving in forty minutes. I've left the return date open.'

Owen smiled. 'Thank you.'

He'd booked the return flight on purpose. Cash was no problem; he still had most of the 30,000 dollars in the money belt at his waist. But he'd spotted two British agents outside. There were bound to be more. And with that kind of coverage, he knew they'd be checking everything – including one-way trips out of here.

He paid for the ticket out of Harry's wallet.

'Gate seven,' the woman said. 'Do you have any luggage to check?'

Owen glanced down at the garment bag he was holding. 'No, thanks,' he said. 'I think I'll keep this with me.'

The young airman rang the doorbell once more. There was still no answer, as there hadn't been when he tried to call from the base. The morning paper was lying on the front steps. Captain Goldman wasn't home, and he hadn't been. Apparently, he had spent the night elsewhere.

Terrific.

He started to turn back to his car. Then he stopped. If the captain wasn't in the house, the NATO report might be. He turned and walked around to the back.

A kitchen window gave to a little pressure. He pushed it up. Surely the captain wouldn't care. If he had to return to the base without the report, after all, he would also have to reveal the captain's white lie.

Sick with the 'flu? Sure he was!

The airman pushed himself up and in through the open window.

The airport in Athens was full of West German agents. Owen recognized three. He had also spotted MI6 at Heraklion. A veritable convention of spies!

And where had they come from, he wondered. Fleming? No. They were on the wrong side for Fleming. Nichols? That made better sense. Nichols and the President in tandem, drawing on global resources.

Owen wondered how long he could get away with this. The world, it seemed, was against him.

He passed through the terminal and took a cab to Omonia Square, where he set off on foot. It was twelve blocks by a round-about route to the Xenophon Gallery. A bell tinkled as he pushed open the door.

The woman who came forwards was grey haired and hand-some, with a pleasant smile and a pair of glasses hanging on a chain at her neck. She seemed out of place in a room full of abstract paintings and free-form sculpture, like a Rembrandt among Jackson Pollacks. Owen knew she wasn't. The CIA had an eye for that kind of detail. Appearance aside, this Rembrandt no doubt knew more about modern art than anyone since Picasso.

'May I help you?' she said.

'Yes, I'm here to see Molly.'

'Molly.' A pause. Then, 'Follow me, please.'

Molly was the gallery's bookkeeper and sat in an office at the back. She also handled identification here at the Athens station. No one went downstairs without Molly's nod of approval.

Owen knew that Molly had known Harry, he hoped not too well. Dark hair, dark beard, in uniform – he *was* Harry Goldman – but he didn't want to press the issue with an unknown intimate friend.

'Harry! What are you doing here?'

He had passed.

He hung the garment bag on a metal rack that was there for office staff coats, then tossed his hat on to the shelf above it. 'I came by to say hello.'

'After all this time?' Molly gave him a doubtful glance. Then she grinned. 'Never mind. You look great. How's the Air Force?'

'Busy in the wide blue yonder.' It was the kind of thing Harry would have said. Cute. And Molly was very pretty.

Pretty, but also smart.

'You look different somehow.' She frowned. Then her face broke into a smile. 'The glasses!'

'You had to notice.'

Molly laughed. 'Vain as ever, I see. I like them. Wrap a sheet around that uniform and you could pass for Euripides.'

Owen sat down on the corner of her desk. 'Euripides wore glasses?'

Molly shrugged. 'He must have. All that writing by oil lamp? How long will you be in Athens?'

'That depends.'

Molly raised an eyebrow.

'On how much red tape you can cut. You may have heard, I'm assigned to Air Force Intelligence.'

'No, I hadn't, but it figures.'

Owen nodded. 'And I'm on priority assignment.' He lowered his voice. '*The* priority assignment.'

Molly looked back at him without saying anything.

'Anne Easton,' Owen added.

A look passed across Molly's face. 'It's terrible, isn't it?'

'Terrible's hardly the word,' Owen replied. 'It's the worst crisis we've had in many a year. If we don't find her soon—' He sliced his throat with his finger and left the sentence unfinished.

Molly nodded grimly. 'I knew something was up when Paul Fleming arrived here. Have you seen him?'

Owen nodded. 'In Heraklion. But listen, there's a file I need to see. I can go through channels if I have to. I was hoping you'd save me the trouble.'

'Which file.'

'Erich Parsons.'

'Sure,' Molly said. 'He's not even classified.'

Owen knew that. It was one of the reasons he had picked Parsons.

'And anyway,' Molly added, 'you know enough to blow this place sky high any time you want to. Come with me.'

Owen retrieved Harry's hat. 'Thanks,' he said. 'I appreciate this.' He picked up the garment bag. 'And so, I hope, will the President.'

Two hours and several steps later, Captain Harry Goldman checked into the Hotel Pandora. He paid for one night in cash.

The Pandora was a clean hotel that offered minimum service at rates to match. Anne would be safe here, alone. It also offered a rear door through which Owen could pass unobserved.

He lifted Anne out of the garment bag, put her down on the bed, and pulled the covers up to her shoulders. She was nothing but a liability now. She was hard to disguise, and slowed him down. As long as he kept her with him, capture was too real a threat. Without her, he could simply go underground. With her, that was out of the question.

He dropped down in a chair by the bed to think through the alternatives. He was on his own, now more than ever before. The toughest assignment of his career gone sour, reversing itself in a brief moment of truth, becoming a different assignment. An unexpected twist of events, but an old feeling: *trust no one*.

On the one hand, Paul Fleming, a man with the power to unleash the worst of both worlds. The CIA and the KBG, working towards a common goal: get Owen! Paul Fleming would never let Owen live as long as he had Anne Easton.

That threat was bad enough. The other was worse. Ed Nichols and all that he represented. Capture. Extradition and justice.

Owen knew what he had to do: dump Anne with some local authorities and disappear. Anything else would be foolish. An unerring instinct for his own safety had kept him alive up to now. And a free man. He could not go against that instinct.

But there was also the question of pride. Professional pride. And commitment. He wanted to *defeat* Fleming, to finish the job, do it right. And Fleming was far more powerful than the local police or anyone else in Athens. Dumping Anne here would be tantamount to handing her over to him.

That was the other thing. He cared about Anne. He could *not* throw her to Fleming.

Yes, a different assignment, tougher still. He had money and his own ingenuity. Nothing more. He couldn't trust anyone now. He was wanted on both sides of a bipolar world; he was sought by the law and the lawless. He was on his own, against all of that. Entirely on his own.

He glanced at the small face sleeping comfortably on the pillow, and he smiled with a new sense of exhilaration. It was an enormous risk, but also an enormous challenge. Against all of that, whatever it meant, he would take Anne Easton home.

And then he would walk away. Richard Owen would simply cease to exist. For ever.

twenty-three

The Pan American ticket agent smiled at the tall, handsome woman who now came to the head of the line.

'Yes, Madame, what can we do for you?'

Owen balanced his purse on the counter, then folded his gloved hands and bent his head slightly to one side. He was wearing a tailored dress suit – no woman his size would ever try to look delicate – and he spoke in a voice that was deep, but soft and pleasant.

He spoke Greek.

'I'm Irena Manalotos of the International Placement Society,' he said. 'I need to arrange for a child to fly to London.'

The man nodded. 'The child will be travelling alone?'

Owen smiled. 'Yes, an orphan boy we've placed with a family in Yorkshire. Unfortunately, we have no one free to go with him at the moment, but one of our representatives in London will meet the flight at Heathrow.'

The man produced a form. 'The age of the child?'

'Four years.'

The man glanced up; he hesitated. 'You understand, we cannot be responsible for him at the end of the flight.'

'Yes, of course,' Owen replied. 'Our representative will be there to take custody.'

The man nodded. 'When do you want him to leave?'

'If possible, tomorrow.'

The man checked the computer set into the counter. Then he glanced back at Owen. 'I can give you a seat on our flight leaving Athens tomorrow morning at ten.'

'Excellent,' Owen replied. He paid for the ticket in cash and left the office.

His next stop was in Piraeus, the port of Athens, at the office of the Kentrikon Lines, which ran passenger ships up into the Bosporus as well as making the regular island tours.

'We'll do what we can, Madame Seiler,' the ticket agent said after Owen explained what he needed. 'How many reservations are we talking about.'

'Twenty-seven people and sixteen animals,' Owen replied.

The man looked up, startled. '*Animals?*'

'We are a circus, sir,' Owen replied with dignity.

'Yes, of course.'

'The wild animals are caged, of course, and the rest are quite tame. Naturally, we expect them to travel as cargo, and our handlers will stay with them.'

'Naturally.'

The man looked at the determined face on the other side of the desk. A lady with a circus and a lot of debts and a chance to play an extra engagement in Istanbul. He had the feeling she'd make it.

'You have quarantine papers for the animals?' he asked.

'We've crossed eight international borders since we left Switzerland two months ago,' Owen said. 'Our quarantine papers are quite in order.'

'And when do you want to go?'

'Tomorrow, if possible.'

'Tomorrow? Twenty-seven people, sixteen animals, and you want to leave tomorrow?'

Owen flashed a gracious smile. 'It's terribly important,' he said.

'Yes, I know. You said so. Well, Madame, I will try.' He cleared his throat. 'There is one other matter. I can't accept your credit. You'll have to pay in advance.'

Owen drew himself up straight in the chair. 'I wouldn't expect you to. I have the money with me. Enough to cover deck passage with one exception. We have an injured child, a boy who will need a cabin. In fact, a cabin for two. The boy's father will be travelling with him.'

From Piraeus Owen drove south to Glyfada, to a small charter airline with a woman behind the desk.

'My son,' he explained sadly. 'We were here on holiday when the crash occurred. He's been in a coma for two weeks.'

'I'm so sorry, Madame Corbel.'

Owen nodded. '*Merci*, you're very kind. But the doctors say he's improved. I can take him home now, and that's why I'm here. Can you fly us to Orleans?'

'Certainly.' The woman smiled. 'When would you like to go?'

'As soon as possible,' Owen replied. 'If you can do it, to-morrow.'

Greek intelligence was checking advance reservations at all ports of exit from Athens. Half a dozen agents were assigned to the airport alone, to study the computer lists, to investigate any reservation involving a young child. It was painstaking, tedious work, almost boring, with nothing but a series of check marks to indicate progress. Name after name discarded. Nothing of interest here.

One of the agents glanced at the next name on his list. His interest revived. He reached for a pile of duplicate ticket forms, found one that matched the reservation. Then he picked up the phone.

A woman answered in Greek. 'International Placement Society.'

'Madame Manalotos, please.'

'I'm sorry, she's not here.'

'When will she be back?'

'Not for another week.'

'*Another* week?'

'Madame Manalotos is out of the country and has been for ten days.'

The agent signalled sharply to his superior across the room. 'You're sure of that?' he said into the phone.

'Quite sure. Could anyone else help you?'

'No thank you, Madame, you've been just the help I needed.'

The Harry Goldman incident came to Ed Nichols' attention via Defense intelligence, where they considered a drugged Air Force officer, recently with the CIA, well within the limits of the unusual circumstances they'd been told to report without delay. Especially when the officer's passport was missing, along with his wallet and one uniform.

Nichols knew the name, as he knew everything in Richard Owen's file. And now, settled into the President's study, on the phone again to his own counterpart in Athens, Nichols knew something else: DIA had reported the incident too late.

'Captain Harry Goldman is still unconscious,' the Greek reported. 'Yet he left Heraklion this morning on an Olympic flight to Athens.'

Nichols felt a surge of conflicting emotions, rage and admiration. 'You're sure it was the same Harry Goldman?'

'Unless you have two Air Force captains of the same name and description with identical passport numbers.'

Nichols sighed. It had to be Owen. He and Goldman had known each other for years. And friendship notwithstanding, the style of the escape was strictly Owen's own.

'Were you able to pick up his trail in Athens?' Nichols asked, and he wondered why he bothered.

'Sorry. He took a taxi into the city and got out at Omonia Square. From there, nothing. However,' the Greek added quickly, 'we have reason to believe he is now trying to leave Greece – *and* that we can stop him.'

Nichols leaned forward.

'Three women,' the Greek said. 'Three names and nationalities, but an identical description.'

Nichols listened to the rest. Three women, each arranging travel for or with a young child. Greek, Swiss, and French. All imposters. Manalotos was out of the country. Seiler and her circus had folded their tent for the year. And no hospital on the Attic peninsula had a young patient by the name of Corbel or any child who fit the woman's story.

Three women, each a diversion. And how many more, Nichols wondered.

Conflicting emotions: rage, admiration, and a growing sense of futility. It sounded like Owen; it *was* Owen, almost without a doubt. But Nichols knew they would never catch him as one of the three women – not in Athens nor London, Piraeus nor Istanbul, Glyfada nor Orleans. For one reason: the three women had been far too easy to find, and Owen would know that, too.

Nichols hung up the phone and leaned back in his chair to think about Richard Owen. Diversion was Owen's style; the obvious was not. Why had he gone to the trouble of setting up three diversions that could be so easily traced? Possibly, to use up the opposition resources.

Professionally, Nichols knew Owen as well as anyone could. He had memorized Owen's file. He had studied his past assignments. He had analysed Owen's techniques and motivation. And he had come to one conclusion, for what it was worth – that Owen would not intentionally betray the CIA.

Owen's loyalty was self-evident, dependable, like a mathematical equation that produced a given solution every time it was worked. It was a loyalty dictated not by idealism, but by the kind of person he was. He would never work for the Soviets; he valued his freedom too highly. He was also the best of his kind, and he had to work for the best. At that level, besides the Russians, there was only the CIA.

Good intentions were no defence in the law – Owen was clearly

186

guilty of kidnapping, probably murder, and possibly treason – but he could not have *known* that Fleming was a traitor. He had to believe he was working for the CIA.

Or did he?

A new thought struck Nichols, and he frowned. Owen had been with Fleming at Knossos, had probably planned to meet him there. When Fleming killed the first policeman he had first called out to Owen. In anger? He had probably thought the policeman *was* Owen. It was *Owen* he'd tried to kill!

Had Owen discovered the truth? Had he *split* from Fleming at Knossos?

A smile spread across Nichols' face as the theory grew towards conviction. Owen, on his own, without the resources of the CIA. That Owen might have to try the obvious; he might have no other choice. And the three women in Athens had each had a child. If there had been a split, it was *Owen* who had Anne Easton. That was good news, because Owen would not hurt Anne. Not if he could avoid it.

A delicate balance, Nichols thought. He wanted Fleming with a vengeance, but he wanted Owen more. Because Owen had Anne. Yet caution was needed. He mustn't force Owen to a corner. He didn't want to precipitate a dangerous choice.

Then another thought struck him, and the smile disappeared. If Owen had split with Fleming, then Fleming must want him as badly as Nichols did! This wasn't a chase, but a contest. Speed mattered. He not only had to find Owen – now he had to do it before Fleming did.

And yet Owen could be *anyone*.

Nichols let out a deep sigh of frustration. Exhaustion and fear. When would this end, he wondered? How would it end? And what would come after that? How far did Fleming's treachery go? How many agents had he turned? Which ones remained loyal to the CIA?

Owen was loyal. Whatever else, he was that. Nichols smiled. In a way, they were on the same side. Then a strange sensation passed through him. It was startling, but unmistakable. Ironic. Incongruous. Reassurance from the most unexpected source.

It was *gratitude* he was feeling. For *Owen*!

And he knew why. He was grateful for Owen's skill, for everything Owen was – a chameleon of a man who could make capture as tough for the Russians as he did for Nichols himself.

Nichols realized he was *counting* on Richard Owen. But for what? What would Owen do now? The answer remained as elusive as the man.

Thank God it was Owen, though, Nichols thought, and not someone else. Against these odds, no one but Owen had a chance.

Molly left the Xenophon Gallery at the usual time. She took a bus home, as she always did. She stopped routinely at the corner market, bought bread and cheese, a packet of cigarettes. She joked with the boy at the counter. She was relaxed; there was nothing special on her mind.

At home, she started to pour a drink, then changed her mind and made coffee. This was no time to blunt her nerves. She had to make contact with Graham. But how? She couldn't. She could only wait, as she had been waiting for hours.

Then the telephone rang.

'Hello?'

'Is Stephanos there?'

Molly's face showed enormous relief, her voice only mild interest. 'You must have the wrong number.'

'Sorry.'

'No trouble.'

The line disconnected at the other end. Molly grabbed her purse and hurried out through the front door. Ten minutes later, she was waiting inside a phone booth and picked up the phone as it rang.

It was Graham.

'Thank God!' Molly said.

'What's wrong?'

'Do you remember Harry Goldman?'

'Of course. Why?'

'He was in the gallery today and talking about Sunflower.'

Paul Fleming was clearly astonished. 'Harry Goldman was?'

'That's just it, I'm not sure. I don't think it was Harry at all.'

There was silence at the other end of the line.

'I could be wrong,' Molly said. 'He looked exactly like Harry – talked like him, moved like him, everything. But after he left, I remembered. Harry was allergic to roses. There were roses on my desk, but he didn't react at all. He didn't even seem to notice.'

Fleming's voice turned cold. 'Repeat every word he said.'

Molly's mind swung back to the moment Harry walked into her office. She left nothing out. The Air Force. The glasses and Euripides. Intelligence work and Anne Easton. The Erich Parsons file.

When she was finished, Fleming asked one more question: 'Did he give any clues to where he was going?'

'No,' Molly said. 'But once I realized he might be an impostor, I made a few phone calls to see what I could find out. There's a Harry Goldman registered at the Hotel Pandora in Athens.'

A reprieve had come from Moscow. Fleming had left Heraklion to a dozen top KGB agents and returned to Athens with Svitsky, aboard an unscheduled plane. He felt sure Owen would come here, too – to the bigger city, with its crowds of tourists for camouflage and its many routes of escape. Now, he knew he'd been right.

Fleming had gone straight to a house near Kolonaki Square, the home of a Soviet diplomat who was on temporary leave back home. The phone was secure here; it had to be. The diplomat was the local KGB Resident.

Fleming used the phone to call his people inside the CIA. He had three at the embassy and one at the local station. The call to Molly paid off.

He hung up the phone, turned to Svitsky and said, 'Owen's at the Hotel Pandora.'

Svitsky nodded. The two of them raced out of the house and into a car outside. Twenty minutes later, they were standing outside Owen's door. A strip of light showed across the bottom. A radio played softly inside.

Fleming produced his pistol as Svitsky stepped back, lowered one shoulder, and flung himself at the door. It flew open. It hadn't even been locked!

And no wonder.

Fleming raised his pistol, swung around in a crouch, then stared into an empty room. Harry Goldman was there, what was left of him – a uniform hanging neatly in the closet. Richard Owen had left him behind. He was gone, and so was the President's daughter.

On his way out of town, Owen stopped by a sidewalk mailbox and deposited a package. In it were Harry's passport and wallet, with 200 dollars to cover the cost of the uniform and the parking charge Harry would have to pay to get his Fiat out of the airport at Heraklion.

It was, he thought, the least he could do for a friend.

twenty-four

Evangelos Panayotides dipped a piece of bread into the *tzatziki* and popped it into his mouth without taking his eyes off his visitor from New York.

'What about the Colombian shipments?' he said. 'They should be more in demand.'

'They should be,' the visitor agreed. 'But some distributors are passing off their Mexican crops for Colombian. That makes all crops suspect. No one's buying anything until this blows over.'

'Which distributors?'

'The Italians.'

'I see.' Panayotides nodded his small, toadlike head. Then he washed down the *tzatziki* with a glass of ouzo and snapped his fingers for a refill.

'It's your decision, Vagele,' the visitor said.

'Yes.' The little Greek picked up his glass and strolled over to the edge of the terrace. The house – his house – was perched on the slope of Parnassus, above the village of Delphi. The view from the terrace spread far beyond the village, to the Temple of Apollo, stark and awesome by moonlight, to the smaller, more serene Temple of Athene Prothene, to the olive grove spreading down the side of the mountain, and to the waters of the bay and the lights of Patras on the other side.

Behind him, the mountain peaked sharply against the moonlit sky. It was from this peak that Apollo once routed the Persian Army by heaving boulders down on the advancing troops – and from this peak that Vagele Panayotides ran an empire so prosperous he could afford to be generous.

Let the Mexican government spray its fields to poison the marijuana; he had no holdings there. The Italians did and were trying to avoid a loss by passing their tainted crops off as Colombian. Let them. Panayotides didn't feel like war.

He took another drink and turned back to his visitor from New York. 'Store it,' he said. 'The stuff keeps. It'll be worth twice as much next year.'

Then he glanced up as the servant reappeared.

'There's someone to see you, *Kyrie*.'

The toadlike face wrinkled into a scowl. 'I don't want to see anyone now.'

'It's a priest. He's at the front door.'

'I don't care if it's the Archbishop! Send him away.'

But the servant persisted. 'He said to tell you his name is Father Phoebus and he knew you five years ago.'

Panayotides' expression froze somewhere between rage and fear. He stood quite still. Then the expression passed, the eyes narrowed.

Father Phoebus was it? What did they want now?

He dismissed the visitor with a gesture and turned back to the servant, a large man who carried a revolver in a holster under his white jacket.

'Tell the good father I'll see him,' Panayotides said. 'But don't go too far away.'

Project Phoebus, a CIA operation with a simple goal – dropping an illegal agent behind the Iron Curtain. Not just behind the curtain, but into the sensitive Karelia Peninsula area, where the Soviets maintained several top-secret defence systems.

The drop had to be made with no chance of a trace back to the CIA. Evangelos Panayotides had obliged with a pilot and a small jet from his large private fleet of planes. He did not do it by choice.

The CIA had the goods on him – not conjecture, like the FBI or Interpol, but documents, *signed* documents, and photographs. Hard evidence. Enough to send Panayotides to jail for the rest of his life.

That was five years ago. And he had *believed* their promise never to use him again. Now, they were back.

He looked at the man who came forward across the terrace, a man wearing the black beard and full robes of a Greek Orthodox priest.

'Father Phoebus.'

Owen nodded.

'What do you want from me?'

'The same thing we wanted before.'

The Greek gestured to a chair, then sat down himself. He leaned back and studied the priest through narrow, heavy-lidded eyes. 'The Karelia Peninsula again?'

'Hardly,' Owen replied. 'No, this time the target is Newark.'

'*Newark!*' Panayotides stared at him, incredulous. Then he threw back his head and laughed. 'You're joking! *Newark, New Jersey?*'

'Newark, New Jersey,' Owen confirmed.

'But *why?*'

'Because Newark is your regular port of entry to the United States. Because you have certain officials there on your payroll and can come and go pretty much as you please.'

The Greek smiled, impressed by the thoroughness of this man. Newark had not come up in his previous arrangement with the CIA. Nor did he care any more.

'That's true,' he said. 'I have had my way at Newark.'

'And *with* you,' Owen added, 'so can I.'

'With *me?*'

Owen nodded. 'I want you on the plane.'

But the Greek shook his head. 'No. I won't do it. I never travel by plane.'

'I know.' Owen smiled. 'A near crash. You haven't flown in three years.'

The Greek stared back at him. There was little, it seemed, that the CIA *didn't* know.

'I'm prepared to pay a rather good price,' Owen added.

Panayotides laughed. 'I hardly think *money* will change my mind!'

'Not money. A *name*.'

The Greek's eyes narrowed.

'The name of the man who betrayed you to the CIA,' Owen said. 'A man who was, and still is, a part of your organization.'

Panayotides leaned forward. The question had plagued him for all these five years. Disloyalty, the worst of all possible treachery!

He spit the words out. '*Who is it?*'

'Will you go with me to Newark?'

The Greek hesitated a moment. Then he said, 'When do you want to leave?'

'Tonight.'

'Tonight?'

'Right now.'

Ed Nichols replaced the phone and sat at his desk in the President's study shaking his head. He knew now where Owen had gone after leaving the taxi at Omonia Square. He had walked into the CIA station in Athens and right back out again!

And this time he'd made a mistake.

He had left a clue. The answer had to be there, in a file drawer marked *P*. Something Owen wanted, and not in the Parsons file. Something else in the drawer *with* Parsons.

Those same files existed on computer tape at Langley. Whatever it was, if it took him all night, Nichols knew he would find it.

He *had* to find it. Owen had made one mistake; it would not happen again.

*

Fleming knew it the minute he saw the file – not Parsons, but *Panayotides*!

He picked up the telephone and called Molly. She called him back from the office in twenty minutes. Yes, a page was missing from the Panayotides file. Molly had also checked with the CIA man inside the Greek's organization. One of Panayotides' jets had taken off from an airstrip north of Delphi less than an hour ago. The Greek himself was on board. With him, two bodyguards and a Greek Orthodox priest.

The plane's destination: Newark, New Jersey.

Fleming knew it was risky going back to the United States before he had Anne Easton. But Owen had to be aboard that plane, *en route* to Newark right now. And if Owen was there, Anne had to be, too.

He knew he had to move fast, get a larger, more powerful plane – one that would not have to put down in between to refuel. He picked up the phone, dialled Aeroflot, asked for a specific agent. And he smiled. It was *Project Phoebus* all over again, but with a new twist this time.

This time, Panayotides was delivering Richard Owen to Fleming.

twenty-five

There was a rumble of thunder as Nichols climbed down from the helicopter, then a sudden burst of lightning that lit up the army trucks parked near the terminal building. Nichols glanced at the sky, now darkened by fast-moving storm clouds, and wondered if Owen had managed to coopt nature's services, too.

Nichols had come to Newark in person. He intended to be there himself when Owen came off the plane – when *Anne Easton* came off the plane. If the plane was able to land here at all.

A man ran forward from the terminal to meet him, leaning into the wind, holding the edges of his raincoat together against sudden, stronger gusts.

'Mr Nichols?' He had to shout to be heard over the roar of a jumbo jet moving into lift-off on the runway behind them. 'I'm John Temple of the FAA. Hell of a day, isn't it?'

Nichols nodded grimly as he shook Temple's hand. 'What do you think?' he said. 'Will the plane have to be diverted?'

Temple glanced at the sky and shrugged. 'Can't say yet. This could pass in twenty minutes. Or, it could get worse. They're having a real blow up in Boston right now. Nothing's moving there but the trees.'

'What's the forecast here?'

'Rain. But we don't know how bad it will be. It's hard to predict what a storm will do.'

Nichols fell into step with Temple, hurrying across the pavement towards the terminal building. Another flash of lightning jagged down through the sky with a sharp crack of sound. In that instant of brightness, Nichols could see faces peering through the canvas covers at the back of the army trucks – two hundred troops from Fort Dix ready and waiting for action.

Nichols wasn't expecting war. He needed bodies to create a tight security shield in the critical areas of the airport. He also knew he might need the expert marksmen among them.

'Meantime,' Temple added as they neared the door, 'you may have a problem with the manager. He's got trouble enough with the weather, he says. Traffic backed up here, aircraft diverted from Boston and elsewhere. He's not wild about your plan.'

'He doesn't have to be wild about it,' Nichols replied. 'He just has to do it. Where is he?'

'Waiting for you in his office.'

Panayotides' servant, who had exchanged his white jacket for a black suit, leaned down to look out of a window on the starboard side of the plane. 'It's American,' he confirmed. 'It looks like an F-15.'

Panayotides nodded. He turned, resigned, to the man in the seat beside him. 'What do we do now?' he said.

'Pray?' The priest shrugged and glanced through his own port-side window. 'There's another one over here.' He laughed. 'Escorts! Just what we needed!'

Fleming raised a pair of high-powered binoculars to his eyes. He swung them across the pavement, then focused on the six trucks at the back of the building.

He turned to Svitsky, who was standing in another window. The building was a highrise apartment a mile from Newark Airport, but it offered an unobstructed view of the airfield and terminal building. They'd arrived here by way of New York, disguised as Soviet crewmen on a regular Aeroflot flight.

But Nichols was here, too, and the whole damn army with him!

'We can hardly go in there,' Svitsky said. 'We need to know Nichols' plans.'

Fleming nodded and raised the binoculars again. 'We will,' he replied. 'But for now, we'll just have to wait.'

Seymour Scott was sitting behind his desk when Nichols walked in. He did not get up.

He was a man of about forty, with receding black hair and eyes that were coldly penetrating behind a pair of wireframe glasses.

'Mr Scott. I'm Ed Nichols.'

'I know who you are,' Scott replied.

His voice was deep and resonant. He might have been a radio announcer instead of general manager of the airport – the man who, more than anyone else, gave orders in this complex mixture of government control and free enterprise. No one person had total authority in an airport, but at Newark Seymour Scott came as close as anyone.

'Then you know I expect your fullest cooperation,' Nichols said.

Scott didn't reply for a moment. He looked back at Nichols, then slowly got up from his chair. 'I know this,' he said. 'I don't take orders from the CIA, and neither does anyone else around here. I don't have the time or inclination to close this airport down. I've got a call into Washington now.'

'Oh, you do.' Nichols was not surprised. 'Then maybe I ought to tell you, I'm not here in my capacity as Director of the CIA. I'm here as a federal marshal. I also have legal sanction to nationalize this airport if necessary under the Emergency Powers Act.'

Nichols reached into his pocket for the letters that verified his statement. He handed them over to Scott, then reached for the telephone.

'What are you doing?' Scott asked.

'I'm expediting your call.'

Nichols listened as the phone rang. Then he identified himself and waited a moment more. A voice answered at the other end.

'I'd like you to speak to the airport manager,' he said into the phone. Then he held it out to Scott. 'It's the President. For you.'

Within thirty minutes, traffic in and out of Newark Airport had come to a halt. Thirteen planes were waiting at the ramps for taxi clearance – and they would wait until Nichols gave the sign to go. Eight more were circling overhead and would soon be diverted to adjoining airports along the Newark routes. The terminal was crammed with irate passengers who were not being allowed to board their scheduled flights, who were, in fact, being herded away from the departure lounges to safer areas inside the main structure of the building.

Outside, activity had also come to a stop. Freight and baggage handlers had been cleared from the airfield. Ground controllers and maintenance staff were permitted only as needed. Otherwise, there were the two hundred troops from Fort Dix.

Newark Airport, Nichols reflected, looked as if it were under siege.

He was standing at a window on the observation deck, looking out at the sheets of wind-driven rain that were sweeping across the pavement. Temple, the FAA man, was at his side.

'Don't worry,' Temple said. 'If you can drive in it, you can land a plane in it.'

197

'That's not much comfort. I don't think I'd like to be driving in this.'

Temple smiled. 'It's still too soon to know if the weather's going to be a problem. We've got forty minutes at least. And in any case, we have our contingency plans.' He glanced across at Nichols. 'So, I gather, have you.'

Nichols nodded.

The Air Force escorts had been Nichols' own idea, his plan originally to prevent Owen from bailing out unobserved over the ocean, or during a wide sweep of the eastern shore. Owen had not bailed out, and he wouldn't now. He could hardly have failed to notice the escorts. There was nothing subtle about a pair of F-15s flying a parallel pattern off your wing tips on either side.

And now the F-15s provided another kind of insurance. If the plane were diverted by weather, they would stay with it. Federal agents and troops were on alert all along the Atlantic seaboard; they could be mobilized with practically no delay.

Yes, Owen was covered. He would not get away. But if the plane was diverted, Nichols knew he could not move fast enough to meet it where it came down.

And he was determined to be there.

Panayotides sat forward in the plane. There was less movement here than in the back, less noise. He felt safer.

Nonetheless, his knuckles whitened as his hands gripped the armrests on both sides of the seat, as the plane began its early descent, down through rain-swollen clouds and turbulence, through darkness unnatural at this time of day.

His eyes shifted to the window on the left, then sharply back again. Low visibility. There was *no* visibility! There was *nothing* out there but dark clouds!

He cursed Richard Owen and closed his eyes, trying in vain to relax. Then he remembered the payment Owen had promised.

It was worth it. He would do this again a hundred times to get the name of the traitor who remained in his organization.

Fleming picked up the phone.

The man at the other end was a ground crewman with twenty years of service at Newark Airport. 'I've got what you wanted to know,' he said.

Fleming nodded. 'Let's hear it.'

'Unless the weather gets worse, they're going to let the plane land. Then they're going to move out of here by car. Two army units in front, two at the rear. Straight back to Fort Dix, where they've got *Air Force One* standing by.'

'You're sure?'

'Positive. I got it from a friend in security.'

'What kind of car?' Fleming asked.

'There's the problem. It's an armoured car. The thing's built like a tank.'

Fleming frowned. It was obvious, now, they could not take Anne in the airport. It would have to be done between Newark and Fort Dix. They could handle the army trucks with dynamite planted on the roadbed, make it look like something Owen had planned. But dynamite enough to stop an armoured car would also kill everyone in it.

And taking Anne Easton home, dead, would not make Fleming a hero.

'Where do they have the passengers?' he asked.

'In the main terminal.'

'What's the security there?'

'There isn't any. But no one gets near the field, or the car, without clearance.'

'Can you get to the car?'

'Probably. I've got a lot of friends around here.'

Fleming nodded. 'Good. Here's what we'll do. I'll send a man in as a passenger. He'll have a package for you.'

'A package?'

'A time mechanism,' Fleming said. 'And just enough plastic to blow the doors on that car.'

Panayotides' pilot switched on his radio. 'Newark Approach Control, this is Charioteer Six. Do you read me?'

There was a moment of silence, then a crackling of static before the reply came through. 'This is Newark. We read you, Charioteer. How's the weather up there?'

'Choppy. Heavy clouds. Nothing we can't handle on instruments.'

'The wind is out of the north-east at twenty-six knots and gusting. Do you have any qualms about landing?'

'None,' the pilot replied calmly. Then he made it official. 'Charioteer Six requesting final approach to Newark on instruments.'

There was a long moment of silence before the response came back. 'Right, Charioteer. Turn left three-zero-six.'

'Left thirty-six,' the pilot acknowledged.

'We're handing you off to the tower now.'

'Roger, Approach Control. This is Charioteer Six out.'

The pilot nodded for the co-pilot to begin a final check of the plane's landing systems and brakes. Then he turned the throttle and banked the big jet into a wide, 306 degree turn.

In the tower, Nichols watched the speck of light turning more to the right with each new sweep of the radarscope. The radio crackled.

'Newark tower, this is Charioteer Six. We just turned on final.'

The man in the headset in front of the radarscope glanced up at Nichols. Then he said. 'We're charting you, Charioteer. Right heading two-zero. You're cleared for runway 4E.'

'Right, Newark. Descending to one thousand feet.'

The man in the headset exchanged a look with Nichols but didn't say anything.

'Brake system?' It was the pilot talking to the co-pilot beside him.

'Okay,' came the reply.

'Landing gear?'

'In place and locked.'

Silence again. Then the pilot: 'We're at two thousand feet, Newark.'

'And cleared for final approach,' the man in the headset said. 'Bring her on down.'

'Roger.'

Nichols and John Temple pulled on a pair of slickers and hurried downstairs by the private elevator. A baggage truck was waiting for them outside. They jumped aboard as the driver put the truck into gear and stepped down on the gas, speeding ahead towards runway 4E.

Nichols wiped the rain from his glasses. His face was flushed with excitement. His palms were sweating. His heart pounded in his chest. He could see that the troops were in position across the field, along the runway. Newark Airport *was* under siege.

And Owen could not get away. Just a few minutes more and Nichols would *have* Anne Easton.

They heard the plane before they could see it, but now it appeared through the low-hanging clouds. It was coming down fast and strong, lined up in a perfect approach to the runway.

'Faster!' Nichols shouted. He glanced across at Temple, who smiled with anticipation.

Then suddenly the smile faded. Temple's eyes widened, his jaw dropped. Nichols' heart leaped in a reflex reaction of fear before his mind could react. His gaze shifted back to the sky.

The plane was dropping too fast! It was coming down at a sharp angle to the pavement.

Nichols heard Temple's cry, two agonized words against a great roar of sound as the pilot put on extra power. *Wind shear!* A dramatic shift in wind speed and direction that struck with no warning at all.

The pilot tried to pull up, but the plane was too close to the ground. It was listing to port. He brought the left wing up sharply, and the right wing dipped too low. The plane rolled back and forth as it roared in close to the runway, as the pilot struggled to bring it under control.

It touched down hard on the pavement. But the nose was up; the wheels touched first. Then the struts that held them snapped off, and the plane came down on its belly. It skidded across the concrete, sending up a huge spray of sparks.

Nichols' heart stopped and his mind rejected what was happening before his eyes. The troops were running for cover. From behind came the shrill pitch of sirens as fire trucks raced towards the plane. And the plane continued to skid, smashing signal lights as it hit the edge of the runway and slid off the pavement, where finally it came to a stop in a deep patch of mud and grass.

The sparks had been doused by the rain. There was no explosion of fire. Charioteer was on the ground and safe.

Nichols closed his eyes and fell back against the seat. He felt weak with fear and relief. Then quickly he pulled himself together. The hatch was opening, the pilot appeared in the door. Then a chute was dropped and the passengers pushed towards it.

Nichols jumped down from the truck and ran towards the plane as Evangelos Panayotides came sliding to the ground. The toad-like face was totally drained of colour. His eyes were wide and staring, in a state of continuing terror. A man in a black suit came next; then another.

Nichols glanced up. A priest in black robes was standing in the open hatch. Their eyes met, exchanged nothing. Then the priest, too, dropped into the chute and came sliding to the ground.

Ben Kaufmann turned to his seatmate as the Eastern jet rolled to a stop at the ramp. 'Nice talking to you,' he said.

'My pleasure.' The other man grinned. 'I have to admit, I never met a professional golfer. Good luck at the PGA.'

'Thanks.'

Kaufmann pushed himself up out of his seat and merged with the line in the aisle. Then the doors opened and people began filing off the plane.

A stewardess had already retrieved his golf bag, a large professional model, from the closet that divided the first- and tourist-class cabins. She smiled as Kaufmann approached.

'I guess you never check these as baggage,' she said.

'No, ma'm.' Kaufmann returned the smile. 'These clubs are my livelihood.'

Outside, palm trees swayed to a gentle wind under a sunlit sky. Miami. The temperature was eighty degrees.

Richard Owen took a deep breath. Then he moved forward, supporting the weight of the golf bag against his back.

The priest at Newark was a servant of Panayotides. Owen had never been near that plane, and neither had Anne Easton.

twenty-six

'They want you at the embassy, now,' Svitsky said.

Fleming studied his face. It told him nothing. But nothing said a great deal. The assignment was over, a failure. Newark had been the end. Patience was a rare thing at the highest levels of government, and in Moscow it had run out.

Fleming stalled. 'Why?'

'I don't know.' Svitsky shrugged. 'They're probably sending you home.'

Home? Where was that? In Moscow? A dacha on the Black Sea? Nice thoughts, but unlikely. Moscow didn't need him now. They would take what he knew and discard him. Or worse. Traitors unmasked were anathema on both sides; once turned, they could turn again. Fleming had no delusions. His value had ceased with his cover. Past loyalty never outweighed present risk. Moscow could not let him live.

He nodded. 'I'll pack a bag.'

After Newark, he and Svitsky had driven to an apartment in Washington a few blocks from Fleming's own. They had tried to pick up Owen's trail without success. And it didn't matter much now.

Fleming had no delusions about the assignment, either. Moscow was right; it was over. He'd been out of contact too long to simply explain it away. Nichols' suspicions had reached an advanced stage. Fleming knew he could not go back. Langley was no more his home any more than Moscow.

He stepped into the next room; he threw the few things he had with him into a suitcase. Then he picked up his pistol.

Svitsky was sitting down, scanning a magazine, when Fleming came back through the door. He glanced up and started to get to his feet.

Fleming fired.

He allowed no time for shock or recognition. The bullet entered neatly, between Svitsky's eyes, and it blew out the back of his head. The force of the shot slammed Svitsky down into the chair. He died there, without knowing what happened.

Fleming picked up the bag and left the apartment, not sure where he was going, knowing only what he had to do. Anne Easton was *still* his only chance for survival. With the President's daughter as hostage, he could negotiate his own future. Nichols would want what he knew – Fleming had no doubt about that – but he needed a position of strength to negotiate for his own terms. Amnesty from the United States and protection from the Soviet Union.

He needed a hostage, Anne Easton. But to find her, he first had to find Richard Owen.

Nichols nodded to the secretary outside the Oval Office, then opened the door and walked in. Matt was behind his desk. He looked up.

Nichols did not say hello. He crossed the room and dropped into a chair. 'Get Elizabeth on the phone,' he said. 'I need to see both of you.'

The President frowned. 'Why?'

'Because I've got an idea,' Nichols said. 'A plan to trap Richard Owen.'

twenty-seven

The big, black-haired man paused for a moment at the door with a metal plaque: *AGVA*. The American Guild of Variety Artists, Washington office. He pressed the button. From inside a buzzer sounded, unlocking the door. He pushed it open and stepped in.

The receptionist looked like a retired showgirl, long retired, with thin hair tinted platinum and teased into a fuzzy mass around her face. She glanced up from her morning coffee and the latest issue of *Variety* spread open on top of her desk.

'Yes, sir?'

The man came forward across the small office. He moved easily, a man in charge of his own life and probably a good many others. His black hair curled neatly back from his face. His fingernails were buffed to a near shine. His suit was clearly expensive. So was the diamond ring on his little finger.

'I'm T. J. Sinclair,' he said.

The receptionist looked up sharply. T. J. Sinclair ran a circus and was the largest employer of AGVA members from here to Hollywood. He was a legend in Washington, an honest-to-God showman in a town full of pale copies. He had *never* come strolling into the AGVA office, nor even called on the phone. He had a staff of lackies to do those errands for him.

'Yes, Mr Sinclair.'

'I want a name and address,' Owen said, knowing that Sinclair never wasted time with idle chat. 'I'm in a hurry. I'm leaving for Europe today.'

Variety said so. The real Sinclair was listed in the column that recorded just such comings and goings by the biggies of the show business world.

'What name?' the receptionist asked.

Owen explained his problem.

Ten minutes later, she had a file in her hand. 'Here it is,' she said. 'George Zvinczk. He lives in Gaithersburg, Maryland.'

Vin-check, Owen wrote phonetically. He noted down the address. 'Phone?'

The receptionist shook her head. 'He doesn't have one.'

That was all the better.

'Thanks,' Owen replied. He dropped the note in his pocket and left the same way he had come.

George Zvinczk was a middle-aged man and balding. His face was deeply lined, with skin hanging loose at his jawline, the result of drink more than age. None of this mattered when he worked; he always sobered up for a job as a matter of principle.

But he had been drinking when Owen arrived on his doorstep. He stared at Owen with eyes that were red and intense with concentration.

'Who did you say you were?'

'I'm Jack Rogers of AGVA,' Owen repeated. 'I'd have called, but we don't have a number for you.'

Zvinczk smiled as he stepped back from the door. 'That's because I don't have a phone. Come on in.'

'Thank you.'

Owen moved a pair of socks from a chair and sat down. 'I have some bad news,' he said.

Zvinczk picked up his glass, a clear liquid drink that might have been water but wasn't. 'Let me have it.'

'The picnic has been cancelled.'

A flicker of disappointment settled into a look of resignation. Zvinczk nodded. 'It figures.'

'But,' Owen added quickly, 'I have another offer for you. It pays twice as much, plus expenses.'

The reddened eyes didn't change. 'I'll take it,' Zvinczk said, and downed the last of his drink.

'I thought you would.' Owen reached into a pocket, then tossed an airline ticket folder on to the bare table between them. Then he added ten 100-dollar bills.

Zvinczk stared at the money. He sat forward, picked it up, and counted it out on the table. His eyes were wide with astonishment, his expression no longer resigned.

'Are you *serious*?'

'Quite serious.'

Zvinczk picked up the ticket folder and opened it. Then he glanced back at Owen. '*Nairobi?*'

Owen nodded. 'A six-week engagement with a circus there.'

'But *me*? Why me?'

Owen shrugged. 'They need a star clown who's not under contract elsewhere.' He leaned forward. 'That's just a down payment, of course. Half of that is expenses. The rest is your first week's pay.'

Zvinczk stared back at him, incredulous.

'You have to leave tonight.' Owen nodded. 'You'll have an overnight lay-over in London tomorrow and arrive in Nairobi the next day. Can you do it?'

'Can I do it!' Zvinczk grinned. 'Are you kidding? For that kind of money, I could go to the moon!'

Fleming strolled into a bar on Fourteenth Street, north of the White House. He was dressed in faded jeans and an old shirt, with a cap pulled low on his brow. The bartender hardly looked up as he crossed the room and slipped into a booth at the rear.

He ordered a beer from the waitress and glanced across at the phone booth. Someone was inside; his calls would have to wait.

The same calls, again, to a handful of former employees who were still loyal to him. They were all he had, and not much. So far, they had turned up nothing to help him find Richard Owen. On the other hand, from what they had said, Nichols was no closer to Owen than he was. And that meant there was still time.

He paid for the beer, took a drink, and picked up the newspaper he'd bought at a corner news-stand. A late edition of the *Washington Post*. The first pages were full of international news, government and politics, nothing of interest to him now. He quickly glanced through the Style and Metro sections. Then, as always, turned to the classifieds.

And there something caught his eye. A display ad in the 'help-wanteds'. A name in boldface type: *Blackjack*.

Blackjack. A CIA project he had once assigned to Owen. A project for which they used the Classified pages as a means of communication. A code name Owen had assumed, temporarily, for himself, and one known *only* to Owen and Fleming.

The format of the ad was as it had been then, but the words were slightly different: *Dealers wanted for BLACKJACK. Excellent Opportunity. Moon Rock Casino. Apply Now Box 745P*.

Fleming smiled. Was it possible? Did Owen want to make a *deal*?

Apply now meant today, or tonight, at 7.45 p.m. He had two hours to clean up and get there if he wanted to be on time. Less if he meant to be early.

And he did mean to be early. If Owen was offering a deal, it might be legitimate. Or it might be another trick. Fleming didn't care. Either way, it would lead him to Owen.

*

Air and Space was one of the nine museums that lined both sides of the Mall between the Capitol and the Washington Monument. Owen pushed through a revolving door and walked in.

It was 7.30, but natural light still poured through the huge windows that rose from the floor to the ceilings of the central exhibit hall. The ceiling was as high as the building itself, with airplanes suspended from it, hanging in mid-air, as if caught in a moment of flight. Among them, the Wright Brothers' *Flyer*, Lindbergh's *Spirit of St Louis*, the Bell X-1 that first flew faster than sound. Other exhibits, on the floor, brought history up to date – *Pioneer 10*, *Friendship 7*, *Gemini 4* – all blackened by the friction of re-entry from space. In another huge hall to the right were early passenger planes. To the left NASA rockets, guided missiles, launch vehicles, and a lunar landing craft.

In between, there were hundreds and hundreds of people.

The museum stayed open until nine at this time of year. It was a popular place with both Washingtonians and tourists. People thronged here. They moved briskly, in no particular pattern. This was not like the National Gallery on the other side of the Mall, where visitors followed the paintings from one room to another, stopping, musing, studying at will. Here the exhibits were positioned precisely to create space and free-flowing traffic.

It was not a place for keeping track of faces.

Owen moved along at his leisure, hands in pockets, relaxed. He was here not to see, but be seen. He did not look at his watch, but when roughly ten minutes had passed, he turned back towards the central hall.

A metal shaft rose up from the floor on one side, to a height of about ten feet. At waist level, there was an opening in the shaft, and inside, for the touching, an exhibit much older than anything else in the building. A lunar sample, a triangle of smooth black basalt brought to earth by astronauts and dating back four billion years.

Owen took his place in the line of people waiting to pass by the moon rock. As he waited, his eyes scanned the crowd. And he wondered what Fleming would do.

*

Fleming had arrived early, had surveyed the exhibit halls and then taken an escalator up to the mezzanine. He picked a place near the balcony rail and glanced over the edge. A black X-15 high-altitude research plane hung even with the balcony level – good cover, Fleming thought.

He raised a camera to his eyes and began snapping pictures as he studied the faces below through the camera's telescopic lens.

Owen arrived early, too, and Fleming could hardly have missed him. A young man in jeans and sneakers, his hair a mass of tight curls, his eyes covered by tinted glasses. And on the back of his T-shirt, a bright yellow flower that might have been a daisy, or a sunflower.

Fleming watched the young man as he wandered among the exhibits, then lined up to see the moon rock. He focused the camera in close. Yes, it was Owen. He was there.

Fleming smiled. He stepped back from the rail, into the shadow of the plane. He did not move to meet Owen.

Owen waited as long as he dared, but Fleming did not make contact. The sky outside was deepening towards night. Owen looked at his watch now; it was 8.15. Then he turned and left the museum.

His car was where he had left it, on the street behind the building. He pulled out into the traffic, driving east. The Capitol came up on his left, its dome brightly lit against the darkening sky, but Owen didn't pause for the view. He made a right turn just beyond the House Office Buildings, heading for the ground-floor apartment he had rented on Capitol Hill.

The sky was darkening but clear, with stars starting to show over the lights of the city. The weather reports were good; a beautiful day tomorrow. Warm and sunny, with no chance of rain. A perfect day for a picnic.

But that was tomorrow.

Owen made a left turn into Duddington Place and pulled the car up to the kerb. Trees and townhouses lined both sides of the street, looking cheerful under the bright yellow glow of crime lights. Owen locked the car, climbed the steps to a front door, then turned around. There was no one on the street, no one moving in either direction.

He unlocked the door and went in.

Elizabeth Easton glanced at her husband, then turned to Ed Nichols on the other side of the room. 'Do you really think this will work?' she said.

They were upstairs in the White House, in the Lincoln Sitting Room, small and cosy with its paisley drapes and matching fabric-lined walls, with its rosewood chairs and French settee that belonged to the Lincoln era if not to the Lincoln family.

Nichols was sprawled awkwardly in a chair designed for someone much primmer and smaller than he was. He shrugged as his eyes shifted from Elizabeth to Matt and back again. 'There's no being sure what Richard Owen will do,' he said. 'I can only repeat what I've told you before. I *think* Owen is trying to bring Anne home.'

Elizabeth sighed. 'I wish I could *know* that—'

'Yes, so do I. But we're moving in a realm of conjecture here. The question is, *why* would he keep Anne with him? Why the *risk*? Without Anne, he could go underground; we'd probably never find him. But with her?' Nichols shrugged and left the question unanswered.

Elizabeth nodded. She was hopeful, but not convinced.

'And frankly,' Nichols added, 'the idea is just outrageous enough to *appeal* to Owen. Returning Anne to the White House. And getting away with it?' He shook his head. 'It fits Owen, all right. But we'll be waiting for him.'

Elizabeth glanced down at the guest list in her hand. 'Which one do you think he will be?'

'It's impossible to guess. The Speaker? A cabinet secretary?'

'The Soviet ambassador?' The President turned away from the window, where his body was caught in silhouette by the lights of the Washington Monument beyond the south lawn. His face took shape as he turned into the softly lit room.

Nichols looked up at him. 'It wouldn't surprise me, Matt, if he came disguised as you.'

'Surely he's not *that* good,' Elizabeth said.

'Almost.'

The President glared at both of them. 'I don't care how good he is. I want Owen caught. First I want Anne, then Owen. After that, if we can, Paul Fleming. But I want Owen caught. And tried. And sent up for life.'

Nichols looked back at his friend. 'Maybe you'd like to have capital punishment reinstated, too.'

Matt Easton was not amused. 'The man's a kidnapper. A murderer. He may be a Soviet spy.'

Nichols shook his head firmly. 'You're wrong about that. Owen doesn't work for the Russians. And he will be caught. I give you my promise on that.'

It was nearly two a.m. when Fleming finally approached Owen's window from the outside. He ran a hand gently around the frame, looking for hidden wires.

They were there, at least two separate systems. Owen was always prepared. There was bound to be at least one more set of wires on the inside. Even if he could get to them, these wires couldn't be cut or dismantled. They had to be shut off.

Fleming stepped back from the window and turned away into the darkness, towards the basement door.

Owen awoke with a start.

There was no sound from the single window that opened to the outside, just a soft buzz from the plug in Owen's ear. And that meant the window was *open*.

He lay quite still, his back to the window, letting his breathing continue as it was. Slow and steady, the breathing of a man asleep. Then he turned his eyes to the clock on the bedside table. The luminous dial was gone. The lights no doubt didn't work either. Someone had cut the electricity at its source.

Four alarm systems wired into the electrical circuits of the house had failed with the flip of a switch in the fuse box in the basement.

But Owen had anticipated electrical failure, either natural or man-made. He had installed a fifth system, undetectable even to a professional eye. It was in the base of the window frame, a tiny alarm operated by battery and activated by movement. It was that alarm that set off the buzz in his ear.

A warning, no more. But enough.

Owen's hand found the switch that was lying under his pillow, then closed around the revolver as a voice came from behind: 'Don't move, Owen. I have a gun.'

Fleming.

Owen didn't move.

A flashlight came on. 'All right, now turn over. Slowly.'

Owen turned over on his back and looked up into the powerful beam of light. Behind it, nothing but darkness. He smiled.

'Hands where I can see them,' Fleming said.

Owen released the revolver and brought his hands out from under the covers.

'Where's the girl?'

'You do have a one-track mind,' Owen said. 'I'm sorry, she isn't here.'

'Where is she?'

'Not here. She's not even in Washington.'

There was silence for a moment. Fleming drew back the flashlight, and Owen could see his face. The features were distorted by shadows thrown up from below.

'Do you think I believe that?' he said.

Owen shrugged. 'Believe what you like. It's not my concern.'

Then suddenly his eyes shifted to a door in the opposite wall. A moan came from the other side of the door! The sound of a child crying out softly in sleep, a sound magnified many times by the silence of a house at night.

A slow smile spread across Fleming's face. He chuckled. Then he started to back away, his eyes and pistol still aimed directly at Owen.

'Don't go in there,' Owen said.

Fleming did not reply. He kept backing, a step at a time, until he was next to the door, solid oak with a brass knob. The house was a hundred years old. Then, for an instant, his eyes turned away.

212

Owen's hand dropped under the covers. 'I'm warning you—'
'Be quiet!' Fleming glared back at him.
Owen watched in obedient silence.
Fleming stuck the flashlight under the arm with the gun, holding it firm, still on Owen. Then his free hand reached for the knob.
It came close, but did not touch. In that fraction of time and space before contact was made, a giant spark was released, a flash of blue fire like the flame from a welder's torch. A sudden, sharp hum filled the room as 44,000 volts of electric power surged up through Fleming's arm.
A sound escaped from his mouth. It was more than a gasp, but not very loud, and cut off almost as it began. His body convulsed. His hair actually stood on end. And his heart stopped cold. Then the spark disappeared, the hum ceased, and Fleming fell back on the floor.
Four blocks away, the lights of the Capitol dome flickered and dimmed. In between, everything went dark. Radios, TVs, the crime lights. A complete power short-circuit.
Owen jumped out of bed, crossed the room in three strides, and dropped down beside Fleming's body. He raised his hand and gave a sharp rap against Fleming's chest. Then he dropped his ear to the chest but heard nothing. He pounded his chest again. This time, the heartbeat resumed. Fleming was alive but unconscious. He would not come out of it soon.
Owen sat back against the rug he had wet down to act as an earth. It was damp, but only that, not enough to make Fleming notice.
A wire ran down from the brass knob to the rug. A second wire emerged near the outside door, ran under the door and across the backyard to a manhole, where Owen had tapped it into the main power lines underground.
There was no need for caution now; the power lines had gone dead. Owen retrieved the wire and used it to tie Fleming up. Then he got up and crossed the room.
The brass knob was harmless now and turned at his touch. He stepped through the door and into the room where Anne slept.
She had slept through it all, as Owen had known she would

when he gave her the last injection. The drug would be easing up now. She would be awake in the morning.

He glanced down at the tape recorder he had switched on from under his pillow. It was still running on a table beside the bed. The only sound on the tape was long past, that single moan that had summoned Fleming far more effectively than Owen himself could have done.

twenty-eight

Elizabeth Easton glanced out over the crowd as she descended the familiar steps that curved down to ground level from the balcony of the White House. She picked out Matt, chatting with old friends, men and women who had been his colleagues when he was still in Congress.

The sun shone down on striped awnings, where White House staff in white jackets served hot dogs and hamburgers, ice cream and cotton candy. There were children everywhere, sons and daughters of congressmen and senators, some clinging to parents, others running across the lawn – playing games, climbing trees, playing softball near the fountain.

Elizabeth watched the children, and the dull ache in her heart sharpened to a stab of pain. Her *own* child wasn't here.

Yet, the mood was festive. Infectious. Square dancers performed a lively routine on a raised platform, to the music of a live country band. Elizabeth almost smiled as a famous senator, well past eighty, joined in. Across the lawn, a calliope was parked on the curving blacktop drive, the tune from its pipes recalling a different era. In between, a magician, a puppet show, clowns roaming the grounds. And hundreds of guests.

There had been so many changes in Congress since she and Matt were there. So many new faces. It was hard to tell the guests from the security guards.

And was one of them Richard Owen? Was he *here*? Could he be here now? *With Anne*?

Elizabeth stopped where she stood. Hope revived, a lifting of spirit, anticipation of joy. Then it was crushed by a force that was almost physical. There was only a chance Ed's plan would work, that Owen would bring Anne home – that he would choose this occasion to do it. A picnic for congressional families. A large-scale party on the White House lawn, with minimum security and swarms of congressmen's children. Ed had planned it that way, as an invitation to the man who had kidnapped Anne.

But Ed gave no guarantees. There was only a *chance* this would work. Elizabeth knew she could not let herself think beyond the moment and what she had to do. Be natural. Behave as if nothing in the world were wrong.

She hurried on down the steps. Faces turned to greet her. Hands reaching out. Friendly smiles. No one knowing about the fear she held inside.

This had to work. It *had* to.

She glanced at Matt and stepped into the crowd. He was standing close by, but facing away from her. She knew he could give her no spoken words of assurance, but she wanted to be beside him. His presence had been reassurance so many times in the past, in crowded rooms with people pressing in. A meeting of eyes or hands, even briefly, brought strength and comfort, a private exchange without marring the public display. She knew Matt needed comfort, too.

But there might as well have been an ocean between them. Voices pulled her one way, another; her progress towards Matt was slow. She smiled at the Ways and Means chairman, shook hands with his dark-haired wife. Turned to another hand. Another voice. Another face.

'And how is Anne?' someone said.

Elizabeth smiled. 'She's fine.'

'She's fine?' Someone else. 'But I read somewhere she was sick.'

'Yes, well—'

Still another voice: 'Nothing serious, I hope.'

Elizabeth's eyes sought Matt but couldn't find him now. She

felt cornered here on the open lawn. Panic was setting in. 'Anne's fine. *Really*. She's much better.'

Sympathetic smiles were distorted by point of view. They seemed hostile.

'It's a shame she has to be sick while she's away from home.'

'A sick child needs her mother.'

'Don't you wish you were *there*?'

'I've been needed here,' Elizabeth answered feebly.

She felt defensive without any reason to be, and angry for feeling that way. Tears stung her eyes, but she held them back. The smile on her face turned painful. Her cheeks hurt. They were starting to tremble inside, as they usually did at the end of a long reception. The muscles of her face were on the verge of rebellion. More than that, her control was about to collapse. She wanted to scream.

But she continued to smile.

She took a breath and fell back on an old technique. 'I'm sorry. You'll have to excuse me. I have something I must tell Matt.'

The bodies parted as they might have for a runner to Caesar. Now, she could see Matt again. He turned and saw her. He smiled, extended an arm.

Elizabeth hurried to him.

'I was looking for you,' he said, and his arm closed around her waist. Gentle pressure, more important than words. 'You remember Les and Susan.'

Elizabeth began to relax. She smiled at the congressman and his wife, a magazine editor, two people she genuinely liked. 'Yes, of course. How are you?'

A conversation began.

At some point while they talked, Elizabeth noticed a clown standing near the ice cream tent, surrounded by dozens of children. She didn't know him by name, only by his familiar appearance – the red plaid suit that clashed with the orange hair, the white face, the red putty nose and the huge, painted-on grin. Her eyes shifted from the clown to the faces of the children around him. And she smiled. The children were enchanted. The clown was as good as she'd heard.

Then a new stab of pain reminded her of her purpose. She turned back to the conversation. Other friends joined them, and they continued to talk.

The orange-haired clown stayed where he was, near the ice cream tent, in the corner of Elizabeth's eye. Once again, she turned to watch him. The cluster of children shifted and, for the first time, she saw another clown at its centre. A traditional tramp clown, done up in a tattered black suit, with soulful eyes painted into a melancholy face. Familiar again, but different. And a clever idea, she thought. The tramp clown was tiny. A midget!

Then without knowing why, Elizabeth looked back at the big clown. His eyes met hers; his expression remained painted in place. But his hand moved. He touched the midget's shoulder with a gentleness that seemed out of place. The tramp clown looked up, then followed the big clown's gaze. The sad face turned to Elizabeth.

The little tramp stood there a moment, then jumped into the air with a suddenness that sent the children into peals of laughter.

He was running, *leaping*, this way.

Elizabeth stood still in a moment of confusion, at the sight of the sad little clown moving with such obvious joy. Moving this way, clearly. To *her*. And she didn't know why.

Then a voice broke over the general din of the party.

'*Mommy!*'

Elizabeth caught her breath as the truth of the moment broke through. She was still afraid to believe. She stared at the painted face, at the familiar motion of the small body in the unfamiliar tattered black suit. Then she dropped to her knees and held open her arms.

It *was* Anne! It was *Anne*!

The crowd stood back, stunned to silence, but Elizabeth no longer cared about public display. She was laughing and crying as her arms closed around her daughter, holding Anne tightly, as if she feared that wishing had caused an illusion, that Anne might fade except for her embrace.

Then Matt was there, too, his arms around both of them. His face mirrored her own. Tears and laughter. No thoughts for image. The crowd simply didn't exist.

Elizabeth caught Anne's face between her hands. Happy tears poured out of the soulful eyes; they smeared and melted the make-up. A smile was there where the turned-down mouth had been. Then she glanced up at Matt. Words failed. A look passed between them. Utter joy. Intense love. Inexpressable relief.

Beside them, an agent switched on his microphone and barked an order. But Elizabeth paid no attention. Across the lawn Secret Service guards jumped to attention, fanning out quickly to pre-assigned positions. But it was already too late.

The big clown had disappeared.

Richard Owen emerged from behind the calliope. The clown suit was gone now, stuffed behind the truck-sized tyres, along with the orange wig and the red putty nose, with the thin rubber mask and the huge painted-on grin. Like the other men here, he was wearing a business suit.

He moved away from the calliope along the curving drive, back towards the iron gate and the freedom beyond the fence. And then what he wondered.

A flurry of excitement arose on the lawn behind him. Owen turned, saw Anne in her mother's arms. And her father's. *Reunion.* His job was done. But he didn't feel free; he felt aimless. He had no idea where he would go from here.

Nonetheless, he moved on. Surprise was no good for moments of stunned inaction – only moments, and no more. He was at the gate now, nodding to one of the guards, passing through. And then he was on the outside.

He picked up his pace as he bypassed the huge building that served as a branch to the White House, as he bypassed the white van he had driven here from Capitol Hill. Then, from behind, came the clang of the iron gate slamming shut. Footsteps running this way. Owen did not look around. It was a clown they wanted, and the white van he had arrived in.

But he didn't slow down, either.

He rounded the corner on to Seventeenth Street, where he'd left the Fiat 124 Spyder, a small sports car with a powerful engine, easy to manoeuvre in city traffic. Another car waited in a church parking lot six blocks away, still another in a hospital lot on the other side of Washington Circle.

Owen cut through the pedestrian traffic, producing the keys from his pocket as he headed for the Spyder. He stepped down from the kerb and came up from the back of the car to the driver's side.

But someone else had stepped off the sidewalk in front of the car – a man in a dark suit, his hand in his pocket and obviously holding a gun. The man stopped in front of the car; he said nothing. Owen turned. Two more men approached from behind.

Then a black car came to a stop beside him, a government limousine. The driver hopped out and came around to open the door.

The man in the back seat smiled, but Owen did not smile back. His shoulders sagged, his face went pale, and life disappeared from his eyes.

This was it, capture. The man in the car was Nichols.

twenty-nine

'Get in,' Nichols said.

Owen did as he was told. He was unarmed against three armed men, and he didn't much care any more.

Nichols nodded to the driver, who pulled back into the traffic, and pressed a button in the armrest at his side.

A glass partition arose from the back of the driver's seat. Owen watched in silence as it locked into place along the roof of the car. He felt no fear, nor even resigned acceptance. He felt numb. He felt dead. Nothing mattered at all.

They turned north on Connecticut Avenue, away from the White House and the government buildings clustered around the Mall. Owen wondered, briefly, where they were going. To Langley?

Nichols didn't say.

He nodded to the glass partition. 'It's soundproof,' he said. 'We can talk.'

'What's the point?'

Nichols smiled. 'I suppose I ought to explain.'

Owen shrugged. He took his cigarettes out of his pocket, lit one, and watched the smoke as it curled in the air.

'The picnic,' Nichols said, 'was a trap.'

'So I gathered.'

'You'll forgive my preening a bit. It's not every day I set a trap for a prey as elusive as you and see it work.'

'Congratulations.'

Nichols produced a handkerchief, took off his glasses, and rubbed at a spot on one lens. 'I couldn't let them have you back there,' he said. 'The President wants your head on a tray.'

No doubt, Owen thought. He wished Nichols would drop the post mortem.

Nichols inspected his glasses against the light from the window. Then he put them back on and turned to look at Owen. 'For myself,' he said, 'I prefer one piece.'

Owen drew on his cigarette. Then suddenly the words sunk in. The President wanted his head on a tray, hardly a stunning announcement. But Nichols, apparently, did not!

Signs of life showed in Owen's face. He turned and caught Nichols' eyes in a direct gaze. 'What are you telling me?'

Nichols did not turn away. 'That I was wrong when I thought Richard Owen kidnapped Anne Easton. Owen died in Oslo. We'll exhume the body, if necessary, as a point of positive proof. As for who kidnapped Anne?' He shrugged. 'I don't know. It might have been Boris Svitsky. Whoever it was got away.'

Owen stared back, incredulous, but he felt alive again.

Nichols gave a confirming nod. 'They have a department for justice down the street from the White House,' he said. 'Justice is not my job. I've got other problems, like an agency full of people I can't trust. That's why I couldn't let them have you back there. I need you now, more than ever. We've got to rebuild.'

Owen laughed softly. 'We've been on the same side all along.'

'Not quite all along. There were days I'd gladly have killed you, if I'd known then who you were. But since Knossos, yes, we've had an identical goal – to get Anne safely home and you safely out of reach.' Nichols glanced out the window, then turned back to Owen, his eyes full of admiration. 'You did a hell of a job.'

Owen dismissed the compliment with a shrug. He had done his job, simply that. Anything less than his best would have been beneath his own standards.

'But you caught me,' he said.

'Only because I had the better perspective. You succeeded in spite of that. You brought Anne home, without any help, with half of the world out to get you. And until today, no one knew where you were.' Then Nichols raised his hands in a gesture. 'Past history,' he said. 'Your new assignment is Fleming.'

Owen smiled. He took a puff on his cigarette and stubbed it out in the ashtray. Then he reached into a pocket, brought out a key, and tossed it across to Nichols. 'I was going to mail this to you,' he said.

'A key?'

'Fleming.'

Nichols stared at the key; then his eyes shifted back to Owen. 'You've got Fleming locked up?'

Owen nodded. 'Trussed up like a turkey and, I daresay, ready to talk.' He gave Nichols the address of the house on Duddington Place.

Nichols stared back for a long moment. Then a smile broke over his face. 'In that case,' he said, 'you can have the night off. We'll start first thing tomorrow morning.'

He handed Owen a different key. Owen glanced at the plastic tag. Room 302, the Executive House Hotel on Rhode Island Avenue.

Nichols pressed a button in the armrest, a pre-arranged signal. The driver pulled into the kerb and brought the car to a stop.

And Nichols extended his hand.

Owen shook it. 'There is one loose end,' he said. 'Twenty-five hundred dollars for a clown by the name of Zvinczk. I promised him six weeks' work at five hundred a week, and I only paid him for one.'

'All right, where is he?'

'In Nairobi by now.'

'Nairobi?'

Owen nodded. Then he grinned and got out of the car.

The hotel was a five-block walk away. Owen entered the lobby, crossed the floor to the elevators, and rode up to the third floor. He unlocked the door to room 302, stepped in, and closed it behind him.

The room looked as if he'd been staying there for days. Clothes, his own size and taste, in the closets and the bureau drawers. Shaving gear in the bathroom. A book, half-read and dog-eared, on the table beside the bed. Extra shoes. An attaché case.

And in the attaché case, new papers. A wallet. Credit cards. A passport and driver's licence. Everything he needed to become the new person he was.

He picked up the passport and opened it to the photo page. And he smiled. A likeness of his own face stared back at him, but nothing else was the same. Richard Owen was dead.

Very thorough. And very funny. Nichols *had* become an insider. He had demonstrated the irreverence necessary for dealing with an insane world.

The name on the passport was Graham.

Dorothy Uhnak
The Ledger 80p

Enzio Giardino is big-time Mafia – the boss of a million-dollar
narcotics outfit, with the Special Investigation Squad on his track.
The way in to the kill is through Elena Vargas, one-time mistress to
Giardino and hard-as-nails hooker ... which makes a drugs case into
a woman's-angle job, and Christie Opara takes up the assignment.
Soon the lady detective and the Puerto Rican prostitute have more
than a little in common ...

'Detective Opara is going to become one of fiction's most popular
police people' SUNDAY MIRROR

The Investigation £1.20

They can call Kitty a lot of dirty names – but they can't call her 'killer'
until The Investigation is over ... Kitty – fascinating, attractive – and
utterly afraid. The world blames her for the wrong kind of love – with
too many men from the worst places. This is a story of passion and
murder, love and detection. One man seeks out the unsavoury
answers that alone could save her ...

'Marvellously real ... the plot twists – ingenious' DAILY MIRROR

The Witness 80p

Billy Everett was a black civil rights leader – one gunshot later he was
a crumpled corpse. The man with the still-smoking gun was a cop.
Detective Christie Opara had seen the real killer thrust the gun into
the cop's hand. Now she had to stalk that killer through the city's
longest, hottest, deadliest summer ...

'Continuously lively and absorbing' SUNDAY TIMES

Douglas Fairbairn
Street 8 80p

Street 8 is on the wild side of Miami. Here the sleepy Florida resort becomes a violent Latin metropolis run by the anti-Castro gunmen fighting for *'La Causa'*. Bobby Mead, used automobile dealer, has a wayward teenage daughter who has friends in this dangerous community, and other problems of his own . . .

'A thunderous *tour de force*' OBSERVER

'Taut, tight, gripping . . . one expects no less from the author of *Shoot*' NEW YORK TIMES

Ed McBain
Fuzz 80p

With the temperature 12 below zero there was nothing good happening in the 87th Precinct – but for the usual quota of muggings, rapes, knifings and burglaries. And then the city officials began to get killed off one by one . . .

'The best of today's procedural school of police stories – lively, inventive, convincing, suspenseful and wholly satisfactory' NEW YORK TIMES

You can buy these and other Pan books from booksellers and newsagents; or direct from the following address:
Pan Books, Sales Office, Cavaye Place, London SW10 9PG
Send purchase price plus 20p for the first book and 10p for each additional book, to allow for postage and packing
Prices quoted are applicable in the UK

While every effort is made to keep prices low, it is sometimes necessary to increase prices at short notice. Pan Books reserve the right to show on covers and charge new retail prices which may differ from those advertised in the text or elsewhere